GRACE NOTES

GRACE NOTES

Charlotte Vale Allen

Thorndike Press • Chivers Press
Waterville, Maine USA Bath, England

This Large Print edition is published by Thorndike Press, USA
and by Chivers Press, England.

Published in 2002 in the U.S. by arrangement with Harlequin
Books S.A.

Published in 2002 in the U.K. by arrangement with Harlequin
Enterprises II, B.V.

U.S. Hardcover 0-7862-4091-1   (Women's Fiction Series)
U.K. Hardcover 0-7540-1820-2   (Windsor Large Print)

The text of this Large Print edition is unabridged.
Other aspects of the book may vary from the original edition.

Cover used by permission of Harlequin Books.

Set in 16 pt. Plantin by Christina S. Huff.

Printed in the United States on permanent paper.

British Library Cataloguing-in-Publication Data available

Library of Congress Cataloging-in-Publication Data

Allen, Charlotte Vale, 1941–
   Grace notes / Charlotte Vale Allen.
      p.   cm.
   ISBN 0-7862-4091-1 (lg. print : hc : alk. paper)
   1. Mothers and daughters — Fiction.   2. Electronic mail
messages — Fiction.   3. Runaway wives — Fiction.
   4. Women authors — Fiction.   5. Abused wives —
Fiction.   6. Vermont — Fiction.   7. Large type books.
   I. Title.
PS3551.L392 G73 2002
   813'.54—dc21   2002020435

This book is for Suzette, who got pushed to the very edge of reason, but refused to go over. And for Suzette's children, Bear, Adam, and Megan, who (like their mother) are very dear to my heart.

My thanks to Lieutenant William Pettengill of the Brattleboro Division of the Vermont State Police for his help.

Thanks, too, to my daughter Kimberly for sharing her knowledge of Brattleboro and for offering useful suggestions.

As always, I'm indebted to my good friend Angelo Rizacos for listening to and reading the work in progress and for his enthusiasm and his always-valid questions.

And, finally, big thank-yous to my editors Amy and Dianne for their faith in my work.

The first email was what Grace had come to think of as standard fare: a note of eight or ten lines saying how much the person — in this case one Stephanie Baine — enjoyed and valued Grace's books. She replied, as she always did, thanking Stephanie for taking the time to get in touch and for her kind comments. It was sincere. Grace *did* appreciate the readers who visited her website and actually made the effort to communicate. Most of the time (based on the site counter at the bottom of the home page) people visited but didn't respond to her invitation to write. It was a phenomenon very similar to bookstore signings, when people would peer at her from around corners but were too intimidated to approach. Something about a live author, someone whose books they'd read, right there in a bookstore in their own town, turned them shy and uncertain. Unless some brave soul marched right up to Grace and started to talk. Then, almost at once, others would follow. But if that first person didn't make the effort, no one would, and Grace would sit for an hour or two, chatting with the store staff while keeping a smile plastered on her face, drinking the coffee they invariably offered and wondering, yet again, why on earth she had agreed to do another signing tour. She hated them, always had. They never changed. The email situation wasn't so very different. Some people clicked on the link and wrote their thoughts on the preaddressed email; the majority chose to visit and leave — the site counter the only clue to their having visited.

Sometimes, staring at the computer screen, Grace wondered about those anonymous visitors. She knew that many of them were abused women who had seen her interviewed on television, or who had read her autobiographical book on the subject. But the largest number of visitors were those who read her fiction. People seemed to find it easier to read about issues within the context of a fictional setting where there was the hope of a happy ending. Everyone wanted a happy ending, even Grace.

The nonfiction audience was quite different, consisting mostly of damaged women and of professionals who found her autobiography a source of insights that no textbook could ever offer — because Grace had been one of the legions of assaulted wives. But she was different. While the majority of battered women stayed on and on, for all sorts of reasons, Grace had escaped three months after the first time Brownie hit her. While he was teaching his Tuesday morning sophomore class, she'd packed up the car and then driven nonstop to her brother Gus's house in Vermont. It had been the one safe place to go, because Brownie, like all bullies, was a coward. And there was no chance that he'd risk confronting Gus, who was bigger and smarter, and who hated men who took their aggressions out on women. He'd disliked Brownie from the moment he'd met him, saying to her, "Be careful, Gracie. I've got a bad feeling about this guy."

The first time it happened, Grace was too angry and too ashamed to tell anyone, especially her older brother. And Brownie was filled with remorse, arriving home the next afternoon with a box of Grace's favorite dark chocolates. She no longer trusted him, but she wanted to believe that his suddenly backhanding her in the middle of very pedestrian conversation was an aberration. For weeks after it happened she marveled at the speed and suddenness of the blow that had come out of nowhere, accompanied by a torrent of enraged shouts, followed by

Brownie stomping out of the house. Yet six weeks later it happened again. No warning, and *wham!* This time she surprised herself with the speed and suddenness of her *own* reaction. She hit him back, hard. A mistake. The subsequent kicks and blows and incoherent shouts hadn't stopped until she was curled into an agonized knot on the living room floor while, upstairs, the baby howled as if she'd seen and heard it all. When it was over, Brownie had gone stomping out of the house, just the way he had the time before.

And after classes the following day, he came home once more bearing gifts and apologies. She ignored him and his box of long-stemmed roses. Enraged and scarcely able to move, she was already planning her escape from this man who'd sworn since Nicola's birth seven months before that he'd never let her go. "I *love* you. You and Nicky belong to me," he said over and over. He meant it. And she believed him — just not in the way she had at the outset. Now she understood that he was one of the deranged types she read about so often in the papers; someone who went to the home of his estranged wife/fiancée/girlfriend and killed her and anyone else who happened to be around; someone who'd see Grace dead before he let her go. She'd become his possession, a chattel. Humiliation closed her throat every time she thought of having to confess (to anyone) that she'd married an attractive, articulate, educated, psychotic batterer.

Clever Grace, resourceful Grace, combative younger sister of the big, but ever-pacific, August Loring the Third, was stuck in a decrepit rented house in a small college town in Pennsylvania with a thirty-four-year-old associate history professor who, with no warning, started taking his fists and boots to her. The shame of it was almost worse than the beatings. That someone as supposedly intelligent as she was, a young woman who'd graduated Summa Cum Laude and had published a dozen articles and short stories in major magazines while still in college, was stupid enough to marry a barbarian, was galling, mortifying. At twenty-three, she'd thought she'd known it all. At nearly twenty-six, she realized that she knew nothing, that she'd been arrogantly living a schoolgirl's fantasy.

So, no matter what Brownie said (and he even wept while delivering his abject apologies after that second attack), she wasn't going to be blackmailed or threatened or cajoled into staying. She was smart enough to be frightened by the man's irrationality, by his violent mood swings, and by the lust he displayed in the aftermath of his attacks, through which she suffered in compliant silence. She wasn't about to say or do anything that might set him off again.

Two weeks later, when the bruises had faded to a sickly yellow and she could take a deep breath without stabbing rib pain, she'd crammed as much as she could into the old Pinto, belted Nicola into the infant seat and ran to her brother. To his credit and her abiding gratitude, Gus didn't say a word. He opened the door, took one look at her, then held her for several long moments, before coming out to unload the car while she got the baby settled in one of the spare bedrooms in Gus's rambling Victorian house.

After countless phone calls, when Gus simply put down the receiver upon hearing his voice, Brownie wrote threatening letters, which Grace threw, unopened, into the trash. Two years later, Brownie divorced her. And that was the end. Except that she couldn't seem to get past the experience. It haunted her sleep; the scenes replayed themselves every time she even thought about the man she'd married. Finally, she wrote it all down in order both to understand it and to be rid of it. Then, satisfied that she'd accomplished that, she sent it off to her agent in New York who called a week later to say, "This is a very important book, Grace." Miles had sounded atypically subdued. "I'm going to auction it." He paused, then said, "I had no idea. I'm truly sorry. Truly sorry." Within a month it had been bought for more than twice the advances she'd previously received. "Whatever else you do, my dear, you will always be remembered for this book," Miles said. "I'm proud to be associated with it, with you."

Hit or Miss was an immediate best-seller. It was, she and Miles agreed, a combination of luck and timing; a subject being aired at just the right moment. Reviewers praised her courage and honesty (she disagreed with the comments about her courage; it was what she'd had to do in order to absolve herself of the lingering sense that she'd somehow instigated the violence, even though intellectually she knew she hadn't — emotionally her guilt and self-blame remained intact for a very long time), and complimented her on the sensitive clarity of her writing.

Her talk-radio and television appearances generated even more sales because no one expected her to be funny. She couldn't help it. Never able to resist an opening, she'd toss off some observation or a self-deprecating comment. They also didn't expect her to be small, or pretty, or easily conversational. "I don't get out much," she told interviewers. It was the truth, but they laughed merrily, relieved at the effortlessness with which they got through what they'd feared would be a tough six- or seven-minute slog over touchy terrain with an angry, humorless woman.

Grace learned quickly how to make those segments count — getting out information about shelters, about breaking the abuse cycle, about freedom. She felt she was somehow repaying the huge debt she owed her brother when she met with groups of women from every conceivable level of the social/economic/racial spectrum, to talk about their experiences and to encourage them to take their children, if they had them, and get away before it was too late.

Finally, after two and a half years of speaking out on the issue, she was suffering from sensory overload. Too many terrible tales; too many bruised, all-but-broken women; too much sorrow; too many deaths; too few happy endings. She had no desire to be thought of as a professional victim, obsessed with what she'd experienced. It was time to go back to being a mother and a novelist, to living her quiet life in the huge converted attic of her brother's house that was her self-contained sanctuary: office, sitting room, bedroom and bathroom. There was even a small kitchen area fitted into the middle one of the three dormers at the front of the house. It consisted of a four-foot-wide countertop upon which sat an electric kettle, a toaster oven, a box of cutlery, and a few plates and mugs. Below the counter was a small refrigerator next to a stool upon which she sometimes sat while she drank a cup of tea and read a book or a magazine, or simply gazed out the window down at High Street three stories below. Up here, contained within the white-painted walls, with a usually gentle light entering from the north-facing skylight, in an uncluttered area she'd furnished with sleekly modern but comfortable furniture, Grace felt safe. At night, she could sit in her bed, which was positioned against the far wall directly opposite the door, and gaze directly up at the night sky.

The second email from Stephanie Baine read:

"Is it really you? Or does someone else answer your email for you? If you do answer your own email, there's something I'd like to discuss with you."

Grace knew at once that Stephanie was in

trouble. Secrecy was all-important to abused women. Their greatest fear was of having it be known that they were being beaten or verbally assaulted, and that people would blame them for being such pathetic losers.

Grace replied at once, saying, "I answer my own email. And no one else reads it. Feel free to write to me."

And so it began.

There was rarely a day when she didn't think about some part of what had happened during the abduction. Two nights and three days of torment and horror had altered her forever and were directly responsible for everything that followed: her parents' abject refusal to accept the truth of what had been done to her (they told everyone, afterward, that she'd been in an automobile accident even though anyone with a brain would have known instantly that no one could have sustained the type of injuries she had in a car crash); her eventual loss of one boyfriend and then another when she risked telling them the truth, and, finally, her nightmare of a marriage. Every single moment of her life had been irrevocably affected by the abduction.

Certain moments — the hammer swinging back before beginning its descent; the bloodied knife taking aim; the glowing tip of a cigarette coming toward her in the darkness — played and replayed until she was sick with renewed terror. It just wouldn't end. And her husband, that odious obsessive, was determined never to allow it to end.

For some reason, in her head she kept hearing Dinah Washington singing plaintively, over and over, "Where are you? Where have you gone without me? I thought you cared about me. Where are you?"

Sitting alone, she'd find herself whispering the lyrics along with Dinah.

>one

In the almost twenty-two years since Grace had fled from her abusive husband, two things had changed significantly. The first was what had happened to the publishing industry. As she'd predicted long before — based on what she saw and heard and read — the smaller, independent houses had vanished, swallowed up by a few corporate giants. And those giants altered forever the way books were published and sold. An editor could no longer make the decision to buy a book and run unilaterally with that decision. Now, everything was decided by committee; profit-and-loss projections and marketability determined whether or not a book could be purchased — regardless of its merits. Prime shelf-space was purchased, and product-placement was the order of the day, whether it was the latest brand of cereal, or a new book. Publishing had become just another, often soulless, bottom-line business.

For Grace, having seen the whole thing evolve, her joy in being a writer was all but gone. There was something too frustrating about dealing, even one-step-removed, with people who couldn't answer the simplest question without first having to consult others, and with having to do battle (via Miles, her war-weary agent) to retain her electronic rights, among many other things. The spontaneity, the excitement had died. She likely would have quit writing books altogether, venturing instead into creating short pieces for a number of websites that had approached her (one even offered to give her an advice column, which was hugely tempting), had it not been for the second change: Gus's being diagnosed ten years earlier, at the age of forty-eight, with rheumatoid arthritis, and his immediate and utter capitulation to the disease.

She would never have believed that her loquaciously witty, tenured, English professor brother would accept a diagnosis as a life sentence. But he did. He *became* his disease. It defined who he was; it dictated the terms of his life; it curtailed his career, his activities and friendships, his thinking, even his range of motion. Ten years later, Gus was, despite her initial and periodic intervention, as close as dammit to a complete cripple. And in very short order Grace had become a caregiver.

Darling Gus had been the best ballroom dancer most women had ever encountered. A physical man, effortlessly gifted at most sports, particularly tennis, he gradually gave up all but the most minimal movement. Because it hurt. And despite all of Grace's best efforts at logic, reason, cajoling, even bullying, her brother wouldn't do anything that heightened the pain that took hold of his joints — elbows, ankles, and knees in particular — and steadily pushed them into impossibly contorted positions. Finally, the once towering, hefty yet remarkably agile Gus was an agonized assemblage of parts gone awry. His once wide shoulders and powerful arms and legs were now those of someone decades older, narrowed and spindly. Frail, always physically off balance, yet mentally undiminished, Gus required almost full-time care. He could be left alone for a few hours during the day, and for most of the night. By default, the night became Grace's only free time, because Gus needed no assistance once he was in bed. (A plastic urinal was close at hand, if required.) But they couldn't manage without help during the day.

Being too young and having too much in the way of capital assets to qualify for Medicare, his personal health insurance didn't provide coverage for what was considered a chronic condition. So Gus was obliged to pay for every aspect of his care — from the nightmarishly expensive prescription medications, to the cost of physical alterations to the first floor of the house (where Gus now resided; stairs being out of the question): grab bars in the bathroom and a special elevated toilet seat; a walker and a portable, folding wheelchair (for visits to sundry doctors) and a ramp to the front door of the house; large-handled eating utensils, and bibs to catch the inevitable spillage. The search just for shoes and socks that would fit Gus's sadly angled feet was endless. No shoe was wide enough, and only diabetic socks were loose enough to pass over toe joints that jutted to one side while the toes had twisted in the opposite direction. Grace intercepted many of the bills and paid them, as well as the property taxes on the house (telling her brother she needed the tax deduction), and most of the utility bills. It had become considerably easier to make these sleight-of-hand adjustments since Gus had given her a power of attorney two years earlier and she'd taken over managing his money.

She also paid for the home help. And they were very lucky to have the two women whose services were offered with grace and affection. Dolly, who came each morning seven days a week and got Gus up, bathed and dressed for the day, was a fifty-something Jamaican woman; sturdy and handsome, intelligent and sensible, endowed with a lovely sense of humor. Grace invariably smiled at the sound of Dolly's lilting laugh and Gus's responsive quips. Once resigned to the reality of his need for assistance, he gave himself over to Dolly's ministrations, savoring the breakfast trays she carried in from the kitchen and discussing with her everything from editorials in that morning's *New York Times* to whatever he'd watched on TV the night before. Unflaggingly cheerful, genuinely caring, Dolly treated Gus in a fond, no-nonsense fashion that usually gave him a good start to the day. Unless he was having a flare. Then his groans could be heard throughout the house as Dolly gave him a sponge bath in his bed, rather than giving him a shower while he sat on the special armed seat in the tub.

Flares could last a day or several weeks. They were impossible to predict. Sudden pain lunged inside the man like something wild. His knees swelled with fluid; he hunched into himself, scarcely moving, unable even to read his morning paper or any of the dozens of books stacked on the bedside table and on the bookshelves next to it. His eyes dark-circled and sunken, he asked for Tylenol 3 or Darvocet three or four or five times in the course of a given day; often his maintenance dose of Prednisone would have to be increased by at least five milligrams. And then, just as suddenly as it had come, the flare would end, and Gus would be wondering loudly where his paper was and making mention of the golf, or baseball, or football game that was scheduled on TV or the radio for that day. At four, he'd tune in to *All Things Considered* on NPR and listen intently until it was time for dinner. Saturday mornings, regardless of his condition, he had to hear *Car Talk*. ("God, I *love* these guys! Who ever dreamed an hour-long show about car problems could be this entertaining!") He'd howl with laughter, even at his worst moments. And Sundays, with the *Times* in a heap at his side, the magazine folded open to the crossword puzzle, which he'd complete later (painfully filling in each blank space with the shaky printing of someone elderly), he'd listen to Garrison Keillor's *Prairie Home Companion*. ("The man's a genius, Gracie; best narratives anywhere. I could live without some of the music, but his humor is unrivaled — never mean-spirited, but always right on the money.") Most evenings, Grace and Gus ate dinner together on trays in the living room and caught the nightly network news with Tom Brokaw, and during the commercial breaks Gus would fill her in on items he'd found of interest on *All Things Considered*.

Six evenings a week (on Sunday nights, Grace helped her brother to the bathroom and then back to his bed where he stubbornly slept in his clothes), Lucia came to reverse the process and get Gus ready for bed. No small feat, since just removing a shirt or sweater (all front opening — pullovers were now out of the question) involved movement of tender, inflamed elbow and shoulder joints that had very little flexibility. As well, there were the attendant illnesses that accompanied the disease and the medications required to address them: kidney problems, opportunistic nonmalignant tumors, diabetes, heart disease, chronic lung congestion, loss of teeth, "tissue paper skin" that tore and bled with alarming ease as a result of prolonged use of Prednisone and, on top of everything else, his hearing had started to go. Great care, firm but tender hands, and tremendous patience were needed in dealing with someone whose disease had, according

24

to his rheumatologist, got as bad as it was possible to get.

Younger than Dolly by ten or so years, Lucia was a big woman with a soft voice that still bore traces of her South Carolina roots, even though her family had left the south when Lucia was twelve. She claimed to hate the Vermont winters but she seemed to flourish in the cold, invariably arriving with a grin as she announced the latest forecast. More deferential than Dolly and somewhat less attuned to nuance, Lucia always spoke to Gus as Mr. Loring (Dolly addressed him as Mr. Gus) and their conversations usually centered on matters of local interest and on the weather. He loved and relied on both women but seemed to relish Dolly's company, perhaps because she was closer to him in age.

For Grace, Gus was pretty much a full-time job. While Dolly had taken over the preparation of his breakfast when she'd first come to them three years earlier, it fell to Grace to prepare the other two meals he received. And there were moments when she stood in the huge, airy kitchen (Gus's first project upon buying the place had been to remodel this room — knocking out the pantry wall and removing its shelves and cupboards, to create a space that took up

most of the rear of the house), hacking vegetables or slamming pots down on the
countertop, muttering away, furious at
having had to tear herself away from whatever work was in progress; angry at always
being at her brother's beck and call. At
those moments, she hated Gus; hated his
utter capitulation to the disease, his needs
and requests, his lamentable lack of health.
Then, inevitably, she'd get hold of herself
and stop. Taking a deep breath, she'd stand
with her hands braced on the counter and
remind herself that Gus hadn't *wanted* to
fall prey to attack by the very white cells that
were supposed to help his immune system,
not destroy it. His pride had taken a terrible
battering; he had to struggle not to succumb
daily to the humiliation of being unable
even to get to the bathroom without assistance.

No one had asked her to do this. She'd
volunteered. Therefore she had no right to
complain. Having, yet again, reasoned
through her anger, she then got on with the
job at hand, more often than not using
humor to ease the situation. In a good Bette
Davis imitation, she frequently delivered
Gus a tray of food, announcing, "Here's ya
din-dins!"

"Oh, yummy!" Gus responded brightly

every time. "Roasted rat, my favorite!"

They both worked diligently to keep things light, to maintain a level of polite civility. Gus had his own anger, and it erupted over silly things that hadn't anything to do with the real cause of his unhappiness. He'd bellow Grace's name at top volume, demanding to know where this or that was. Hearing him shout, she'd go taut as baling wire, wanting to race down the two flights of stairs from the attic and ask him why the hell he couldn't use the intercom; it was why they'd had it installed. But of course she knew why. Every time he gave way and used one of the many gadgets Grace provided to make things easier for him, he was conceding another measure of defeat. Eventually, he'd take to using the intercom just as he'd taken to using the speakerphone and the walker; just as he'd accepted the daily help of two hefty women who dressed and undressed him, bathed him like some gigantic infant, and cooed over how nice he looked (freshly shaven, or rigged out in newly laundered flannel pajamas). For both Grace and Gus, each day brought new and different compromises, paid for in this realm's coin: anger.

Yet twenty-two-year-old Nicky had no trouble at all dealing with either one of them. She treated her uncle as she always had, calling him Dad and sitting on the foot of his bed to spend an hour, or two, or three bringing him up to speed on her life, asking why he didn't call so-and-so and invite him or her to visit (knowing full well that Gus didn't want any of his former friends or associates to see him in his present condition) and politely accepting his illogical reasons for refusing to return calls or extend invitations. And when Grace was fuming with impatience or anger, storming about the kitchen or stomping up the stairs, Nicky would say, "Chill, Mom. Go for a walk or something. You're taking all this way too personally."

It *was* personal, of course, but Nicky had a gift for defusing moods and situations. She was, in fact, gifted in dealing with people in general. She had her uncle's innate social ease (hence his great success as a teacher) and the kind of pale-skinned, dark-haired, fine-featured beauty that would guarantee her an attentive audience. Nicky was kind, generous, smart, and a housekeeping nightmare. Things stayed where she dropped them — on the stairs, in the living room, the kitchen, the floors of the upper hallways, and on every surface of her room. She was chaotically disorganized, could never find her wallet, or her keys, or some item of clothing she just had to wear. She was equally disorganized about money and didn't consider coins or dollar bills actually to *be* money. So at least once a week, Grace went through the house, collecting Nicky's belongings, sorting them for the wash or the dry cleaners, and culling coins from pockets and purses, even plastic or paper bags from the local markets. She'd convert the resulting (considerable) collection into five- or ten-dollar bills and leave them on Nicky's dresser in her room — which was as typical of Nicky as the living room was of Gus.

Previously Gus's bedroom, Nicky had taken it over five years earlier when Gus could no longer manage the stairs. Grace, her friend Vinnie, along with Gus's friend Jerry had moved all of Gus's things down to what had been the den. Then they'd moved Nicky's furniture from her old room into Gus's far larger one. When everything was in place, the three had congratulated themselves on a job well done. Nicky's new room looked great.

But not for long. Now strings of fairy lights ran around the perimeter at ceiling height and burned night and day; mosquito netting hung in a graceful gauzy sweep above her never-made bed; books and magazines were everywhere as were mounds of clothing, shoes and underwear. Her ancient teddy bear (one side split and leaking stuffing) and her tattered blankie lay next to her pillow (she often slept with the blankie draped over her head); the armchair was piled high with clothes, school papers-in-progress, more magazines, random shoes, dirty socks and a variety of scarves. The dresser drawers were always partway open, their contents hanging over the rims: lacy bras and thong underwear Grace couldn't conceive of wearing (squirming every time she even thought about it); body stockings and tights, sweaters and blouses and still more scarves. There were trails of burnt incense on the bedside table, along with clots of candle wax. Used tissues were everywhere — except in the wicker waste basket — and every surface, except for the desk, bore a substantial weight of perfume bottles, hair care products and cosmetics. Nicky even put candles on top of her computer monitor.

With a sigh, Grace would spend an hour or more setting the room to rights, but within ten minutes of Nicky's arriving home — outerwear dumped on the floor in the front entryway — the mess would begin accumulating again.

Grace too often felt ready to pitch a screaming fit. That fit was so close to the surface, so nearly palpable that she felt fairly pregnant with it: this ever-swelling entity that lived and grew hourly, daily, weekly, inside her body. This was not what she'd had in mind for her life, she thought regularly. She distinctly remembered *having* a life, but it had been subsumed under the weight of her brother's needs and her daughter's unheeding carelessness. She longed for time alone, time without the demands of others placed upon it. It was never going to happen. Certainly, matters would improve once Nicky graduated from college in another semester and pursued her dreams of getting into radio or TV production in either Boston or Manhattan, depending on the offers that came in once she started sending out her résumé. If the offers weren't to her liking, she planned to work for a year, then go to graduate school. Either way, she was, she said, "Getting out of Appalachia north." There were moments when Grace thought Nicky's absence would be unbearable; but, at other moments, Grace couldn't wait for her to go. There would be far less for her to do, fewer demands on her time; she might actually get back a facsimile of a life. But in the meantime, turmoil was the order of the day.

31

In a silent, resigned sweep, Grace would clear the mess (deeply grateful to Velma, who came twice a week to clean the place from top to bottom), and then escape upstairs to her self-contained world at the top of the house to work on the computer for an hour or two, answering email or trying to concentrate on the current novel she had been writing for the last year and a half (and which, she thought with rueful regularity, she might well be writing for the rest of her life if she didn't somehow manage to get a substantial chunk of uninterrupted time).

The computer had replaced the traveling she'd once done, the trips she'd taken to Europe or Asia; the ten-city book tours she'd hated but which, in retrospect, seemed like glorified working vacations. She traveled now on the Internet, did any necessary research online when possible, and dealt with a steady flow of email from friends and from readers. The computer, along with the videos she rented weekly to watch with Gus (he loved movies as much as she did, fortunately) were brief, regular holidays she took from her life. Both Gus's body and her life had become grossly distorted things.

>two

Sometimes, staring blankly at the screen, Grace marveled at the wayward passage of her life. First had come the revelation at the age of six that both she and Gus were adopted, not the natural-born son and daughter of Lydia and August Loring Junior. That information might have thrown her into a tizzy had it not been for Gus's matter-of-factness in the aftermath of her being told.

"I remember when they brought you home," the then sixteen-year-old had told her. "I was pretty excited about it," he'd confessed with typical Gus-like candor. "They'd been talking about it for months, so I was ready. I didn't even mind baby-sitting. It was fun, except when you cried for three hours and nothing would get you to stop. But the thing is, you were so *complete*, Gracie. I don't know what I was thinking — that you'd come in a pod or something, like a tadpole, or in one of those big thingies like *Invasion of the Body Snatchers* — but it never occurred to me that babies were actual, small people. Anyway, it's not a big deal. They should've told you sooner, but they don't really understand how smart you are. And even though it's a complete cliché, it's great to be someone people wanted and not some pain-in-the-ass natural-born they're stuck with for all time."

So there was that, and Gus, typically, made it okay.

Then there was Gus's "outcoming," as he called it. Lydia and August Junior went crazy. "They basically told me never to darken their doorstep again." Gus laughed. "So Gothic, so typically overdramatic. As if I was suddenly going to show up at the country club with a troupe of drag queens in full regalia and disgrace them. I haven't lived at home for eight years," her then twenty-six-year-old brother had told her over lunch when they'd met up one Saturday at a restaurant outside Hartford, roughly halfway between the family home in Connecticut and his new teaching job at the college in Vermont. "Anyway, I always hated the country club — all those red-faced, self-important businessmen in their weekend finery of lime-green trousers with hot pink jackets, and the overpermed wives in Lily Pulitzer prints and Pappagallo shoes. Bad food, endless nonsensical conversations about people with mortifying nicknames like Tweezie and Thumper."

Grace had laughed. She felt exactly the same way about the club and its members. But to Lydia and August Junior the club was proof of their status, their social acceptability. It was sad because, to Grace's mind, they were decent, albeit misguided, people. "I'm sure it'll blow over by Christmas," Grace said confidently.

Gus had shaken his head, saying, "It'll never blow over, baby sister. Their kind of people just don't have children with aberrant tendencies."

He was absolutely right. They never spoke of Gus again. It was as if he hadn't ever existed. If Grace mentioned him, she received a frosty look from her father and a wounded one from her mother. And sometimes, weirdly, Lydia would segue in — seemingly picking up where she'd left off in some previous conversation — saying, "and after all we did for him." As if personal preferences could be defined by the type of upbringing one's parents had provided; as if a certain level of wealth were a verified determining factor in heterosexuality.

There was no comeback to this. And Grace gave up trying to bring Gus back into the family when — home from college for

Easter — she told their parents of Gus's ascent to full professorship at the age of thirty. She received only the usual glacial look from August Junior and the imperiled deer-in-the-headlights look from Lydia. Anyway, by this point, she was in trouble with them herself. They hated the way she dressed (it was 1974 but her parents were trapped in a time warp and wanted her in country club clothes); they hated the music she played (they dined to Mantovani albums); they hated, but tried to pretend they didn't, the two published pieces she proudly showed them.

"You really should be taking business courses," her father said. "There's money to be made on Wall Street."

It was useless trying to explain that she had no desire to enter the corporate world. The fact she'd been writing since the age of twelve and had always declared her intention to be a writer was of no consequence. Gus and Lydia believed she'd grow out of this "phase," come to her senses, and get down to the serious business of making money.

Her marriage to Brownie, though, was more than acceptable to her parents. They were fully prepared to overlook the less than salubrious fact that a professor had been having an affair with their student daughter, because James Harris Brownell came from a fine old Main Line Philadelphia family. He knew how to dress and what to say; his social skills were impeccable. He was so acceptable, in fact, that when it came time to run from the man, Grace knew her parents would send her right back to him; they'd tell her to stop making such a fuss, to behave like a proper wife, and they'd even personally escort her to his door. Which was why she ran to Gus, because her older brother had a first-hand acquaintanceship with the real world and didn't believe that wives were chattels or property of any kind that could be maltreated at will because a marriage license permitted it.

So complete was her parents' approval of him that, until he remarried, Brownie regularly phoned August Junior and Lydia, who commiserated with him on Grace's terrible behavior, and blamed her entirely for the failure of the marriage. "You've got to take the good with the bad," her mother said. "That's a wife's job."

"So I should just stick around and let him beat the shit out of me, then rape me for good measure? Have I got that right?" Grace demanded, furious.

"I wish you wouldn't swear," Lydia had said unhappily. "It's probably why James was so upset with you."

After that infuriating call, Grace phoned home far less often. But she did take Nicky down to Connecticut to see Lydia and August Junior once or twice a year, and never spoke ill of them in her daughter's presence. They were the only grandparents Nicky had; Grace wanted the child to have some sense of personal history.

By the time she was twelve, however, Nicky was reluctant to visit.

"They're so, like, prehistoric, Mom," she'd complained. "It's depressing, kind of. I mean, I don't want to hurt their feelings or anything, but all they do the whole time we're there is tell me I shouldn't do this, or I shouldn't say that. I'm amazed you and Dad" — referring to her uncle Gus — "didn't take drugs or anything. How could you stand them?"

"Actually, we couldn't," Grace confessed, and then went on to give Nicky an edited version of hers and Gus's life with Lydia and August Junior.

Mightily affronted, Nicky declared, "That's the worst thing I've ever *heard!* Half the kids in my school are gay. What's the big deal?"

"Half?"

"Okay, so maybe only a third. But who cares?"

"Your grandparents do."

"Well, that's just sick. Okay? Dad's the coolest of all my friends' parents. Everybody loves him. I can't *believe* this! You don't just throw people *away!* I hate them! I'm never going there again as long as I *live!*"

"You don't hate them, Nicks. You just don't agree with them. And that's fine. Neither do I."

"No, I *hate* them. You couldn't *pay* me to go there again!"

As it happened, it was a moot point. A chimney fire in the early morning hours five days later burned the house to the ground. Lydia and August Junior died in their beds of smoke inhalation.

With the exception of an old, fully paid-up life insurance policy on Lydia that named both Gus and Grace as beneficiaries, and the homeowners coverage which also, oddly, listed them as the proprietors (a subsequent title search revealed this to be the fact: ownership of the Darien house had been put in their names many years before and, no doubt through some oversight, had never been changed), the rest of the estate went into trust for Nicky. Literally overnight, the twelve-year-old was enormously wealthy. Except that she couldn't touch the money. She was to inherit one third of the estate at the age of twenty-five, another third at thirty, and the balance at thirty-five. The trustees would pay out tuition and maintenance costs, but they'd have to be petitioned for funds for any other purpose.

Nicky was heartbroken at hearing of the deaths and stayed home from school for the four days prior to the funeral, curled up on the window seat of her room, clutching her ancient teddy bear and sobbing as she gazed out the window. Nicola was, at bottom, a good-hearted, generous and caring girl. These qualities, combined with her stunning good looks, made her very lovable. Luckily, her lack of domestic skills and her hopelessness with money rendered her human. She was, at times, intellectually sophisticated, charming, poised and always interested in the people around her. At other times, she was perilously close to being a ditzy airhead, oblivious to the chaos she regularly created, capable of fussing for hours over which pair of shoes she should buy. It was a given that everyone in the shoe store would be asked their opinion. It was further given that all those present would leave the place feeling lifted for having encountered the amusing, good-natured young woman. Nicky was irresistible. She was also often blind to what went on around her, so preoccupied was she with her friends and her exhausting social life, and with clothes.

Her wardrobe was so extensive that it occupied not only the closet in her room, but it also extended to one of the guest rooms. In fact, the spare room was completely filled with clothes, shoes, cosmetics, sundry hair care products, handbags, coats, boots and perfumes. She was the quintessential consumer, always on the lookout for what she considered to be a bargain and for what Grace considered to be outrageously overpriced. Some of her daughter's acquisitions were staggeringly expensive. Others were the essence of taste coupled with practicality, like the Range Rover the trustees permitted her to buy on her sixteenth birthday, and which was often used to get Gus to a medical appointment when the other household vehicles couldn't handle the snow and iced-over roads. Since the money Nicky spent was her own and made only a partial dent in the annual maintenance income from the trust, Grace tried to refrain from commenting when Nicky heaved through the front door, loaded down with yet more purchases. The Fates had been kind. They'd created a consumer and provided her the wherewithal to indulge herself.

And sometimes, Nicky tuned in to what

was going on around her and demonstrated a responsiveness that redeemed her utterly. When she'd seen her mother sorting bills into piles on the kitchen table one afternoon a year or so earlier, she'd stopped to ask, "What's all that?"

"Doctor's bills, the running tab from the pharmacy, insurance premiums of several varieties, property tax bills for the car and the van, telephone, cable, utilities. Stop me any time."

"Those are all Dad's?"

"Most of them. Being sick ain't cheap, Nicks."

"Let me see," Nicky said, picking up the monthly pharmacy bill. "Wow! Five bucks a pill? What is this stuff, gold?"

"Actually, for a year after he was diagnosed, Gus did take gold injections. They worked."

"So what happened?"

"They stopped working."

"Too bad, huh?"

"Very too bad."

Nicky looked over at her mother. "What about Dolly and Lucia?"

"What about them?"

"How much do they get?"

Grace told her, and Nicky whistled. "That is a *ton* of money!" she exclaimed.

"It sure is," Grace agreed.

"Tell you what," Nicky said, looking toward the window as if doing mental arithmetic. "You know how hopeless I am with my checking account."

"That is a true statement." Grace smiled.

"I'll just tell the bank to put some money in Dad's account every month. Okay?"

"Okay, Nicks. That'd be a help. Thank you."

"But don't say anything to him about it. Okay? He'll just get all pissed off, the way he does. And who needs that?"

"Nobody in this room."

Nicky offered her mother one of her heart-stoppingly spectacular smiles, the kind that turned male legs to Jell-O and made females wonder why someone so gorgeous had to be so goddamned nice that you couldn't even hate her. "C'n I ask you something?" Nicky said after a moment.

"Sure. What?"

"Didn't you guys ever want to know who your real parents were?"

"I had moments. Gus never did. We made a pact when I was eight that we'd never try to find out. We decided that we were descended from royalty and it was best to keep that a secret."

"Be serious. That's little-kid stuff."

43

"I am serious. We agreed that having each other was enough and we'd never go looking. That way we couldn't be disappointed."

"But what if all this time some poor woman was looking for you, the baby she had to give away?" Nicky's eyes began to fill. This was a girl who wept over dog food commercials.

"She'd have found me by now, Nicks. It's not that hard to do these days."

"You think?"

"I think."

"Okay. I've got homework, then I'm gonna go hang with Migs." And off she went, leaving behind her shoes, a sweater and two tubes of lip gloss.

How did she *do* that? Grace laughed, dropping the lip glosses into her pocket as she considered the truth of what she'd told her daughter. In fact, she had wondered about her birth parents, and about the circumstances that had led them to give her away. But the more she'd thought about it, the less inclined she'd become to know. An anomalous response, definitely. Still, she trusted both her brother's and her own instincts. It was best not to know. Besides, as she'd told Nicky, if their parents had wanted to find them, they could have, quite easily, because she and Gus had both been born in

Connecticut and adopted through the same agency. That much had always been known. She did think it might have been interesting to know if anyone in Gus's birth family had had rheumatoid arthritis. But since there was considerable debate about whether or not it was an inherited disease, and since Gus had no children to whom he might have passed along the genetic marker — if, indeed, one existed — there wasn't much point to speculating.

A week later, the first monthly transfer had appeared in Gus's account, in the amount of three hundred dollars. Grace was very touched. The money would cover the cost of her brother's Celebrex, Cumadin and Prednisone each month. Most of Gus's savings, and his share of the sale of the Connecticut house, were long gone; his insurance premiums came to more than eight thousand dollars annually; his pension plan had been seriously depleted by heavily taxed premature withdrawals; and he wouldn't be eligible to begin drawing early Social Security benefits until he reached the age of sixty-two. Grace's own accounts had suffered as a result of her efforts to help her brother, and only a new book would bring her any income. She just couldn't, though, get enough uninterrupted time to finish the work in progress. Her royalties on the previous books weren't sufficient to cover the monthly expenses, and most of her inherited money was gone, too.

Staring now at the contents of the open hard drive, Grace quietly broke into tears. She felt trapped.

>three

Grace couldn't bring herself to open the folder that contained the sections of her new manuscript. She finally had a couple of free hours to get some work done and she couldn't get started; merely thinking about it made her feel queasy. Aversion, rich and ripe as imported cheese, overwhelmed her. She hated the idea that she *had* to write, that she had no other means of earning money. If she had any other skill that would bring her an income, she'd pursue it without hesitation. *I hate my life,* she thought, her fingertips poised on the keyboard. *I* have *no goddamned life. I'd like to run away, spend a month sitting on a beach, take a cruise to Alaska, get in the car and just drive — leave behind the caregiving, the demands, the need to keep working.*

This was stupid, self-indulgent. She knew that once she opened a file and reviewed where she'd left off, she'd be fine. She'd slide back inside the minds of the characters, relocate the tempo of the narrative and where it needed to go, and get to work. It was always that way. Yet she simply couldn't open the folder. Could not.

After staring blankly at the Apple in the upper left-hand corner of the monitor for a minute, she let her gaze wander over the contents of the open hard drive. Nicky had pasted *South Park* icons on a bunch of her files: Cartman glowered at her from atop the system folder; Kenny stood guard over a file full of business correspondence; Mr. Hat represented a file labeled "Ideas." Perhaps a couple of games of Tetris would focus her. Sometimes, it did, and she was able to get to work after fifteen or twenty minutes of that, or of a few hands of computer Solitaire. Some years back, she'd read an article in the *Wall Street Journal* that explained why Tetris was the most popular computer game, ever, among women. Something about its orderliness. The one part she remembered in particular was an interview with a business-woman from the midwest who was on a flight into Kennedy when the plane began a slow loop over Manhattan. "I Tetrissed the skyline," the woman said. Grace had laughed in delight and relief over the article, glad to know she wasn't the only grown woman addicted to the game. It was, in a way, like being given permission to indulge her sense of order by lining up falling blocks of various forms so that they meshed and disappeared off the screen. She could play for hours and had felt guilty about that, until she'd read the *Journal* piece.

As she was about to surrender and double-click the Tetris icon, the finder began flashing to indicate she had email. Always pleased to get mail — in any form — she pulled down the finder menu to get to the Messenger window. The inbox contained two items of spam and something from the woman who'd wanted to know if Grace answered her own email. She had to smile at the notions people had about writers, the idea that authors had glamorous lives, with staff to handle the mundane chores. Only a handful of writers made the kind of money that allowed them lavish lifestyles, airbrushed author photos, and personal assistants.

Dealing with the spam first, she got the full headers showing, then pulled up the page source. That done, she copied the entire document and went to SpamCop to paste it into the waiting box and file a report. Then she deleted the spam and looked at the genuine email.

Subject:
Date: Thurs, 21 Dec 2000 10:09:26 -0500

From: Stephanie Baine
<baine_stephanie@spotmail.com>
To: Grace
<gloring@homecable.com>

Dear Grace:

Thanks for writing back to me so quickly. It's taken me a couple of days to get myself to the point where I could write to you about this. I know it's going to sound ridiculous, but my problem has to do with New Year's Eve. Every year my husband insists that we have a big party to celebrate the occasion, even though he knows it's the toughest time of the year for me. I'd rather go to bed and sleep through it, wake up when it's finished. But he's invited more than thirty people here for that evening and there's no way I could get out of it now, especially since he basically threw out a blanket invitation to the whole neighborhood.

This is very difficult to talk about, but the thing is, I was abducted on New Year's Eve when I was sixteen and held captive for several days. It was a very bad experience, with a lot of injuries, and ever since then this time of the year has terrible associations for me. My parents never wanted to hear about it and they told everybody I'd been in a car accident, and my husband always says I'm overreacting, that I'm a drama queen. I'm thirty-three now and I still have nightmares and flashbacks about the whole thing, so I don't think I'm overreacting, but maybe he's right. I don't know what to think anymore; I just know that I can't stand even thinking about having a party that night. On top of all that, my parents just arrived this morning for Christmas and they're staying until January first. So I have to deal with them too. And they give me just as hard a time about the party every year as Billy does.

I have a really nasty headache, the same one that I've had for the last two days. I went into a quiet room to lie down and try and get rid of it, and my parents pounced on me. My Dad said that I should not be lying around in the middle of the day. I tried to tell him that I was sick, and get this, he says that wives aren't allowed to get sick. Then my

Mom tells me that I'd better not be starting my annual meltdown because I have less than 2 weeks left to get ready for my party. She told me to get myself together and keep everybody happy.

I'm feeling so panicked that I can barely function. I'm really fighting it, but being out today, seeing all the ads for New Year's parties, really got to me. I almost feel like I'm back in time, and it's going to happen all over again. I know that's totally stupid and impossible, and I've told myself that a million times now, but it's not working.

If you have any suggestions on how I can get through this thing, I'd really appreciate it. Thanks for reading this long rant, and thanks for writing Hit Or Miss. It's helped me a lot. I like your other books, too. You're a wonderful writer and I'm amazed that you'd take the time to talk to me.

Sincerely, Stephanie

Grace immediately fired off a reply.

Subject: re

Date: Thurs, 21 Dec 2000 10:22:21 -0500
From: Grace Loring <gloring@homecable.com>
To: Stephanie Baine <baine_stephanie@spotmail.com>

Dear Stephanie:

Before I can make any suggestions, I need to know if you ever got any professional help in the aftermath of the abduction. Were the police involved? Was there a court case? Once I have a few mo re details, I'll be able to give you a specific reply. Please know that I won't judge you, but I honestly can't advise you without more information on what happened, and without knowing whether or not you've talked about this experience with others.

I do think your parents have pretty strange ideas about marriage. What does your father do, anyway? And what does your husband do?

Best to you,
Grace

Her curiosity well piqued, Grace wondered what kind of people would refuse to acknowledge the truth about a crime against their daughter, or to console a ravaged child. Answer: the Lydia and August Junior type of people, the ones who believed it was a wife (or child's) duty to obey, even to get bashed. But what sort of husband would insist on having a party on a night he knew had horrific associations for his wife? Not a very nice one, she thought, having already developed a set of negative reactions based on the scant information Stephanie had provided about him. The woman had told more about her parents than she had about her husband.

Anxious to see what Stephanie would say in her reply, Grace went downstairs to make a cup of coffee and to check on Gus.

Subject:
Date: Thurs, 21 Dec 2000 11:12:26 -0400
From: Stephanie Baine <baine_stephanie@spotmail.com>
To: Grace <gloring@homecable.com>

Dear Grace:

Aside from my parents, two boyfriends and my husband, I've never talked about what happened. As for the police being involved, after it happened I decided to go to the local station. I didn't want to tell them everything so I just told them that this guy was bothering me. He lived on our street and was always in trouble with drugs and fights. Everybody was afraid of him. Anyway, the police paid him a visit, but basically nothing happened. Then two days later when I got home from school my cat was dead outside our front door. That really scared me, because he'd said that if I told anyone what he'd done he'd kill my whole family, and after I found the cat I believed him. My parents said it was my own fault I got so badly hurt, because I should have fought harder. I was stupid to get myself abducted, and maybe that's true. But he put a knife to my throat and made me get into the trunk of his car and I don't know how I could have fought against that.

I never made it home after the kidnapping. I was in his car, he was driving me somewhere, I don't know where, and we were in the vicinity of the military hospital. I played dead, and when he relaxed his grip on the knife that he had, that's when I jumped out of the car. That's the last thing that I remember before I woke up in the emergency room and could tell them who I was. My parents came, once they were called and I said that I was in a car accident. They believed that story, although looking back, I don't see how they could. I was 16, so the hospital wasn't allowed to tell them any different, even though they knew what had happened. I didn't tell them the real story until a few years later. I've thought about this so much and wondered how they didn't figure it out long before I told them, but I think that they didn't want to know.

So, the answer to your question is no. I haven't really talked to anybody about this. I've been too ashamed. Everybody's outside, so I have a few minutes of peace and quiet. I don't think my husband loves me, have thought that for a while now. But I always had my parents telling me that I was crazy to think it, and he would tell me the same thing. I even said to him once that if he loved me then he wouldn't act like he did, and his response to that was to say that I was committing emotional blackmail. So, all this time I was convinced that I was the one with the problem. My Mom would accuse me of hating men because of what happened to me, and to stop taking it out on Billy. He would basically say the same thing. I'm sure you can tell that I'm very confused. Most of all, I'm worried sick about this New Year's Eve party, and I'd be so grateful for any suggestions.

Thanks for listening to all this. I really appreciate it.

Love, Stephanie

PS: My father was in the military but he's retired now. And Billy's also in the military. But he's going to be retiring in a few months and going into the private sector.

Grace got up and walked around her attic room, thinking, looking down at the silk-on-silk, four foot by six foot Persian carpet she'd bought some ten years earlier — a gift to herself to celebrate the sale of a book. It occupied the central area of her huge aerie, with nothing on it to distract the eye: predominantly orange-red, it had border designs within border designs, five in all, until the central panel gave way to a delicately interwoven floral design in cream and green, with touches of pink and red. It was an exquisitely complex piece whose colors altered in hue, depending on how the light struck it. Even on the dreariest days, it seemed to glow, relieving the modern starkness of the white room with its white furniture. The only other item with any color to it was her blue Mac G3, to which she now returned to write a reply to the troubling email.

Subject: re
Date: Thurs, 21 Dec 2000 11:42:14 -0500
From: Grace Loring <gloring@homecable.com>
To: Stephanie Baine <baine_stephanie@spotmail.com>

Dear Stephanie:

You were very brave and very resourceful to rescue yourself. And I can't believe your parents bought into the car accident story. You're right: they obviously didn't want to know the truth. But blaming you was so wrong. I really can't understand parents who wouldn't console their child under those circumstances.

What you've got to do right away, Stephanie, is call your local rape crisis center and talk to someone; you need to start getting these memories out of your head and into the air so that they'll begin dissipating and lose their freshness. Once you get some perspective on what happened, you won't relive the experience every time you think about it. You can call a crisis center in complete confidentiality; you don't even have to give your name. But please do it. You have to start talking about what happened.

In the meantime, try to stay out of everybody's way as much as possible. Don't engage in arguments with your parents or with Billy. I'll think about the party and get back to you soon.

Please know that I'm very sorry for what happened to you. It wasn't your fault. Nothing you did caused it to happen. What became of this psychopath, anyway? And could you tell me more about your husband? Knowing that both your husband and your father are/were in the military explains a lot. Men in the police and the military seem to have the worst problems with domestic abuse.

Best to you, Grace

After closing her Internet connection, filled with anger on Stephanie's behalf and with an odd energy, Grace went downstairs to say good-night to Gus. He was dozing, an open book propped on the reading pillow she'd got him from the Levinger's catalog sitting on his chest.

Placing a bookmark between the pages, she put the book within his reach on the bedside table, and set the pillow next to him on the queen-sized bed as he came awake and looked over at the time on his bedside clock.

"Nodded off," he said with a wry smile. "I'm getting to be a regular old poop, Gracie."

"Never," she said, sitting on the side of the bed, thinking how sad it was that his mind was still young and active, that his humor remained intact, while his body had completely betrayed him. Before the disease made its presence known, her brother had had a wonderful life, with close friends and a long-term, happy relationship with one of the sweetest men ever to walk the planet, who just happened to be a state trooper.

Jerry was entirely closeted on the job because he believed that his life would have been made hell by the men with whom he worked. A few of them had achieved near legendary status in the profoundly heightened degree of their homophobia. There'd been an incident on Halloween several years earlier when a young trooper had pulled over a car with a broken tail-light. When he'd seen the occupants up close, in full drag and makeup, he'd flown into a rage, hauling the driver out of the car and pounding his face to a bloody mess with his nightstick until the passenger pulled him off and dragged him back to the cruiser where he'd shackled him to the steering wheel with the trooper's own handcuffs, then used the cruiser's radio to call for backup. The guy he'd beaten senseless happened to be a deputy district attorney from Montpelier, and his friend was a Boston cop. The trooper was fired the next day and later convicted of aggravated battery. A sympathetic judge sentenced him to a year's house arrest, knowing he'd probably get murdered in the prison system, and a year's community service. The state ultimately agreed to what was rumored to be a huge out-of-court settlement with the victim, and picked up the tab for his initial hospitalization and several subsequent rounds of reconstructive surgery.

It was Jerry's unshakable conviction that the most violently homophobic guys were the ones who were terrified by their secret attraction to other men. He was probably right. The guy the young trooper had beaten so violently hadn't even been gay. The two men had been returning from the liquor store and were on their way to pick up their wives at a nearby motel before heading off to a Halloween party. If the mere sight of a guy in drag could make someone so crazy, it was, Jerry reasoned, plain good sense to be careful on the job.

As Gus had begun to deteriorate, he'd sent Jerry away. Amazingly, Jerry understood and backed off. But he still phoned regularly and dropped in at least once a week, with a book or some fresh-picked strawberries — a small offering of one sort or another. And Gus's involuntary smile at the sight of him confirmed what both Grace and Jerry had known all along: that the man was the love of Gus's life and sending him away was for Jerry's sake, not his own. Gus did it, hoping that Jerry would find someone healthy, someone who could move around under his own steam and didn't require big, strapping women to get him up and dressed. But it was six years later and Jerry hadn't found anyone else. Grace didn't think he was looking; she thought Jerry, too, had lost the great love of his life. And he was never going to give up on Gus.

"I've started emailing with a young woman," Grace said. "There's a horrible history. She was abducted on New Year's Eve when she was sixteen. I don't have all the details, but it sounds really bad. Now she's got a husband who insists on having a party every year on that night. Sounds like abuse to me."

Gus gazed at her for several moments, then said quietly, "Don't get involved, Gracie. It's a mistake."

"How can you say that?" she asked, instantly on the defensive. "More than half my life has been about *getting involved*."

"You don't know this woman," he said

reasonably. "She could be anyone."

"That's ridiculous. She's a young woman in trouble. I'm trying to help her, that's all."

"Don't be obtuse. It's very definitely about getting involved, and I think it's a mistake. You could get embroiled in something."

"Embroiled?" she repeated, getting up from the bed. "For God's sake, Gus! You're making me sound like some sort of idiot. I'm simply trying to help someone who's in trouble. It's what I've always done." She was so angry that she wanted to hit him.

"I just think it's a mistake," he said quietly. "I'll drop it. Could you give me one of my Cumadin?"

Knowing he wouldn't discuss the matter further, she found the prescription vial on the bedside table, got one of the pills and popped it into his mouth, then held the glass for him so he could sip some water through the straw.

"Thanks. How's the manuscript coming?" he asked.

"It isn't," she said curtly, then at once felt guilty. "I keep intending to do some work but wind up playing Solitaire or Tetris for hours instead."

"A little avoidance, huh?"

"A lot. Sleep well," she said, bending to

kiss his forehead. "See you in the morning."

"Thanks. You, too."

She turned off the light, pulled the door half-closed, and went to the kitchen where she stood gripping the rim of the counter as she looked around the room that had once been the warm hub of their lives, trying to get herself under control. Telling her not to get involved, as if she was some dimwit who couldn't recognize a cry for help when she heard it. But Gus was always giving her advice. Why, this time, did it so infuriate her? Could he possibly be right? No! She didn't think so.

She hated living in a state of fear, but couldn't find a way out. There'd be stretches of several hours when she'd be free of it — reading a good book, or watching a movie that completely held her attention — but once the book was put aside, or the movie credits began to roll, she'd feel it again: that sense of impending danger, of something horrible just waiting to happen.

But as bad as the days were, the nights were worse. Every awful thing that had ever happened in her life had taken place at night. Night was her enemy, her undoing. She couldn't sleep for more than an hour or two without taking meds of some kind, or a few drinks. Even then,

65

there was no genuine rest because of the night-mares, the endless re-enactment of some moment, or entire scenes, from those days and nights in the warehouse. The thick, repellent odor of burned coffee; the reek of her body's waste; the smell of him. *Knives and hammers and needles; rats, insects, darkness. Heavy metal rock music that played at such a volume that the walls and floors seemed to tremble. And, ceaselessly, drumming on the tin roof high above, the rain, the constant, pounding downpour. The endless, maddening rain.*

>four

Still rankled by Gus's warning the night before, Grace wondered if it was possible that this was a scam. She found it hard to believe. It would have to be one of the most elaborate ones ever conceived, she thought, as she re-read that morning's email from Stephanie. No one could fabricate things like this, Grace decided. The truth lay in the small details, the behavior of the people that Stephanie described. Still, Grace didn't even know where the woman lived. There were facts that needed clarifying.

In the meantime, there was Christmas to get through. On the twenty-fourth, Dolly and Lucia each received the customary check within a gift card for a week's pay. Both were so touchingly grateful that Grace wished she had more to give them.

As for the holiday itself, the family celebration had, for a long time, consisted of nothing more than a special dinner — this year it was a roasted chicken (none of them liked turkey) with an apple onion stuffing that Nicky loved so much that Grace always baked an extra panful wrapped in foil, along with mushroom gravy, mashed potatoes, and roasted winter vegetables — and a token exchange of gifts. Nicky gave Gus an exquisitely soft, near weightless cashmere cardigan which he stroked appreciatively; Grace received a Louis Vuitton wallet ("Yours is falling to pieces, Mom"). Nicky accepted her presents which, since the age of twelve, she'd insisted couldn't cost more than ten dollars, and thus represented a terrible shopping challenge for her mother who confessed, "I cheated a tiny bit this year," as she gave her daughter the card announcing a year's subscription to *Movieline* magazine. ("It's the *best!*" Nicky declared happily. "Thank you!") And from Gus, also via Grace, Nicky got the French editions of *Elle* and *Vogue*. ("Total heaven, Dad! Exactly perfect.")

After dinner she left to go see Migs, taking with her a large duffle bag crammed with presents. There was a copy of *Look Homeward Angel* and a volume of Anne Sexton's collected poems from Gus for Migs, and a gift certificate from Gus and Grace for her mother. "She needs a lot of stuff," Nicky said, trying to downplay her constant generosity to her childhood friend. Migs and her mother, who was a clerk at the courthouse, lived in a tiny, three-room apartment over a gift shop downtown on Main. Thanks to Gus, Migs was a full scholarship student at the college. And thanks to Nicky, she got to do and to have things her mother could never have afforded. "You really think Migs's mom will like the jacket?" she asked her mother before leaving.

"I think she'll have a meltdown over it, Nicks. It's gorgeous. Say hi and merry Christmas for us."

Subject:
Date: Wed, 27 Dec 2000 09:12:26 -0200
From: Stephanie Baine <baine_stephanie@spotmail.com>
To: Grace <gloring@homecable.com>

Dear Grace:

I hope you had a good Christmas. It was the usual horror story here. Billy gave himself a nice new set of knives, and just gave me money. We went out for dinner and he pulled some stunts in the restaurant, so I wound up not eating. Naturally my parents ignored it all. My mother told me to stop being such a drama queen and eat my dinner.

Thank you for saying it wasn't my fault. All I've heard for the last seventeen years is how stupid I was, how I should've fought him off, how I should have done this, done that. But the truth is, I couldn't do anything. He had a knife and I was terrified.

I know it's good advice, but I don't think I could phone up and talk to a total stranger. What if Billy found out? I'd be in even bigger trouble then. But if it's confidential, as you say, then maybe I'll give it a try. I'd like to talk to someone, it's just that I'm scared about doing it. Whoever I talk to might think the same way my parents and Billy do, and blame me for being so stupid.

We're going to a neighborhood party tonight. I'm definitely not in the mood. But my friend Sandy will be there. She's great and always makes me laugh. Now if I could just get rid of this headache, I'd be happy.

You may have gathered that I don't have the best marriage in the world. The truth is, Billy never passes up an opportunity to remind me of what happened. He's always leaving knives around, or calling me in because there's some show on TV about bugs, or rape, or missing girls. He loves tormenting me with the details. I think he thinks I actually liked what happened. But that's too sick.

Last night, after I wrote to you for the last time, I got into an argument with my Dad about politics. My Dad is almost Fascist he's so conservative, and I'm not. He even said to me and I'll quote, "You have the nerve to call yourself a Catholic." I am so surrounded by lunatics, it's not funny. I finally told him not to talk to me anymore because he has never learned to treat me with respect. He was pissed, but he did leave me alone. I was never good at standing up to him, but since I started writing to you I'm getting better.

My mom wanted to go shopping today but I told her that I'm just too tired and emotionally drained to spend the day at crowded stores. She's quite unhappy with me at the moment, but there's nothing I can do about it. When I told her that I didn't want to go out, and the reason why (dread of the party), she told me to cut the psychobabble. Then Billy chimed in, saying that he wished that she was staying longer, and she told him that she couldn't because I don't have any time for her and she gets bored. I'm so mad! I had to tell Billy off in a big way. He got right in my face this morning and screamed at me because I asked him to stay out of the kitchen while I cleaned. I got right back in his face and told him to never scream at me again. He skulked off, but the three of them are all in the other room together, sending barbs my way whenever they get the chance. It's an insane asylum. I'd love to be rid of all this turmoil.

Sorry to vent again. If I'm bothering you, just say so, and I'll back off.

Love, Steph

Subject: re
Date: Wed, 27 Dec 2000 10:42:14 -0500
From: Grace Loring <gloring@homecable.com>
To: Stephanie Baine <baine_stephanie@spotmail.com>

Dear Steph:

Your household does sound like a lunatic asylum. What's wrong with these people? Why are they always on your case? Fill me in, please. I'd like to know more about your parents, and about you. Do you work? If so, at what?

I've been giving it a lot of thought, and I think the only way to handle the New Year's party is to decide you're going to have a great time. Go out and buy yourself a fabulous outfit and some great shoes, even new makeup. Have your hair done, get a manicure. Keep telling yourself you're going to have a good time, and you will. Maybe you could get your friend Sandy to go shopping with you, since you enjoy her company and she's not always on your case.

Is Billy violent? That concerns me, because I don't want to give you advice that will set him off. Is it just verbal/psychological abuse, or does he get physical? And where do you live? I'm trying to get a more accurate picture, but it's difficult when I know very little about you.

I can understand your father being right-wing. That seems par for the course for men in the military. But what's up with your mother? It sounds as if her primary purpose in life seems to be upsetting you, messing with every part of your life, interfering, making excuses for your husband, demanding attention. Try very hard to ignore her. She acts as if you're the mother and ought to be looking after her; and if she can't get what she wants she throws tantrums. Seriously, I don't want to offend or upset you, but this is a very unwell woman.

I'll be waiting to hear from you.

Best, Grace

PS: Your call will be completely confidential, but you have got to call the crisis center. You need some support closer to home, and you need it right away. You'll get it, I promise, if you phone. Trust me on this. Just take the first step.

While making lunch, Grace thought about Stephanie's family. Her mother sounded certifiable, and her father came across as a typical military martinet, running his household as if it were a battalion under his command. Billy, though, remained pretty much of a mystery. Abusive, obviously older than Stephanie if he was soon to retire from the service, and obsessed with what had happened to his wife years ago. These three people seemed to be sadists who enjoyed tormenting the young woman. Clearly Stephanie had fallen into a pattern of victim behavior and had been putting up with all kinds of abuse for a long, long time — if she even recognized any of it as abuse. It was very hard to break the habit of assuming bad treatment was your due. There was always some way to assume the blame, because it just had to be your fault if the people who were supposed to love you treated you badly. So you'd spend hours on end analyzing every last thing you'd ever said or done, tracking backward to pinpoint the words or behavior that had made loved ones turn against you. A maddening, frustrating exercise that could never provide answers because, in retrospect, everything you'd said and done was subject to negative interpretation — if you were the one doing the interpreting. Other people wouldn't see any of it, of course. The interior, personal fallout from abuse was insidious.

With Gus's bib thrown over her arm, Grace carried the tray into her brother's room. It was such an old-fashioned setting, with its antique cubbyholed, lion's-footed desk, its gleaming mahogany highboy with the brass drawer pulls, the damask draperies framing the window, yet somehow essentially Gus. He valued the past, loved the solid beauty of well-crafted furniture, but also appreciated the technology of the present, especially television — the proof of that being the twenty-one-inch Sony that sat on a sturdy swivel base that Jerry had bolted to the wall facing Gus's bed.

Leaving the tray on the desk, she motioned her brother to sit forward while she grabbed some extra pillows and arranged them behind him. He always seemed to find the most awkward positions for himself, so that the bulk of his weight was heavily centered on the base of his spine; or he half-sat and half-lay on the bed with his head and shoulders at an angle that guaranteed he'd have neck pain. Along with everything else, he had osteoporosis and his body was slowly, visibly starting to twist to the right. Why couldn't he get into the habit of sitting up properly? Surely he couldn't be comfortable. But he'd stay for hours in these impossible positions, often dozing off while the radio played nonstop in the background, then, upon awakening, he'd groan and complain of neck and shoulder pain.

He was at times, she thought, like an outsized child: careless with his damaged body, seemingly unaware that he was adding to the damage by not making an effort to sit or lie down properly. The terms of his life were dictated by his body, but his revenge (or something) seemed to be in his relative disregard for its well-being.

Aware that he was eyeing her assessingly as she placed the Velcro-fastening bib around his neck, she reached for the tray and set it across his lap.

"Grilled cheese," he said happily. "My favorite."

"I know."

"What's up, Gracie?" he asked, working

to open the paper napkin from the tray. Something as simple as unfolding a napkin represented a challenge to fingers that were little more than contorted, strengthless appendages.

"Nothing's up."

"Oh, something's chewing away at you, all right," he said knowingly, pushing the top of the napkin into the neckline of the bib. "You've got that look."

"What look?" The sight of his hands made her stomach rise threateningly. His nails needed to be trimmed. She made a mental note to phone the woman who came once a month to cut his finger- and toe-nails. At the beginning, Grace had kept his fingernails filed. But as the muscles disappeared from his body and the strength left his hands, she had to stop. She found the boneless-seeming, rubbery feel of his fingers creepy. The same held true of his arms and legs. For the first couple of years, she'd applied moisturizer to his skin, to keep it supple. But the long-term effects of the drugs, particularly the Prednisone, made it far too easy for his skin to tear, and he always had bruises, just-healing gashes, great purple patches of blood that had collected just beneath the surface. When confronted with the unavoidable evidence of more wounds, she'd find herself unfairly, even irrationally, blaming him for his condition, so she left it to Dolly who, with infinite tenderness, cautiously applied Moisturel to Gus's bath-warmed body three mornings a week.

"The semi-angry look of preoccupation," he said calmly, "of wishing you were somewhere else, doing something less menial."

At once she felt guilty; tears began collecting in the corners of her eyes. "I'm sorry, Gus," she said, dropping into the graceful Queen Anne chair next to his bed. "It's just that I can't seem to have a good run at anything because I keep having to stop . . . or anticipating that I'll have to stop, which amounts to the same thing."

"That simply isn't the case," he said reasonably. "We've been over this at least a hundred times. There's Meals On Wheels. I can handle opening a paper bag and unwrapping a sandwich, and Lucia is more than able to put a foil container into the oven for twenty minutes, or however long those things take."

"Right. Mystery meat on sandpaper for lunch, with butter and mayo on the side in cunning little unopenable packets, followed by a swell dinner of imitation turkey with faux gravy and frozen peas. Or mac and cheese with not one but two sides of wilted broccoli. I don't think so."

He smiled, his hand poised to pick up half the cooling grilled cheese sandwich. "That's why they pay you the big bucks, kiddo. Such a way with words. You make it all sound positively delectable." He managed to pick up the sandwich half, saying, "Just remember it's about choices, Gracie. Any time you need a break, take one. But don't make me the focus of your anger and discontent. Okay? I may be crippled, but I'm not stupid. It doesn't make me a happy little camper to know you're stomping around here with a big grudge and a matching attitude."

Ashamed, she said, "You're the least stupid person I've ever known. I really am sorry. The truth is, I'm probably a Tetris junkie and need to join a twelve-step program." She stood up, kissed the top of his head, said, "Eat. I'll be back shortly," and went to the kitchen. She stood looking out the wide multi-paned back window at the snow-covered garden, her entire body hot with shame. "Pull yourself together," she whispered, her breath fogging the window. "This isn't fair to him. Okay. Okay," she whispered. "Have your coffee and your sandwich and get it into one piece, you miserable wretch."

Why was she like this? she wondered, as she ate without tasting the food. When had she become so angry about something she'd gladly volunteered to do at the outset? Maybe, she silently answered herself, when five or six years after the fact, reality kicked in and you realized it wasn't temporary. Maybe you'd thought of it the way most young people think of old age: as if it's a virus you're not going to catch. Dumb, really dumb.

"You know what?" Nicky said that evening after dinner while they were loading the dishwasher.

"What?" Grace asked automatically.

"I think you need to go see Vinnie."

"Oh, my God!" Grace turned to look at her daughter, saw Nicky's eyebrows waggle meaningfully, and broke out laughing.

"Go ahead and laugh, but it's time."

"I can't believe my own daughter is standing here telling me I need to go get laid!"

"It would never occur to Dad, but it sure has occurred to me. You've got to take the edge off, Mom. You're like this alarm clock that's set to go off."

"More like a detonator. Anyway, for all I know he's not even around." Grace put another plate into the machine. "He's probably still in the city."

"Oh, he's around," Nicky said.

"How would you know that?"

"As it happens, I passed his car on Route 9 this afternoon on my way home from Putney."

Grace looked again at her daughter. Vinnie's car was unmistakable: a mint-condition '55 Thunderbird. "Really?" Suddenly, Grace felt lighter.

"He was making the turn into Maple Valley," Nicky went on, "and it didn't look as if he was just arriving. The car was clean, which means he's been here for a while."

"He hasn't phoned."

"Oh, pul-ease! Have you phoned *him?* Ten bucks says you haven't. You're so — *fifties!*"

"That is correct. I am of a generation that waits for men to call us. We do not call them."

"Get over yourself and phone him. Go hang out and see what he's been working on lately. You guys always have fun. You *love* Vinnie, for heaven's sake."

"We'll see," Grace said with feigned indifference.

"Such a mother thing to say."

"True." Grace poured detergent into the dispenser wells, then closed the dishwasher door. "It's what I am, after all."

"Poor Gracie," Nicky crooned, putting the

dish towel on its hook, "unappreciated mother and caregiver. Go see Vinnie *Il Magnifico* and let him show you his etchings. You know you're crazy about him, and he's not exactly casual about you. Go pose nude again for him. You know you got off on it." Laughing gleefully, she raced out of the kitchen before Grace could offer a comeback.

With a shake of her head, smiling, Grace finished tidying the kitchen. She could hear Lucia saying good-night to Gus. Another day gone. Heading up the stairs, Grace wondered if there'd be an email from Stephanie waiting.

Subject:
Date: Thurs, 28 Dec 2000 21:18:22 -0100
From: Stephanie Baine <baine_stephanie@spotmail.com>
To: Grace <gloring@homecable.com>

Dear Grace:

I do trust you. After I got your email this morning I did it. I made the call. My parents were out shopping and I had a couple of free hours, so I did it. The woman I talked to was very nice. I guess I thought it would be like talking to a shrink, that she'd just listen without making any comments. But she was friendly and very sympathetic and said a lot of the same things you've said. It was really hard, but I told her some of what happened when I was sixteen, and then I told her about my parents and Billy and how they all basically blame me for the whole thing. My phone pal (I don't know what else to call her) thinks the three of them are lunatics, just like you do. She was very easy to talk to but by the time I hung up I had a monster headache and had to go lie down for a little while. Now I'm pretty shaky and even more scared than I was before. Sorry.

I'm so stupid. I thought I'd told you we live in Arlington, VA. We're near DC so Billy can commute to work. My parents are from N. Carolina, which is where I was born. After college I did social work, but Billy made me quit. I know that makes me sound like a huge loser, but it was easier not to fight any more over it. My dad's retired and my mom has never worked. No way my dad would've let her, even if she'd wanted to. You may have noticed that the men in this family are very controlling. I'm sick to death of it, and of them.

I guess Billy does get kind of physical, nothing major. Now that I think about it, he does. He's "accidentally" bashed me in the head with one of the cabinet doors, or bumped into me so I crashed into a piece of furniture, or fell down some stairs. Stuff like that happens pretty often and he always smiles and says, sorry, it was an accident. Mostly it's verbal. And with my parents here and all three of them on my case, it's no wonder I've got nonstop headaches. I have been being lectured for the last hour on all of the usual topics. I finally told them that I had had enough, that I wanted to have a calm night, and that if they weren't going to let me have one then I was leaving. That did the trick. They went to bed. I hope you're still up, because they have me in such a state that I'm broken out in hives. They actually told me that they thought I was nuts and should see a shrink. I got the lecture about how they've never seen anyone get so upset over such a fun holiday, etc. Then they honed in on me and delivered the zinger: they expected me to be up and happy at midnight, and to sing Auld Lang Syne. I just started laughing, I couldn't help it. I wish I could videotape all this and send it to you. Talk about fodder for a novel.

I loved your ideas and I'm going to go shopping tomorrow and get my hair done and have a manicure. Sandy's going to go with me. It'll be fun. We always have a great time.

Thanks so much for your advice and for caring. I already feel better, stronger.

Love, Steph

Subject: re
Date: Thurs, 28 Dec 2000 22:02:13 -0500
From: Grace Loring <gloring@homecable.com>
To: Stephanie Baine <baine_stephanie@spotmail.com>

Dear Steph:

Good for you! I'm so proud of you for taking the first step. Now you'll have some support close to home. And I'm sure your new phone pal told you that you can call any time. Right?

Actually, as crazy as your parents are, you really could benefit from some time with a shrink. You need to be able to talk about the things that have happened to you, get the horror out of your system and start letting some fresh air into your brain.

About your job, how and why did Billy make you quit? You've got to be bored, staying home alone all day — when your parents aren't around. By the way, those two would give anyone migraines and/or hives, from the sound of it. One of these days you're going to have to put these people at a distance. As long as they're around telling you how stupid and inadequate you are, you're never going to able to start rebuilding your self-esteem.

Let me know how your day goes with Sandy. I'll enjoy the outing vicariously. If I want to do any serious shopping, I either have to go to Boston or make a trip down to Manhattan (which is an overnight venture, because I hate driving at night, so I usually stay at my agent's apartment.)

Anyway, congratulations on making the call. Sometimes, doing the right thing is terribly hard. But in the end, you'll be glad you did it.

Here's a hug,

Grace.

"I understand you're in the vicinity, and I was wondering why I haven't heard from you."

"*Gracie!* I was just thinking about you." She could hear the pleasure in Vinnie's voice.

"Thinking, but not phoning."

"Oh, now, you know I hate to be presumptuous."

"What's presumptuous about picking up the phone to say hello?"

"What time is it?"

"Coming up for ten-thirty."

"Still early. I could drive in, be there inside half an hour."

"Not tonight," she said with less edge to her tone.

"Okay. Tomorrow. I'll come pick you up

before Gus's nap time, say three-thirty. That'll give me a chance to have a visit with him, then you and I will come back here. I'll make my famous pasta, ply you with a nice robust burgundy, and then jump your delectable little bones."

She laughed loudly.

"Which part was funny?" he asked.

"All of it."

"Oh! Good. So, then, when we've recovered from our strenuous post-dinner activities, I'll drive you home — unless you're interested in posing. Are we on?"

"I don't like to make it too easy for you."

"R-i-g-h-t," he drawled. "I might go back to the locker room and spread salacious rumors about you. Then the day after tomorrow the entire high school will be talking about how easy Gracie is, how she puts out for the boys."

Again, she laughed loudly. She hoped Gus couldn't hear and that Nicky had her headphones on, because they both knew there was only one person who could elicit this kind of laughter from her. Her face was flushed and she felt better than she had in ages. "You would, too."

"I've always been the kind to carry tales of my conquests back to the troops. It keeps their morale high."

"I'm hanging up now. I'll see you to-morrow."

"Bet your sweet cheeks you will! I'm going to start finding errant tube socks and boxers right now, so the place is immaculate — just for you."

She laughed once more and put the receiver down as Nicky appeared in the doorway, grinning.

"So, when're you getting together?"

"Tomorrow. Were you listening?"

"Are you kidding? The entire *neighborhood* could hear you laughing. Get serious!"

"You're very smart," Grace said, admiring her daughter. Nicky's beauty was both a perpetual surprise and a reward. "And so nice to look at."

"Whatever. Okay. I'm glad you guys are getting together. I'll hang here tomorrow, maybe have Migs over. We'll make dinner."

"Which means I'll have to renovate the kitchen."

Nicky made a face. "You're such an ingrate," she said, putting her hands on either side of her mother's waist and leaning in to kiss her. " 'Night, Mom."

" 'Night, baby girl. I love you."

"I know. You, too."

After a few seconds, Grace turned back to

the screen to see that there was a new message in the inbox.

Subject:
Date: Thurs, 28 Dec 2000 22:20:22 -0200
From: Stephanie Baine <baine_stephanie@spotmail.com>
To: Grace <gloring@homecable.com>

Dear Grace:

You're going to lose so much respect for me when you hear this story. Anyway, Billy had been bugging me to quit for a while, and I didn't want to. I had made some great friends, loved my job, etc. Plus, I had my own money which was important to me. Anyway, they moved our office to a poorer part of town so that the clients could get to us easier. Billy had a fit, warned me I was asking for trouble. One girl in our office did get threatened, but that was all. This guy showed up in the lobby with a gun and threatened to shoot her if she didn't expedite his case. We had security guards, they handled it, and nothing ever came of it. I told Billy about this, and he said I had to quit. I said no. One night, I was coming out of work, and he had hidden in the back seat of my car. He put a knife to my throat and asked me did I want to be a crime victim all over again. It was dark, he disguised his voice, and for a minute, I didn't know it was him. Then I heard the laugh and knew. He raped me in the back seat of the car in the parking lot of my office. He said this was what I was asking for, and worse. I quit the next day, terrified. I know how awful and weak that sounds, but I was still so frightened then of everything. I'm a lot stronger now, but I still have way more fear than I should.

I've never told anyone about this. I hope you're not too disgusted with me.

Thank you for the hug. I needed that.

Love, Steph.

Subject: re
Date: Fri, 29 Dec 2000 09:12:13 -0500
From: Grace Loring

<gloring@homecable.com>
To: Stephanie Baine
<baine_stephanie@spotmail.com>

Dear Steph:

I now have confirmation (as if I needed it) that you're married to a very sick fellow. The sooner you get away from this man the better. It's hard to feel calm and functional when you're trapped in a house with someone you fear and dislike; someone who's capable of doing what he did to you in that car, to get his way. Trust me. I've been there. You don't know whether to kill him or yourself. The minute he's gone, the relief you feel will be overwhelming.

As for your new phone pal, most women are going to be sympathetic to you because so many have been in your position. Accept her help and don't worry about being judged. Some experiences are too big just to go away altogether; they're always there in a corner of your brain and sometimes a visual, a smell, anything, will trigger and revive them. But they can be put into per-spective and relegated to the past, where they belong. Could you please stop beating yourself up for being human — in spite of your hor-rible parents and your horrible hus-band. It's a bit of a miracle that you're as whole as you are. Give yourself some credit for surviving — both the experience at sixteen and this marriage. By the way, how long have you been married to Billy?

Your mother sounds like the Prince of Darkness in a skirt — determined, at all costs, to mess with you. Just re-member that you have rights and you can exercise them. If you want and need to, throw the whole gang of them out. You're stronger than you realize, and you're going to make it out the far end just fine.

Let me know how things go.

Another hug, Grace

five

Alvin Steinberg was fondly and misleadingly known as Vinnie (people invariably expected him to be a slickly dressed, gold-chain-bedecked Italian) to almost everyone who'd ever met him — with the notable exception of his ex-wife, who referred to him in scathing tones as *That Man*. Six-foot-three and perennially ten to twenty pounds overweight, he had a mass of curly red hair, a great brush of a mustache, pinchable Santa Claus cheeks, blue eyes electric with intelligence and humor, and huge, clumsy-looking hands that were responsible for arguably the finest pen-and-ink illustrations done anywhere in the past thirty years. His work appeared in magazines that ran the gamut from cartoons in *The New Yorker* to the cover of *Rolling Stone*. Every gallery show he'd had for more than twenty years was a sellout before the doors opened, and some of the wealthiest people in the world had a Steinberg piece in their collections.

He could, with only a few lines, create an image that would make you laugh aloud in delighted surprise. He could also, through intricate cross-hatching and lines fine as silk thread, make an image of such detailed depth and shading that the viewer was drawn to study the piece in something akin to wonderment. He could dash off a caricature, or produce a portrait, both capturing the essence of the subject. His illustrations for children's books guaranteed they'd achieve best-seller status. The demand for his work was such that he regularly, regretfully, had to refuse commissions.

A dozen years earlier, as a favor to Gus, his former roommate at Yale, Vinnie had agreed to spend a semester as resident artist at the college. The hefty, gregarious man had been such a hit with students and staff that after his stint, any time enrollment was slipping the headmaster put in a call and Vinnie would come up to spend another semester teaching at the small college.

After his first stay, finding Vermont appealingly "other" from the Manhattan he'd known all his life, he bought a three-acre property with a dilapidated barn in Maple Valley, and often spent a month or two there, toiling on his never-ending renovation of the barn. He and Grace had met seven years earlier when she, too, had been enlisted for a term at the college — as resident writer.

Grace loved the man the first time she'd heard him laugh, which happened about twenty minutes after they were introduced at a faculty get-together the afternoon of the first semester. One of the older professors, (always fondly introduced by Gus as "The crusty yet benign Arlen Jasper The Fourth") told the following joke:

A man boards an airplane and takes his seat. As he settles in, he glances up and sees a very beautiful woman heading straight toward him. Lo and behold, she takes the seat beside his.

Eager to strike up a conversation, he blurts out, "Business trip or vacation?"

She turns, smiles and says, "Business. I'm going to the annual Nymphomaniac Convention in Chicago." He swallows hard. Here is the most gorgeous woman he has ever seen, sitting next to him, and she's going to a meeting of nymphomaniacs!

Struggling to maintain his composure, he calmly asks, "What's your business role at this convention?"

"Lecturer," she says. "I use my experience to debunk some of the popular myths about sexuality."

"Really?" he says. "What myths are those?"

"Well," she explains, "one popular myth is that African-American men are the most well-endowed, when, in fact, it's the Native American Indian who is. Another popular myth is that French men are the best lovers, when actually Jewish men are. However, we have found that the best lover in all categories is the Southern Redneck." Suddenly, the woman becomes a little uncomfortable and blushes. "I'm sorry," she says. "I shouldn't be discussing this with you. I don't even know your name!"

"Tonto!" the man exclaims. "Tonto Goldstein! But my friends call me Bubba!"

A veritable gusher of laughter erupted from Vinnie's mouth. Tears streamed down his round cheeks and he bent almost double, his big body all but convulsing. Everyone automatically laughed harder in reaction to him. Grace did, too. It was a silly sexist joke, yet she found it hilarious. What had captivated her in the aftermath of its telling was the wonderful purity of Alvin Steinberg's response. He wasn't afraid to laugh, and he'd surrendered himself utterly to it. Watching him mop his eyes with a crumpled hankie, she'd thought he was the most overtly generous human being she'd ever encountered. And she just had to find out how someone got to be middle-aged and still managed to keep their best qualities intact. Vinnie should, by rights, have been smug about his accomplishments and mean-spirited in the way that hugely successful people so often tended to be. Yet he wasn't. He had a child's gift of unselfconsciousness in his appreciation of humor, of people, of ideas, of conversation. He was a bona fide enthusiast, the first she'd met, and she'd hovered close by his side, studying him appreciatively as he chatted jovially with some of the professors, until at last he turned to her, saying, "So, where should we eat? You in the mood for dreck-to-go or hellishly chic?"

"Hmmn. Let's compromise and do Chinese."

"I knew I was going to be crazy about you. Come on. Make nice to all the goyish boys and girls and we'll go eat. I'm fainting from hunger here."

"I'm a goyish girl," she said. "And why are you talking like an immigrant all of a sudden?"

"I'm the child of immigrants. You think it doesn't rub off? And listen here to me, cupcake. Gus is goyish, no two ways about it. He's such a wasp you could get a stiff neck just looking at the guy. Not that I don't love him, because I do — dearly. He's a *mensch*. But you. You're Jewish. What? Nobody ever said that to you before?" he asked, taking her hand in his as they headed to the parking area.

"As a matter of fact, no."

"A shiksa you're not," he stated. "Those big haunted eyes, the thick curly dark hair, the stereophonic laugh. Jewish! I know these things."

"You could be wrong."

"Never! Let me give you a little lesson, sweetcheeks. Oy, I could bite you. You know that? Okay. So, Vermont is goyish. Skiing and farting around in the snow is goyish. This college is goyish. Arlen Jasper One Vee is beyond goyish, a category all his own. You, you're so smart you give off sparks. Also funny and argumentative. Therefore, you are *Jewish*. So what'll we eat? You like scallion pancakes? I love those. And lemon chicken. We'll go in my car. I'll bring you back for yours later."

"I'll follow you," she'd said. "I don't like driving at night. I don't see well in the dark."

"Ah! Okay. That's fine." He had chucked her under the chin with one pudgy hand and said, "Such a cutie. Who knew Gus's sister would be a Jewish cutie?"

"Evidently no one."

"Hah!" he bellowed, his red curls bouncing. "Just for me, you've been waiting."

"Hah!" she echoed. "Don't hold your breath!"

"See!" he said happily, waving a finger in front of her nose. "Jewish!"

Captivated by his energy and bounding enthusiasm, she went home with him after dinner that evening. He was the first man she'd made love with since escaping from Brownie who didn't leave her feeling somewhat suicidal for having been stupid enough to be gulled by her hormones into a dismal sexual encounter. This was different. Warm against the broad wall of his chest, cradled by the curve of his arm, she listened to him put words, in lieu of inked lines, into a lengthy description of her endless assets. "Next time, you'll pose for me," he told her. "I'll get every detail down on paper. It'll be the best work of my life." He won her trust with his patience, his exclamations of delight — in everything about her — and his absolute lack of expectations.

Later, driving back into town at near two A.M., her hands sweaty on the steering wheel as she concentrated on the winding two-lane, unlit highway, she couldn't stop smiling. She'd found someone she just might be able to love.

Vinnie arrived at the house promptly at three-thirty the next afternoon.

101

"Whoof!" he huffed, wrapping Grace in a bear hug and lifting her clear off the floor. "Hello, hello, hello! You couldn't have called me sooner, cupcake?" he asked, setting her down and gazing into her eyes.

"Your fingers are broken?" she countered.

"Are yours? What's with you, you couldn't pick up the phone? Never mind. Where's your crazy brother?"

"In the usual place. Go on. He's been waiting for you."

"Where's the little shiksa?" he asked, looking up the stairs.

"Not home yet. And why is Nicky a shiksa, but I'm not?"

"The father," he said patiently. "The goyish father. These things show. She's got princess habits, but the style is Preppy Handbook."

"Get in there and see Gus." She gave the man a push. "We'll discuss this later. I'm just going to check my email."

"Computers, feh."

"They're only 'feh' because you don't have one."

"Shows what you know."

"You got one finally?"

"This we'll also discuss later." He started down the hall, bellowing, "Gussy, I'm here, *tsatskeleh!* Have you missed me?"

Dear Grace:

Sandy and I had a great day. We shopped in the morning, and I got a cute black dress and new black heels. We had lunch and then I got a haircut and we both got manicures. I haven't had one in forever, so it was fun. Then I came home and started to feel a little weird, which is why I'm writing to you instead of doing what I should be doing. I'm trying to do the things that you told me to, like concentrating on how much fun this party is going to be, but I'm still having trouble. I had such terrible nightmares last night, and I feel so out of it. I'm sure part of it is that I'm overtired, but I'm also having those panicky feelings again.

I've been going over all the stunts Billy has pulled over the years. I have a hard time standing aside and seeing how crazy he is, because before Billy entered the picture, I had both of my parents pulling the same shit. My Mom actually blamed me for traumatizing the first jerk that dumped me over what happened. She asked me how did I expect him to handle the news that I had been hiding what happened to me the whole time that we were dating, he was just a kid, and not able to handle such upsetting news. I reminded her that we were the same age, and I was the one who had done all of the suffering, not him. That's when I got the eye rolling and the speech about how I had no mercy for anyone but myself. My mother is just so out there as far as Billy is concerned. If I have to hear one more time how lucky I am he doesn't beat me and gives me all his money, I'm going to scream. I wonder what she'd do if I told her no he doesn't beat me, but he has raped me, and more than once in the four years we've been married. Probably blame me, as usual. One reason that I think that my mother and Billy are so enthralled with each other is that they both hate women. She's always talking about how rotten women are, can't trust them, etc. I'm sorry to be rambling and dredging up ancient history. I'm in bad shape. I'm scared, sad, any negative emotion there is. I'll be so happy when this is all over and Billy is gone. He and my parents can have each other!

Up until the time that I was attacked, my parents adored me, trotted me out, a la Jon Benet. They would have people over for dinner and try to make me dance or play the piano, which I always refused to do. After the attack, they were done with me. I can't imagine what was going through their heads, because I could never feel that way about kids if I had them. I'm trying hard to stay sane, but every last thing that this trio has done is coming back to haunt me, and there's lots of material there, trust me. I just wish I knew why, what it is about me that makes these people behave this way. Thank God I have you to listen to all of my nonsense. I'm in one of those moods where I want to go to sleep and not wake up.

Sorry for all the whining. After the first of the year I'm going to get in touch with a lawyer and start the machinery going to get a divorce. You've made me face the fact that I don't have a real marriage here. I don't know what it is, but I do know it's sick.

Thanks for listening and for giving advice and hugs. I'm so grateful.

Love, Steph

At the barn, several hours later, Vinnie asked, "What's up, Gracie?"

"Nothing's up."

"Don't kid a kidder. Spill."

"I've been emailing back and forth with this young woman in Virginia, trying to give her some feedback and encouragement."

"Battered?"

"Abducted and raped at sixteen. Her parents said it was her own fault; she didn't try hard enough to get away. She's married to a guy who didn't want her to work, so to drive his point home, he hid in the back of her car and when she came out of work and got into the car, he raped her."

"Nice guy."

"A prince. I'm urging her to bail out, and fast."

"Good call."

"Gus thinks I shouldn't get involved. For some reason, the fact that he thinks it pisses me off."

"Oh, you're just pissed off in general."

She leaned on her elbow to look at him. "Why do you say that?"

"Please," Vinnie said quietly, with a smile. "I've seen you, what, half a dozen times this year? Which for starters is a whole lot less than usual. And for seconds, every time I have seen you, you've been quietly seething. I think taking care of Gus is turning you into a mental case. You need a break."

"How do you suggest I might manage that?"

"Hey! Don't start a fight. This is me." He stabbed a forefinger at his chest. "I don't do fights. It's what drove *That Woman*" — his smile widened — "so crazy. She *loved* fights, lived for them; they validated her in some cockamamie way. Who knows? She picked the wrong fella, that's for sure. Just talk to me here. Make nice." His big hand reached out to stroke her hair with typically gentle appreciation. "What's to stop you from coming back to the city for a week or two with me? Have long lunches with your shiksa girlfriends from college, see your agent, get one of those two hundred dollar haircuts, buy some clothes, sleep with Uncle Vinnie every night."

She had to smile back at him. "Uncle Vinnie. That's adorable. So, tell me. How do you propose I pay for the lunches and the haircut, the clothes?"

"You've got money."

"It's going fast, Vin. Do you have any idea what it costs just for Dolly and Lucia? Then there's the meds, the doctor visits, the this, that and the other. Our food bills are astronomical. The cost of heating that house has gone sky-high, almost triple what it was two years ago. Then —"

"Okay," he cut her off. "All this I know. And last year it wasn't an issue. Why all of a sudden is it an issue this year?"

She lay back and gazed up into the dark depths of the raftered ceiling high above. "Gus doesn't have a whole lot of money left, aside from his pension. And he's frightened of spending what he has and winding up penniless. I've been paying more and more of the bills, but my income's slowed down because I haven't managed to finish a new book. I'm starting to feel tapped-out and trapped, and that makes me angry. The fact that he doesn't fight the disease makes me angry. His posture makes me angry. That he sleeps in his clothes if Lucia doesn't come makes me angry. *Everything* makes me angry. I'm manufacturing it like some hot new product. I know it's wrong, that I don't have the right. But I can't get control of it. I love my brother, Vin. I *adore* him. But he's *become* rheumatoid arthritis. It's that stupid line. You know? If you look up the term in the dictionary, you'd find a picture of Gus."

"There are fighters and fighters. My ex, may she rot in hell, is the confrontational type; one of the ones whose adrenal gland thrives on dissension. Then there's the type who take adversity and stand it on its head. I don't get along with the first type. I'm okay with the second type. And whatever else he might be, Gussele isn't a complainer. That has to count for something."

"It counts for a lot."

"So, okay. Take a break. Never mind the lunches. And I'll cut your hair. I'm good with scissors."

She laughed and flipped over to lean on his wide, smooth chest. "Why didn't you call me?"

"Because the last five times you've been all tight and angry, and I don't like you that way. Not that I don't like seeing you, because I do and you know it. I could look at you night and day without stopping, for maybe an entire week. Then, of course, I'd fall on my face and be hospitalized. But I don't like seeing you with your shoulders all hunched and your face like a prune. If you let me, you know, I could help you fix the situation."

"It's not up to you to fix anything."

"As if that matters. I *want* to, and because you won't let me, *I* get all hunched and prune-faced. And what good does that do anybody? We wind up with two *mieskeits* shlumping around. Which is very attractive."

"God, you're going immigrant again!"

"Hey! Sometimes it works."

"It always works."

"So come back to the city with me for a couple of weeks. I'll drive."

"When are you going back?"

"I was thinking the end of next week."

"Let me think about it. Okay?"

"Listen, sweetcheeks. Nicky can handle things for a week or two. You might have to buy new appliances and have the kitchen linoleum replaced, but otherwise she'd probably love a chance to prove she's up to it. Gus has the helpers. They'll all manage without you. Take a break! Do it for yourself. Do it for me. It's been a long time since you came to the city."

"Almost a year. I will think about it." She looked over at the clock. "I have to go home."

"For why?"

"I just do, Vin. Give the shtick a rest and take me home, please."

"What is it now, six years, seven? You know how many times you've spent the night here? Never, that's how many. The world would come to an end if you rolled over, tucked your little hands under your cheek, the way you do — so cute — and went to sleep? People know where you are. What's so important that you can't stay?"

"If I knew the answer to that, I'd stay. I don't *know* why."

"You don't trust me?"

"I trust you absolutely. You're the only man I'll ever trust for the rest of my life. It's not about that."

"It's about something."

"Sure, it is. But the psychoanalysis will have to wait, Vin. I need to go home."

With a big sigh, he said, "So fine. We'll get all dressed up again and I'll take you home."

"It's not that I don't want to stay," she said, thinking about how cold it was outside. "I do. But there's something significant . . . I just have to go."

"But you'll come back to the city with me?"

"I'll *think* about it."

"We could go dancing with Miles and Leigh. That was fun."

"Better than fun. I do want to. Let me sort things out."

"So we're halfway to a yes," he said, sitting up and reaching for his robe, his eyes on her.

"At least."

"I'll phone every day and nag."

"Oh boy! The famous Jewish whine."

"Of a splendid vintage."

"Home, I'm going."

"Home, you are going. Right after we talk about Sunday night."

"What's Sunday night?"

"You are so *farklempt*. It's New Year's Eve. I told Gus I'd organize the booze. Jerry's coming, a few people from the college."

"How few?"

"Six, eight." He shrugged.

"When was this arranged?"

"A week or so ago, when we talked."

"Nice of everybody to let me know."

"I'm letting you know now. So put on that gray silk dress with the neckline down to there, do a little something with the hair, and we'll have fun."

"Gus *agreed* to this?"

"Matter of fact, it was his idea."

"He's so sweet," she said softly. "How can I be so angry with someone so sweet?"

"Want to know what I think, *maideleh?* I think you're angry with you. Gus is just something externalized you focus on. Soon as you figure out what it is about yourself that makes you so mad, it'll go away and you'll be fine. So you'll wear the gray dress?"

She wiped her face with the back of her hand and said, "Yeah. Just for you. Now, home. Okay?"

He lifted her chin, gave her a kiss, then said, "Home. Okay."

. . . He's been tormenting me for the last twenty minutes or so. I've not responded, but he hasn't let up. I finally left and told him to go to hell. I'm so tired of this shit. He's getting desperate now that I'm not responding to his taunts. If he ever goes to sleep, I'll be back. He's leaning over me trying to see what I'm doing. What a creep! Wish me luck, and I'll talk to you soon. Damn, I didn't need this tonight. I really hate him.

I have to write this email while I'm still able. If I wait too long, I won't do it. He's not here, so I can tell you the unbelievable stunt that Billy pulled last night. I decided to sleep on the sofa and he tried to pull a fast one on me. Before I even knew what was happening, he had me on the floor, said he was going to cheer me up. I told him to get off me, but he kept telling me that he knew I wanted him and was just out of practice, his words. To make a long horrible story short, he got that kick that he so richly deserved! Of course, this is all my fault, according to him I'm emotionally disturbed and he was just playing around, but I think that all men are rapists. He almost had me believing him. I told him that if this ever happened again that I would scream and call 911. That shook him up but good. I don't know if he really would have hurt me or if he honestly thought that he was just fooling around. He's stupid enough to believe that. Nevertheless, I was hysterical after I finally got rid of him. He's been on his best behavior today. I don't know what's next, I'm starting to be afraid to even think about it. This is so humiliating, but I had to tell someone, I'm still so shaken up.

He apologized for his behavior last night, one of his typical apologies complete with razor attached! He told me that I was driving him crazy because he feels like he has no control over me anymore. Can you believe this guy!?? And then he tells me that he'll never touch me again, he knew that I was frigid when he married me and he'll have to live with it. And for the clincher, he says, Are you sure that you're not having an affair online? What a total fool! I'm no longer afraid of him. He's not dangerous, just incredibly stupid.

When darkness fell, she tended to get a little crazy. Her fears assumed enormous proportions, and there were evenings when she was so frightened that she couldn't eat. She'd try, but the food would immediately come back up. The sleeplessness and lack of nourishment would give her blinding headaches that even prescription drugs couldn't touch. She just had to wait out the pain, huddled on the sofa, wrapped in blankets — even at the height of summer — in the dimly lit living room. The curtains drawn, every door and window locked; there were motion sensors that flooded the property with light when movement was detected. It didn't deter the raccoons, who almost nightly activated the lights. She'd peek out through a slit in the curtains, watching as they paused on their way across the back garden, as if affronted by the sudden illumination. She'd laugh softly at the sight of them, surprised each time to discover that she was still capable of laughter, of being amused. The intrepid family of four would turn toward the house as if fully aware of her, as if affronted by her, as well as by the lights. Then they'd lumber out of sight. God, but she admired those raccoons — their surly independence and determination.

She hated living this way, hated the chronic fear that was, she thought, like scoliosis in the way that it bent her spine and curtailed her forward momentum. She had to make it end, and there were ways to do that. But even in her contemplation of some small freedom, her fear had the upper hand and kept her captive. She was afraid of almost everything, even the steps she'd have to take to escape.

six

Subject: re
Date: Sat, 30 Dec 2000 07:14 -0200
From: Grace Loring
<gloring@homecable.com>
To: Stephanie Baine
<baine_stephanie@spotmail.com>

Dear Steph:

From the sound of it, your parents have devalued you totally and made you believe you're substandard in every way. And because they're your parents you've accepted their judgment of you as stupid and worthless. By the same token, you've put up with Billy for four years because your parents told you to. And because of the shame factor, feeling that you had nowhere to run, you've stayed. You have to understand that you've been turned into a shame factory. Your parents started it, and Billy has carried it on with their approval. So to recover from this, you've got to stop taking responsibility for the behavior of this hateful trio. That means you don't get ashamed and you don't go into self-blame mode. You've got to try to get some indignation working for you; it'll move the fear aside and make you see things more clearly. Obviously, something just wouldn't let you keep on anymore, so you reached out (to use NYPD bogus cop-talk) for help. And you will get it.

You need to talk every day with your phone pal about the things that've happened to you. Until you air it all, every time you think back, you'll relive those experiences. Until you get the horrors (and shame) out of your head, you're going to keep on devaluing yourself because the pattern is so well established. None of this happens overnight, but it does get better.

Billy obviously gets off on putting you down, hurting you. It's a form of power. And anything someone else does that makes another person feel less than she is, is just wrong.

Given that he knows what you've been through and that he seems determined to re-enact it repeatedly makes him a nasty fucker. Sorry, but it does. You really need to get away from these people. Once this party is out of the way and your parents have gone home, you can set the wheels in motion.

So, Steph, take it easy tomorrow if you can. Lock yourself into the bathroom and take a nice, long bath. Do your best makeup, get dressed, have a drink, and enjoy yourself in spite of everything. You deserve to have some fun. And your friend Sandy's going to be there, too. Right? Stay well away from your parents; stick close to the people you like, and you're going to get through this without incident.

We're having a small gathering here tomorrow, a few friends in for dinner. But I'll be thinking of you.

Hugs, Grace.

She hit the "Send" button and watched

her email disappear from the screen. Then, without really knowing why, she created a new folder, named it StephMail, and dragged all the emails she'd received from Stephanie into it. That done, she sat back, comparing the two angers she felt. One was general and had to do with Gus and her feeling of entrapment; the other was specific and concerned this young woman and her frightful trio of relatives. *Take* my advice, she told the StephMail folder, *and* have a good time tonight. Don't let these people defeat you.

The idea that Stephanie didn't seem to understand what constituted abuse bothered her terribly. It happened far more often than people realized. Beat someone down long enough, either physically or verbally, and it starts to feel normal. Daily life comes to consist of the expectation of some form of hurt, and that's routine. A day without hurt is abnormal, not routine. She wanted to show up on Stephanie's doorstep in Arlington and kick Billy in the balls, then bash the parents' heads together. She itched to retaliate on Stephanie's behalf and had visions of herself playing an uncostumed version of Wonder Woman — giving these people some serious hurt of their own to think about. Right! she thought, shaking her head. This almost-forty-eight-year-old, hundred-and-ten-pound, five-foot-four-inch Wonder Wretch was going to wreak havoc on a trio who were undoubtedly bigger and stronger and meaner than she. But she longed to be able to strike some sort of blow on Stephanie's behalf.

It could never happen. She was using the only weapons she had at her disposal: her wits and her experience. And Steph was listening, taking it seriously. She'd already taken the first step and called the crisis hotline. Getting this woman to acknowledge and comprehend her victim status was going to be hard because she'd been most effectively brainwashed into believing she was a chronic, unjustified complainer.

Gus's voice came bellowing up the stairs, and that anger that was general moments before became focused. Her stomach knotted and she whispered angrily, "Why the hell can't he use the damned intercom?" as she closed the browser window and went stomping downstairs to see what he wanted. Maybe she should spend a week with Vinnie in New York, get a little distance from the ongoing stress of seeing to Gus's needs.

But what good would a week do? She needed a month, two months, maybe forever. And she thought again, guiltily, of the inevitability of Gus's death. He might survive another five to ten years, give or take. But with such a seriously compromised immune system, it was unlikely he'd make it to sixty-five. This wasn't going to be how she lived the rest of her life. And why was she even thinking about Gus dying? She adored her brother, always had, always would. If he could only make some small effort on his own behalf — adapt to the tools she acquired (the intercom, for example), and just sit up properly, things would be easier for both of them. Was that such a lot to ask?

. . . That fool was his usual creepy self last night. Really pulled a number on me, brought up something that only the two of us know about. He was trying to see what I would do if he taunted me with the worst thing he could think of, but I didn't give him any satisfaction. I just stared at him for a minute, told him that he was truly depraved and went upstairs for the rest of the night until he went to bed.

I had a terrible migraine this evening. I took some Excedrin and rested. It took a couple of hours for me to feel human again. When Billy came home I told him that I had a bad migraine. He didn't say anything, and a few seconds later, walked up behind me and clapped his hands in my ear. I yelled at him and he turned it all around on me. I'm so serious, can't take a joke.

He got nervous last night when your email came in. He guessed it was you because I wasn't on the computer at all last night until you chimed in. I spoke too soon, the fool just snuck up behind me. Fun time is over. I'm going to distract him and I'll be back later.

Arriving at his bedroom door to see Gus lying with his head and shoulders almost hanging off the bed — risking a fall that would do him serious damage — Grace had to admit it *was* too much to ask. You couldn't change people, couldn't make them handle things the way you would, couldn't make them think with your brain instead of their own.

"If you tell me you're comfortable, I'll have to do you an injury," she said with a helpless smile, coming around the side of the bed to help him sit up. One hand flat in the middle of his back keeping him upright, she straightened the pillows, saying, "Okay. Now scooch over a bit. You're right on the edge."

Grunting with the effort, he shifted maybe two inches over, then sagged against the pillows. "I've always liked being right on the edge," he said wryly, his eyes closed to conceal whatever pain the slight movement had caused.

"You've always liked being a smart-ass," she countered. "What were you shouting about?"

"Would you do me a favor?" he asked, opening his eyes.

"Sure. What?"

"I need a Darvocet and I can't reach the bottle."

"Don't you think you should wait until you eat something?"

"Just give me the pill and skip the inquisition. Okay?"

"Okay," she said, reaching for the pills. "Bad night?"

"Not my best."

"Think you're starting another flare?"

"Hope not." He opened his mouth and she deposited the pill on his tongue, then held the straw steady while he drew water from the glass in her hand. It took him two tries to get the large red pill down. Then he sank back and closed his eyes. The darkened room had the stale smell of sleep and the subtle reek of decay that only she seemed to notice.

Dolly would arrive in twenty minutes or so to work her magic, clean and feed Gus and make him laugh. She'd spray Febreze on the sheets when she made up the bed, and for a time the room would be faintly perfumed. Then, by evening, Grace would once more be aware of the odor of decay.

"Need anything else?" Grace asked, keeping her eyes averted from the urinal perched atop the small waste basket beside the bed. Everything was bothering her this morning.

"No, thanks."

"Okay." She touched his arm lightly and went to the kitchen to hit the "on" switch for the coffeemaker. It would take fifteen minutes for the full pot to brew, so she went back upstairs and slid into her desk chair, determined to get some work done. But she couldn't even look at the file. She double-clicked on the Solitaire folder and started a game, aware of Nicky's habitual slow-awakening down the hall: the muted music from the clock radio, the creaking of the old wide, tongue-and-groove floorboards as Nicky moved about her room. The house was a factory, Grace thought. The morning shift was starting.

. . . Yesterday was not a great day for me. I ended up going on a 45 minute crying jag. I haven't done that in a long time. I feel so weak, but at least it happened now, and not while the idiot was at home. He would have loved that. I'm still hanging in there, but this shit is wearing me down night after night.

Billy was trying to be nice this morning, I think he realizes that he went too far last night, and that I'm not going to take it anymore. However, I still had trouble being civil to him. I'm really angry about all of the stuff that he pulled and one morning of being just passably civil is not going to do the trick. I'm sure that by tonight he'll be up to his old tricks anyway. That's his usual pattern.

He just went outside to take a walk. I guess he got tired of being angry without an audience. The only reason that I'm doing everything right is because you showed me the way to! I don't think he'd go postal on anyone else, he saves that all up for me. He's so nice to strangers it's unbelievable. How twisted is that? I'm still so shaky even though I won this round. I don't know how to stop it. He's outside, but my hands are shaking so bad*ly* that I can hardly type. I should feel great, and I do to an extent. But I can't seem to shake the panic that sets in every time one of these episodes occur*s*. It makes me so angry at myself. Do you think that there's hope I'll ever stop panicking?

"I think it's a great idea!" Nicky said, pouring soy milk into her coffee.

"How can you drink that?" Grace asked routinely. "It's the most disgusting stuff."

"You don't think cream is disgusting? Your arteries are probably clogging as we speak. And don't change the subject. I think you should take a week or two and go hang out in the Apple with Vinnie. It'll be the bomb."

"Not even going into the matter of Gus, I can't not work for a whole week, let alone two. And then there's the email."

"You'll take your Powerbook, plug your modem into Vin's phone line. Why are you making such a case for not going? A break would do you good. You're getting kind of snaky."

"Snaky. That's nice."

"Well, you are," Nicky said reasonably. "I know how hard this is for you, Mom."

"Do you?" Grace gazed at her daughter for a few moments. "I guess you do."

"What's with you and Vinnie, anyway?" Nicky asked, pouring oat bran flakes into a bowl and adding some of the soy milk. "You guys are crazy about each other. But he's over there and you're over here. I mean, okay, I understand how you feel about Dad. But don't you *want* to be with Vinnie, at least more than every so often? I don't get it. He's rich, he's funny, he's beyond talented, and he's not terrible looking."

"Damned with faint praise."

"Well, he's not Brad Pitt, but he is cute in a kind of woolly mammoth way."

Grace laughed loudly, daily more convinced that her daughter would one day take up writing. Her flair for mad description was exceptional.

Unfazed, Nicky chewed away at her cereal. After a pause to drink more of her soy milk-stained coffee, she said, "Go hang out with Vinnie. You'll have fun, and you'll learn some new Yiddish expressions. What was that word you came back with last time that I loved so much?"

"Farshtunken?"

"Nope. That one's good. But it's the other one. Remember we nearly peed our pants laughing?"

128

"Oh god! *Fartrasket!*" Grace started laughing again. Nicky joined her.

"Can you *stand* it?" Nicky gasped. "A word that sounds like rat farts and means decorated! What an insane language! Too great! Go hang with Vin," she ordered, putting her bowl in the sink before taking one last slug of her coffee. "I will look after the ranch, tend to the cowpokes, feed the cattle and keep marauders at bay."

"What's with the John Wayne routine?"

"Seemed fitting." Nicky shrugged, then glanced over at the clock. "I've gotta get going."

"Promise me you're not driving into the city."

"I *told* you. I'm leaving the car at the train station in Stamford. There are *four* of us. Nothing *bad* is going to happen. We'll catch the ball dropping in Times Square, then head back to Lucy's place for some sack time, and I'll be home by tomorrow night. If it gets way late, I'll come back the morning after. But I'll let you know. Okay? You are *such* a fusser!"

"Hey! Have you any idea what a crush the city's going to be? It's prime-time crime night."

"Oh, poetry." Nicky rolled her eyes, then flashed a smile. "Chill. We'll be fine."

"Phone me when you get to Lucy's."

"Okay. I'll phone you. God! You'd think I was twelve years old." She pressed a kiss on Grace's cheek, snatched up her backpack and keys and raced out of the kitchen to collect the large bag she'd left by the front door.

"Think you've got enough luggage?" Grace called.

"I haven't decided yet what I'm going to wear," Nicky called back, dragging the duffle bag out onto the porch.

"Have fun!"

"You bet!" Nicky said and closed the door.

She'd left a bracelet, another lip gloss and twelve cents on the kitchen table.

Unbelievable, Grace thought, laughing softly as she scooped up the change and dropped it into the half-filled jar on the counter.

. . . Billy has been calling me all day, probably trying to see if I'm online or not. I didn't talk to him though. I just said that I was too busy, which actually was the truth. I dread his homecoming tonight, I could tell from his voice that he's pissed. I guess that I wasn't nice enough to him this morning. He was really awful last night. The usual mind games that he loves to play with me. I never let him see that I was afraid of him though, and eventually he lost interest, which was wonderful! And get this, the idiot told me that we should have a baby to get us back on track. That's what started the war last night. He was livid when I burst out laughing. I don't know what tonight will bring, but nothing could be worse than last. I did tell him that I would call the police on him if I had to and that put the fear of God into him.

The whole day long Grace was preoccupied with vague worries about Nicky driving with her three friends into Manhattan instead of taking the train, and equally vague worries about Stephanie. It was pointless, she told herself. She had no control of anything beyond the front door, and not a whole lot more control of anything inside this house.

As she studied the gray silk dress, sniffing it before deciding it was okay but needed to be pressed, she had to reach deep inside herself to find any enthusiasm for the coming party. She just wasn't in the mood and would have to fake it. Or maybe the presence of people she liked would elicit her best self, the one who could enjoy listening to the clever banter of a roomful of educators, an artist, and one very smart state trooper.

She was turning into a terrible curmudgeon, mean-spirited and ill-tempered. Nicky had called her snaky. What was happening to her? she wondered, daring to confront her reflection in the bathroom mirror. When had she developed such jagged edges, such antipathy toward so many people and things? Was this really the fallout of too many years spent caregiving? And could she, with any legitimacy, blame anyone but herself for the choices she'd made? No, she could not, she told her mirror image. Stop grumbling and take your shower, wretch!

. . . He's such a sadist. As he's going up the stairs last night, he said, I don't know why you're so mad. I was making jokes about cigars, not anyone putting a knife inside of you. I could seriously strangle him. How am I supposed to close my eyes now that he's brought that memory into the open? I told him way too much. I am a fool for ever trusting him. I had those little voices warning me not to marry him, but I pushed them out of my head. I'm having trouble keeping it together. All of it self inflicted. I've been having these intrusive flashbacks and have a hard time sitting still. I know a big part of it is because when I get overtired, it's harder to keep the horrors at bay. I've sat in the same room for the last two hours with him and he hasn't said one word. As soon as I came out here to write to you, he followed me out to visit. I made him leave, he's such a sneaky creep!

He grabbed me just like the last time. Only this time, I threatened him and he backed off. Of course I had to listen to the usual stupidity of how he'd never force me to do anything, and I need professional help. God, I hate him! He twisted the whole thing around and made it seem like I was just overreacting, all he wanted was to be with his wife, etc. I'm just so relieved that I got away from him.

Jerry arrived early with two shopping bags full of food. "I actually found sugar-free truffles for Himself," he told Grace, giving her a hug after setting down the bags and removing his coat.

"That's fabulous!" she declared, always taken by the look, the scent and the feel of this man. Off duty he wore wonderful clothes, subtly styled and of beautifully textured fabrics. Tonight he had on black gabardine slacks and a black cashmere V-neck over a gray silk shirt. He smelled pleasantly of Obsession; his dark hair was cut short and side-parted. Even in winter he seemed to have a bit of a tan that emphasized gray-blue eyes framed by enviably thick black lashes. "You look great," she complimented him.

"You look pretty great yourself. You should wear makeup more often, and I like your hair up. High heels, too. Very swank, Gracie. I just want to put a couple of things in the fridge and a couple of other things in the oven. Okay?"

"Sure." She led the way to the kitchen and leaned against the counter, admiring him as he removed items from the bags. "You brought a lot of stuff," she observed.

"I was hungry when I hit the stores. Always a mistake. Leftovers will mean you don't have to cook for a day or two, what with Dolly and Lucia off until Tuesday."

"What is all that, anyway?"

"We've got some cold poached salmon in a very nice lemon dill sauce, some stuffed mushrooms for appetizers and some mini *quesadillas*. There's also a caramel mousse for dessert. What's everybody else bringing?" he asked with sudden concern.

"No idea. This is Gus's doing. I didn't even know about it until Vin told me last night."

"Is he coming? I love that guy."

"He's coming. And he loves you, too."

"Really? That's good to hear. You never really know with straight people."

"That's crap," she said mildly. "And since when does Vinnie qualify as 'straight'?"

"This is true. Artists are exceptions to all the standard rules. How come you haven't run off with him yet? He's crazy about you, you know."

"I've certainly thought about it. I'm crazy about him, too."

"Think harder. Is that Angel you're wearing?"

"It's Nicky's. I sneaked some. Delicious, isn't it?"

He was about to say something when Gus bellowed from his bedroom and the doorbell rang simultaneously.

"You go see Himself while I get the door," she said.

"The truffles now or later?" he asked.

"Up to you, my darling."

"This is going to be fun," Jerry said, beaming. "Like old times."

"Just like old times," she echoed, heading to the front of the house.

seven

The living room was an environment Gus had created entirely by himself, and over the years they'd simply updated items — like the carpeting or the upholstery on the furniture, or a new lampshade — whenever necessary. The walls were painted a pale matte gray, the high ceiling was creamy white, and all the wood trim was a deep, glossy red. A deeper gray thick pile carpet covered the floor, and the windows were concealed by oversized white wood shutters. Brass lamps cast golden pools of light and tonight a fire danced behind the simple brass fire screen. To Grace, this room was Gus as she'd always known him: solid and comforting and warm, enclosed by brilliance.

There was a moment when she sat perched on the arm of the sofa, eating the exquisite poached salmon with some of the savory, top-crisped potato-and-onion casserole that Annette (Mrs. Arlen Jasper IV, affectionately referred to by everyone at the college as The Wife Of) had provided, when

137

Grace felt herself suddenly distanced from what was going on. As if attached to a zoom lens, her vision shot backward in space and she saw the room and the people in it from a point well beyond normal viewing range. It was very like studying a photograph. She was large; it was small, yet minutely detailed. And she examined every aspect of what she saw, with clarity and with something close to sorrow.

There in the wing chair near the fireplace sat her brother, all rigged out in gray flannels, with a red cardigan over an Oxford cloth blue button-down shirt. No shoes, just a pair of the outsized white diabetic socks she ordered twice a year from a specialty place in Manhattan; his crooked feet propped on the ottoman, which was upholstered in the same soft wide-wale charcoal corduroy as the chair. A tray across his lap, he gripped a fork between the flat of his thumb and the outside edge of his forefinger and ducked his head to get the food into his mouth. He'd already spilled a fair amount down his front. Jerry would lean over from time to time from the companion chair and, without comment or fanfare, blot the spills with his napkin. That was selflessness; that was love: quietly mopping up the mess of someone you cared for.

On the off-white settee opposite the wing chairs, Arlen and The Wife Of were eating, and drinking a richly aromatic Burgundy that had a faintly fruity aftertaste. Between bites and sips, they were chatting happily to Genevieve Gallant who had brought four bottles of the superb wine. The unspeakably elegant French professor (who always looked good and had never been seen in jeans) sat next to her considerably younger, rather rough-hewn husband, Paul, who was just completing his doctorate in psychology. Tonight, Genevieve was in a pale green silk lounging outfit of loose trousers and flowing top; her shoes were low-heeled, dark green suede, exquisitely simple — as only the most expensive items can be. A long string of lustrous pearls falling alluringly over her full breasts and a narrow diamond wedding band were her only ornaments. Her honey-colored hair was coiled into a chignon that sat gracefully at the nape of her neck. Perfection with legs, Grace thought; so quintessentially Gallic, with her pouty lower lip and hooded brown eyes, her straight, well-shaped nose. She'd probably driven males wild all her life, with those ample breasts, that narrow waist and her long, long legs. Yet she was gracious always, and instinctively generous. If you admired something of hers, often she would respond, "You would like it?" and offer to take it off there and then and give you the item in question. Disarming, sexy even in her mid-fifties, and brilliant, too; happily wed for a decade to a man almost twenty years her junior. Anyone could see that Paul adored her; his eyes acquired a glow when he looked at her. Yet he was never possessive; he never crowded her, never appeared to resent the attention she drew. That was trust. That was love: being sufficiently mature to allow someone the space and freedom she needed in order simply to be herself, without being threatened or undermined by the attention she received.

Beside Grace on the sofa (in the same off-white fabric as the settee and usually covered by a flannel blanket to catch Gus's spillage, but removed for the occasion) sat Vinnie, resplendent this evening in a black watch plaid suit that looked surprisingly good on him, with a white turtleneck pullover and new black glove-leather Bally loafers. When he wanted to, Vinnie could look like the wealthy, successful man that he was. Rarely, though, did he want to. He seemed happiest in baggy-bottomed, paint-stained jeans and T-shirts, usually imprinted with some hilariously rude comment. (Grace's favorite was the one that read: This is the farkatke T-shirt you get for going there and doing that). Next to him sat May Blake, the head of the biology department, a plain-looking woman with wispy blond hair who dressed badly (tonight she wore a sadly limp, short-sleeved, ill-fitting, full-skirted, navy-blue rayon dress with an uneven hem, and strappy black high heels that were startlingly sexy but completely at odds with the dress). May's plainness was redeemed by remarkable, electrically charged green eyes that missed nothing. She wasn't a particularly kind woman but she was always fair, and Grace liked her for that; she'd long-since grown tired of well-intentioned people who merely observed but never acted. May was an activist. If she saw a wrong, she'd do anything and everything to right it. She was the moral force of the college, the one people counted on to make unbiased judgments. And she did. It was May who'd instituted the system of fines for students who took staff parking spaces or left their cars improperly parked, sometimes for days. It was she who'd brought the college's rules into line with the times and asserted that positions had to be taken on student drinking, on date rape, on drugs, on everything pertinent to an ever-evolving value system. To be willing to tackle the status quo, to be fearless in confronting the establishment to make things better for others, that was love.

May and Vinnie were talking about some article they'd both read in the *New York Times* earlier in the week. May was heatedly insisting that the downfall of the country was imminent, if the president's current moves were anything to go by. "We'll wind up set back a hundred years, with hanging judges, coat hanger abortions, and legions of disenfranchised people out on the streets — homeless, broke and ineligible for welfare because, naturally, people just *love* being on welfare so much that we simply can't allow them to have it. Better the poor, the mentally ill, the grossly underpaid should just die on the streets. The agenda benefits primarily middle-aged white businessmen. Women and children, ethnic and sexual minorities, none of them count. *They* don't make *campaign* contributions. The man is a transparent puppet," she fumed. "And in typical right-wing philistine fashion, he cloaks it all beneath the supposedly benevolent mantle of Christianity. The evil people do in the name of Christianity —"

"May, sweetheart," Vinnie interrupted, "you're preaching to the choir here. I didn't vote for the *gonif*. I'm one of the bleeding heart liberals the philistines despise, because we're such do-gooders, such mugs, such suckers for a good sob story."

"Let's change the subject," May said. "I feel an ulcer starting."

Knowing when to make peace for the sake of preserving someone's calm and dignity, that was love. Vinnie was a wise, caring man. He could be touchingly self-effacing, cloaking his generosity in humor. Grace felt choked by the welling affection she felt for everyone present.

Gus had this evening unerringly elected to surround himself with people possessing unusual resources, each capable of displaying personal passions. Her brother was a smart man; he knew people, could see past surfaces to the rich veins of treasure underneath. What did he see, she wondered, when he looked at her these days? *What* do you see when you look at me, Gus?

She continued studying those present from her distant vantage point. Mechanically eating, she tried to locate herself in the picture, but couldn't. She felt disconnected, ineffably sad. Another year was ending and a new one that would only bring more of the same was about to begin. She was forty-eight; better than half her life had already passed, and she seemed to be doing no more than treading water, trying frantically to keep from going under.

Nicky hadn't phoned from the city. But that was typical. She'd phone in the morning to say she was sorry, she'd forgotten. And at twenty-two, as she pointed out so often, was it fair to ask her to check in like an adolescent to let her mother know her whereabouts? Nicky was a grown woman, responsible — in her own haphazard fashion. Forgetful sometimes, self-indulgent sometimes, but never mean, never unkind, never anything less than completely loving.

It was after eleven, and she wondered how Stephanie was doing, if she was managing to have some fun at her party. Grace truly hoped so. Pleasure was so elusive when you were constantly on guard, waiting for the next blow to fall, the next verbal assault. *"You're so fucking stupid! You can't do one god-damned thing right! Moron!"* Heard enough times, you started believing you really were stupid, incapable of putting one foot in front of the other just to get across a room. Insidious torture. A power game on an evil level. The harm a man did to his wife or child was insignificant, nothing more than a wrist-slapping offense in a courtroom over-seen by a benevolent, understanding male judge. Yet if that same man committed these offenses against a woman or a child unrelated to him, he'd get a stiff prison sentence. In spite of all the rhetoric, the countless editorials and endless news reports of yet another husband killing his wife and children before killing himself, a man could still perform acts of sadistic bestiality upon his wife or children, or both, and a judge would give him probation and order him to attend anger management classes. *Anger management classes!*

Her appetite suddenly gone, Grace got up and went to the kitchen where she scraped the remains of her meal into the garbage before putting the plate in the sink. The thirty-two cup coffeemaker was happily gurgling away like a merry mechanical child, very pleased with itself. Half a dozen desserts were arrayed on the table, along with plates and cups and cutlery.

Stopping at the window, she looked out at the night. The sky was absolutely clear, punctuated by the Morse code of glittering dots and dashes; signals sent from unthinkable distances. Dead stars, gone hundreds, even thousands, of years, transmitting ghost light to a still-living planet that was, perhaps, nothing more than a pinprick in the fabric of the universe.

"What's with you, sweetcheeks?" Vinnie asked from behind her.

Focusing on his reflection in the window, she said, "I'm considering infinity and the human capacity for good and evil."

"A little heavy for the occasion, don't you think?"

"I'm feeling a little heavy," she said, shifting her gaze back to the limitless night sky. "I don't even know why. I was sitting in there, looking at everyone, thinking what fundamentally good people they are —"

"— and feeling defective by comparison," he finished for her.

Turning, she looked up at him. "How do you know that?"

"Because I do. It's ten to twelve. Come back and watch TV, count down to the new year with the rest of us." He took her hand. When she didn't move, he tugged, and she let him lead her back to the living room where Jerry was pouring champagne for everyone while May turned on the TV.

"Get your bubbly!" Jerry said, holding up a magnum of Moet & Chandon.

Vinnie got two flutes from the sideboard and Jerry filled them, smiling, while in the background a frantic voice-over shrieked, "Okay, there's the ball! It's about to start its drop!"

146

Everyone looked at the screen as the crowd in Times Square began counting down, a roar of sound accompanying the descent of the illuminated ball. Four, three, two, one. *"Happy New Year!"* they all shouted, except for Grace who, to her horror, looked up at Vinnie and erupted into sobs.

Vinnie pushed a handkerchief into her hand and she quickly mopped her face as the group formed a loose circle. With Gus at its apex — Jerry's hand on one of his shoulders, May's on the other — holding hands, they sang "Auld Lang Syne." Then kisses were given and received. The Wife Of took Grace into her arms, held her with a motherly warmth that brought back Grace's tears, and whispered, "You're a good woman. Happy New Year, Grace dear."

Grace clung to Annette for a long moment, at last able to whisper, "Thank you."

Then Paul hugged her with surprising tenderness before looking searchingly into her eyes. "I hope the new year is kind to you, Grace," he said before kissing her cheek and handing her off to Genevieve.

"Ah, *chérie*," she murmured, holding Grace to her cushiony bosom, *"tu es trés gentille, trés ardente. Je t'adore, vraiement.* 'Appy New Year."

"Je t'adore, aussi, Genevieve," Grace re-

plied, accepting and returning the kisses on each cheek the woman gave her.

And so it went, the softly uttered sentiments, the good wishes, the embraces, until Grace at last bent to kiss her brother's cheek and he kissed her in return, then smiled happily, saying, "Good party, huh?"

"Wonderful," she agreed, kissing him again before going in search of Vinnie as Jerry shut off the TV and switched the CD player back on.

In a far corner of the living room, Vinnie shielded Grace from view as she wept into his chest. "Sha, sha, sha," he murmured. "It's okay." Setting down his glass, he pulled the handkerchief out of her hand and dried her face.

"I can't believe I *did* that!" she croaked, mortified.

"It's nothing," he said, blotting her face. "So you've shown people who already knew it that you're not superhuman after all. What does it matter? Do I get *my* kiss finally?" Without waiting for a response, he kissed her on the mouth, then chuckled. "Like a little kid's, that face. Like you lost your best friend, or your dog."

"I've never had a dog."

"So your best friend, then. Whatever."

That won him a soggy smile. "You're my

best friend," she said. "And you look so nice tonight, Vin. Have I lost you?"

"Not a chance. I'm a forever kind of guy."

"That is so corny."

He shrugged. "Maybe. But true. And you — *shainkeit*. A man could get ideas about a woman in such a dress."

"Oh boy! Here we go again with the immigrant shtick. Listen, you want to spend the night?"

"No."

"No?"

"What're you, crazy?" He laughed. "Of course I want to. What about Gus?"

"He won't mind."

"So it's because the shiksa Princess is in the city?"

"Maybe. I don't know. Anyway, you can help me clean up later."

"Hah! Ulterior motives. I *knew* it!"

"Hah! You're *wrong,* 'cause I didn't even think of it until just now."

"Fine, so we'll clean up. In the meantime, dessert we haven't even had yet. Happy New Year, Gracie." He gave her another kiss.

"God, I hope it's better than the last one," she said fervently.

"It will be. My promise."

"I wish it was up to you, Vin. Then I'd have no doubts at all."

Subject: just checking in
Date: Sun, 31 Dec 2000 16:24:18
-0300
From: Stephanie Baine
<baine_stephanie@spotmail.com>
To: Grace
<gloring@homecable.com>

Dear Grace:

I was in the kitchen trying to get last-minute things ready for the party this afternoon and Billy was up to his usual tricks. He tried to scare the heck out of me. Came up behind me and clapped his hands as loud as he could. I whirled around and smacked him. Then, I said oh sorry, didn't know it was you. What a creep. I refuse to let him get to me. He started to tell me why a shotgun is such a favorite weapon among Southern men, but when I asked him why, he lost interest. Score one for Steph! I can't wait for the day he marches out of here for good! I'm hanging on by a thread now because I'm tired, couldn't sleep at all last night. I'm so panicky right now. I'm almost sick I'm so shaky. If I didn't have so much stuff to do for this stupid party, I'd

150

seriously consider staying in bed with a handful of Xanax and a good book. I've already gotten yet another lecture from Mom about improving my attitude and being grateful for all the stuff I have. I told her that I feel like I'm falling apart, and she says, Well, you have no reason to feel that way. I don't know which of us is crazier. She just left to go get changed, so now I can tell you what Billy said. He told me that all I needed was a good fuck to get rid of my nightmares. He's such a pig.

No one would believe the shit these people come up with. I informed him of my Mom's expectations for midnight - the champagne toast, etc, and he says: Oh, I can't drink because I may be called in to counteract terrorists. I couldn't help it. I broke out laughing! And he says: What are you laughing at? I just said if you only knew!

I was wondering if I should take another Xanax (I had one around noon) to make my heart stop racing, but I don't want to turn into a zombie. I was putting stuff away, and Billy says oh

151

why are your hands shaking? I told him that I was starving and made him fix me a snack so that I could keep working. I decided not to drug myself out, so now I can safely drink. The fool has been pulling nonstop stunts. He went out to run an errand, and came back with all these party favors, which we already have a ton of. He dumps them in my lap, and says go through these, and winks at me. I just handed it all back to him and said you go through it, I'm in the middle of something. He wasn't pleased, but left me alone for five whole minutes. He's been in rare form the entire day. I got him good after one of his stunts. He came up behind me to scare me again, and I dropped one of those big plastic coke bottles right on his foot. That was the end of that! He even tried to start his whispering shit again, but I told him I'd call my parents in to listen if he that kept up. He was starting to panic at this point because none of his usual stunts were working.

I went upstairs to get away from everyone and only planned to stay a few minutes, just say some prayers and get my head on straight. I ended up passing out cold and woke up with Billy on top of me. I kicked him straight across the room, told him to get out and let me rest or I'd start screaming. He looked at me like I was insane, but he hightailed it out of there. He called me all kinds of terrible names and left to go running! I went back to sleep, and this time I locked the door. I'm worried about what I'm facing after my parents go home.

I'm planning on taking up permanent residence on the couch from tonight on. I don't trust him at all anymore and can't stand being around him. These stunts today were his worst yet. I'm still shook up by the incident in the bedroom, but I'm also proud that I stood up to him. I'm sure he's in shock that I didn't freak out or cry, any of the things he expects me to do.

I'm sorry to go on and on this way, but I'm so nervous about tonight. Wish me luck, Grace. This is really rough.

Love, Steph

Subject: me again

Date: Sun, 31 Dec 2000 17:22:18 -0300

From: Stephanie Baine <baine_stephanie@spotmail.com>

To: Grace <gloring@homecable.com>

Dear Grace:

Sorry to be writing again, but I need a sanity break. I've been called about every evil thing in the book tonight! I don't know what got into the three of them except that they can't stand the fact that I've grown a backbone. I've already informed Billy that I'm sleeping on the couch tonight. He hasn't responded yet, except with a smirk, but I'm holding my ground. Speaking of butcher knives, my damned parents left one laying on the counter the entire day. I kept asking them if I could put it away and they kept saying no, they might need it later. So every time that I walked out here, I had to stare at it. You'd think that at least my Mom would have pro-tected me. She knows about my knife trauma.

In spite of my brave act, Billy's succeeding in shaking me up. He's watching something really vile, and keeps turning up the volume really loud. What a complete and total prick! I'm still ignoring him, but then my Mom comes in to complain about how "uppity" I've become. I laughed and reminded her that I wasn't going to take any more name calling or criticism, and she says, See what I mean. Then she starts in about how rotten I am to Billy, how I could have never survived her life. She then tells me how great I have it and do I know how lucky I am to have had only one bad thing happen to me in my life. She says at least I didn't get killed and I need to start appreciating what I have and be grateful. She told me she doesn't have it in her to care about anyone, that she has no clue what it means to want to help anyone and be nurturing, and that's why she loves Billy so much, because they're just alike. She started crying, begging me not to take him away from the family, he's the son that she always wanted, and couldn't I just try with him. Then she tells me that I've never had to struggle a day in my life,

I've always had money, etc., and why can't I just get over the "past unpleasantness" and enjoy my life. I had nothing to say, there's no reasoning with her. She said she had a hard time believing Billy is as bad as I say, because he's always so nice when she's around and treats her so well, and she'd give anything if I could just offer her some kind of proof. I asked her what about my word, but she basically told me that that wasn't good enough. She's mentally ill, that's all there is to it. I walked out on her. I've never done that before, but she made me so angry. She and Billy have probably been talking and plotting the way they always do, and they've figured out that someone has been helping me learn not to be a doormat anymore. He doesn't know that I have you to help me, he'd die if he did, or kill me, I don't know which. Whatever it is, neither one of them is happy about the fact that I'm changing.

I've just about made myself sick obsessing over my mother's stupidity. I've been thinking about everything that she said and at first it didn't really bother me, but as it started getting dark, the time I always go nuts anyway, it began getting to me. I ended up so angry and panicked that I had to go throw up. I guess I'm not as strong as I thought I was. I'm recovered somewhat now, but I still feel dizzy and nauseous. People are going to start arriving in an hour or so and I wish I was locked in my bedroom, sleeping.

Please don't be mad at me, Grace. I know I'm being a total wimp, but these people are insane and I don't know how to deal with them.

Love, Steph

Subject: sorry
Date: Sun, 31 Dec 2000 18:05:18 -0300
From: Stephanie Baine <baine_stephanie@spotmail.com>
To: Grace <gloring@homecable.com>

Dear Grace:

Sorry to be flooding you with emails.

This'll be the last one, I promise. But my mother had to come back for another round. I'm so sick of her nonsense. She is just so out there as far as Billy is concerned. This time I got the lecture on how lucky I am he doesn't beat me and gives me all his money. I want to scream. I wonder what she'd do if I told her no he doesn't beat me, but he does rape me, is always having these "accidents" where I wind up getting hurt. She'd probably blame me, as usual. Then she started in on "the change in my behavior" and asked me if I was having an affair online. I broke out laughing over that one. It's definitely occurred to her that I've been talking to someone, she doesn't know who, just some bad influence like Sandy. God help me! She's in the doorway, if you can believe this, still screaming that I never listen to her, don't respect her, blah, blah, the usual bullshit about poor wounded Billy, and how no one outside the family could ever understand how <u>he's</u> suffered all these years, putting up with me. Then, and you're not going to believe this one, she tells me that if I can't find a way to be happy with him, maybe I should come home and live with her. I'm in shock, reeling from being screamed at just minutes before thirty people are due to arrive, and then she wants me to move home? No way in hell!

I guess you can tell how much I'm looking forward to this party. I won't bother you again tonight, and I really hope you're not angry with me for venting this way. It's a nuthouse here. You're the only sane person I know right now, aside from Sandy, and I think the world of you. You've been so kind to me. You'll never know how much I appreciate it. They'd have dragged me off to the mental ward by now, if it hadn't been for you. So thank you for listening.

Love and happy new year,

Steph

>eight

Vinnie was a tidy, quiet sleeper and scarcely moved. Grace was grateful, because she had serious problems sharing a bed. It made her panicky, even claustrophobic. Fallout from Brownie. The effects of her brief marriage were long-term. She had learned to accept them and years ago had stopped trying to go back to who she'd been before Brownie took his fists to her. There could be no going back. She'd taken a detour on her personal evolutionary path and since leaving him had traveled cautiously down a new road. Speaking out, fighting back had undone most of the damage, but not all of it. When she least expected it, some residual fear made itself felt. Something as simple as sharing a bed, even with her own daughter, was impossible. Those nights when the then two-, or three-, or four-year-old Nicky had awakened from a bad dream and wanted to climb into bed with her mother were nights when Grace didn't sleep. The child's slightest movement jolted her, flooding her system with adrenaline. So Grace either read or lay for hours watching her fearless child dream her way through the night.

Now she lay on her side, looking at the uncovered window. The earlier clarity of the night had given way to an angry wind that whipped through the branches of the old oak outside, and sleet threw itself against the glass in irregular gusts. By morning, everything would be coated in a layer of ice. Only the sturdiest of vehicles would be on the roads. A good day to stay indoors. With Dolly and Lucia off until Tuesday, Grace would make Gus's breakfast. Vinnie, she was sure, would be more than willing to help Gus to the bathroom, get him cleaned up and dressed.

But this sudden storm was a prime example of why she couldn't go off to spend a week or two in the city. If the weather was bad, Nicky would be left on her own to care for her uncle. And while she didn't mind fixing his meals, she was understandably squeamish about his other needs. To her, Gus was Dad. She just couldn't handle more than the cosmetic, non hands-on part of caregiving. Grace could barely manage the other parts of it herself when circumstances left her no alternative. So, no. A trip to the city with Vinnie would have to wait until spring.

"Why aren't you sleeping?" Vinnie asked in a whisper.

"I can't."

There was a long silence. Then Vinnie said, "You mean that literally, don't you?"

"Unh-hunh."

"And that's why you'd never stay the night with me."

"That's why."

"You should've said so. I'd've understood."

Turning toward him, she rested her head on her arm, saying, "I wanted to believe I could get past it. I hoped I could. You're the one I'd *want* to be able to sleep with, Vin."

"I'm sorry, Gracie." He found her free hand and held it. "I'll go flop in one of the guest rooms."

"You don't have to do that —"

"It's fine. You need to get some sleep, and I'm one of those bears who can hibernate in any old cave."

"Now I feel terrible."

"Gracie, Gracie," he chided softly. "What's to feel terrible about? You haven't done anything to me."

"But . . ."

"Listen, *maideleh,* nothing was promised. Did you sign papers on this? Did I? No. A lot of people in this world sleep in separate bedrooms. So now, when're you going to tell me what's up with you?"

"I can't . . ."

"You know something I discovered a long time ago? In the dark you can say anything."

She thought about that for a moment or two and decided he was right. Somehow being unable to see his face clearly, yet anchored by the sound of his voice and his proximity, gave her a rare confessional opportunity. "I feel guilty and rotten and angry and hopeless," she admitted in a rush. "I didn't used to be this way, Vin. Yesterday I was actually thinking about Gus dying."

"For sure you'll go to hell now. But you know what? I'd be seriously worried about you if you'd never thought of it. Grace, the man is dwindling away, getting eaten up from the inside out by his own immune system. How could you *not* think about it?"

"But I thought of it in terms of my own freedom, Vinnie. That makes me —"

"Human, is what it makes you. You are *such* a Jewish mother! Oy, the guilt, the guilt. Don't worry," he quoted the punch line from one of his favorite jokes (How many people does it take to change a light bulb for a Jewish mother?), "I'll just sit here in the dark."

Her laugh was muffled as she blotted her

163

face with the hem of the pillowcase. "He's my *family*, Vin; he's all I've got except for Nicky. And by summer Nicky will be somewhere else, living her own life, leaving lip glosses and clothes and nickels, dimes and quarters all over the place." She laughed again at the image, then quickly sobered. "I feel so resentful sometimes, being stuck here, fetching and carrying, cooking when I don't want to. And now, like some kind of monster, I'm waiting for him to die so I can have a life again."

"You want him dead, Gracie?"

"No! But . . . sometimes, yes — at moments when I think of all the things I could do, the places I could go. Then I'm just sick with shame at wishing my brother were dead so I could do what *I* want to do. I hate my pettiness, my selfishness. He hasn't done anything to have me feel that way about him.

"The thing is, I know a break would do me good, but I'd still have to come back and deal with him deteriorating week after week. And what do I do when it reaches the point where I can't manage anymore, when he needs more care than I can provide for him? I could *never* put him in one of those *places*, Vinnie. I couldn't let him be warehoused, and probably mistreated by people who don't know him or care about how special he is. Just parked somewhere to die, surrounded by underpaid, uncaring strangers. But that time is coming closer every day, and on the one hand I want an end to this, but on the other hand I could never do that to him." She paused to take a deep breath, then said, "Maybe you're right and I am Jewish, the way I'm *kvetching*."

He chuckled and squeezed her hand. "Let me ask you something, Gracie. All those people tonight, One Vee and The Wife Of, Jerry and May, Genevieve and Paul, you think they don't know how you feel? Gus and Nicky, Dolly and Lucia, you think none of us knows how you feel? *Everybody* knows. And you know what? We all think you're the least selfish, least petty person we know. Why? Because we're not sure any of us would have the strength to do what you've done for Gus. Of course you get a little *meshugah* now and then. Anybody would. This is tough; no question. But if you could swallow a little of your pride, you'd get help. Would it kill you to admit you can't do it all and accept some help?"

"You're talking about money and I can't —"

"What do you care if it's money, or if it's people giving their time? Are *you* the only one allowed to show love for the man?"

"No, but —"

"Grace, let people help. It doesn't make you less of a person; it doesn't mean you're weak or a failure. It simply means your plate's so full that stuff is spilling on the floor. Jerry would help in a heartbeat, and don't think for a moment that Gus would refuse him. He's long-since past the shame, past not wanting Jerry to see him twisted like a human pretzel. Jerry's shown him time and again that it doesn't matter.

"And May loves to cook. She said tonight that she'd be happy to double up on the portions she makes and bring over some backup meals for your freezer. Paul is dying to discuss Dostoyevsky with Gus, which would mean company for him, not to mention intellectual stimulation. There are all kinds of people at the college who'd actually *like* to be able to do something for their friend. But you've put it out there that no help is needed.

"Look, Gracie. You made a choice and you've honored it. But a wise person knows when to admit she's taken on something that's grown to be more than she can handle. Let. People. Help. You don't have to do this alone."

"Okay. I'll try."

"Is there more than just your pride involved? Are you maybe trying to prove something?"

"Maybe I am," she said truthfully. "Not proving specifically, but repaying. Gus gave me and Nicky a home when we had nowhere else to go. He's been the only father Nick's ever known. I owe him a lot."

"Giving yourself a nervous breakdown by way of compensation seems a little excessive, wouldn't you say?"

"You think I'm having a breakdown?" she asked, shocked.

"No. But you're headed down the right road. At the rate you're going, Gus is going to outlive you. Keep on the way you are and you'll fall apart. You need to admit that this has become too big for you, and let people in. Gus needs it. You need it. Nicky needs it, too."

"That's scary," she said, caught by the idea of being broken down, like some machine gone horribly awry, its inner parts not meshing properly, screws and wheels seizing for lack of proper maintenance; the entire thing in danger of shuddering to a complete stop.

"You should see it from the outside, looking in. It's scary. You're *oysgemutshet*."

"What's that?" she asked.

167

"In words of one syllable: worn out. So I'm going now to bunk down across the hall, and we'll talk more in the morning. Okay?"

"Okay."

"Are you sorry we had this conversation?" he asked.

"A little," she admitted. "I feel like a whiner. Other people have it way worse."

"True, they do. But you are not now, nor have you ever been, nor will you ever be 'other people.' A couple of days from now, you'll be glad you got it off your delectable chest." He leaned across, gave her a kiss, and said, "I love you, Gracie. Sleep." Wrapped in the afghan he grabbed from the foot of the bed, he went to the door, stopped and added, "Stop thinking so much. Give your head a rest." The door opened, closed quietly, and he was gone.

Subject: re: sorry
Date: Mon, 1 Jan 2001 07:46 -0400
From: Grace Loring
<gloring@homecable.com>
To: Stephanie Baine
<baine_stephanie@spotmail.com>

Dear Steph:

I hope things went well and that you

managed to have some fun last night. I also hope the insane trio left you alone and that you were able to stick close to Sandy and your other friends, and that this is the beginning of a new era for you.

I had kind of a mini-meltdown at midnight. I guess things just caught up with me and I got a little teary. Otherwise, it was a lovely party. Gus reads people so well and he has wonderful friends. Everyone came with tons of fabulous food and good wine. And we all ate and drank way too much.

Try to keep your cool and don't rise to anything your parents or Billy say to you. Just blow it off, ignore it, and do whatever needs to get done. First chance you get, talk to your phone pal again. Make it a daily habit. She's going to help you more than you know. And when you feel ready, talk to a lawyer about getting out of your marriage. You might also give some serious thought to divorcing your parents while you're at it.

Do let me know how things went.

Hugs, Grace

Nicky called just after ten that morning, to say, "Sorry I didn't call last night. It was wild. Tons of people showed up at Lucy's. Her parents had friends over, too. They had a swing band, plus the party was catered. The best food! Little lobster thingies sort of like egg rolls but way better, and these kind of tart things with curried chicken. I ate like a complete pig. Then, around eleven, we all headed down to Times Square. It was the bomb, Mom! Everybody screaming like crazy. It was like a monster venting session. Total freedom to shriek your heart out. There was this one guy near me who was howling, *'Happy no fear!'* and this girl, she just stood there, all by herself, crying. I grabbed her and said, 'Come hang with us,' and she looked — rescued. Complete sweet-heart. Her name's Gin Holder and she's a senior at Yale. How cool is that? I told her about Dad and Vin being Yalies and she was psyched. Thing is, her mom died two weeks before Christmas and her dad's away on business. She's an only like me and didn't want to be alone, so she got on the train and came into the city. We adopted her on the spot, and took her with us to the bar at the Algonquin for a drink after, then brought her back to spend the night. We didn't get home to Lucy's place until almost three. So what about you guys? How was the party?"

"It was great. Jerry brought fabulous food. We watched the ball drop on the tube at midnight."

"Cool. Did you see me in the crowd?" Nicky laughed.

"I actually looked for you."

"I knew you would, totally knew it," Nicky said warmly.

"Well, you were right. Chalk one up for the kid. So when do you think you'll head back?" Grace asked. "The roads are bad here, Nicks. A lot of black ice."

"I'm pretty wiped, so we'll probably wait and come back tomorrow. Okay?"

"Sure. Given the weather reports, I'd prefer you stayed off the highway today. The forecast for tomorrow's good."

"How do you spell relief?" Nicky laughed again.

"Just check in with me later, will you?"

"Okay. How's Dad? Did he have a good time? Did you?"

"He had a very good time. And Jerry put him to bed, did the whole thing, while Vin and I cleaned things up."

"Wow! That's a major first. Listen, I'd better go. We're heading over to the Plaza for lunch."

"I love you, Baby Girl Brownell. Happy New Year."

"Love you, too. Happy New Year, Mom. Give Dad and the Vinster my love."

After the call, Grace went upstairs to check her email again. Nothing from Stephanie. The poor woman was probably exhausted after her ordeal the day before, Grace reasoned, and went back downstairs.

Vinnie was giving Gus a shower and over the rush of the water, she could hear the two of them laughing. It was probably the most fun Gus had had in the bathroom in a long time. While he was accustomed to Dolly, Grace knew he found it an ongoing source of humiliation being bathed by a woman. Not because he disliked women, but because it pointed up his helplessness. Vinnie was performing exactly the same routine, but was telling jokes and doing his immigrant shtick throughout, and Gus was howling with laughter. Smiling, she tidied the kitchen, then stood for a minute or two at the window, admiring the way the sunshine refracted off every frozen surface.

Subject: How are you?

Date: Mon, 1 Jan 2001 22:14 -0300
From: Grace Loring
<gloring@homecable.com>
To: Stephanie Baine
<baine_stephanie@spotmail.com>

Dear Steph:

I hope everything's all right, and that you're just recovering from the pre-party nonsense with Billy and your parents, and the party itself. Please drop me a line when you get a chance and let me know how everything went and how you're doing. I'm a bit concerned at not having heard from you.

It's been a pretty quiet day around here. Nicky's spending an extra night in the city with her friends and we're working our way through the left-overs from the party.

I forgot to wish you a happy new year, Steph.

Hugs, Grace

She couldn't remember when she'd stopped

thinking exclusively about her own death (lured by its promise of peace yet fearful of its prematurity — she really didn't want to die) and started thinking instead about his, wishing for him to die slowly, in agony. Not that she still didn't think about dying herself. But creating detailed mental scenarios of the many ways his life might be brought to an end offered antidotal moments that were almost as effective as prescription drugs. Sometimes she could use up as much as two hours formulating some new scenario, absorbing with pleasure the imagined pain contorting his smug features as his big body was slowly, methodically butchered. Her favorite private screenings included shots of castration or evisceration; an ice pick being driven into his ear or into his brain via an eye socket. With grim satisfaction, she witnessed his prolonged demise, nodding at the rightness of it. God forgive her, but he deserved *to die.*

>nine

Nicky phoned just after eight the next morning to say that she and her friends would be catching the nine o'clock train back to Stamford. "We're going to drop Gin off in Westport, so don't worry if I'm not home until later."

"What's 'later,' Nicks?"

"I don't know. It depends. Just don't worry."

"If you get a chance, check in and give me a status report. Otherwise, I'll worry. You know me."

"Mission control to Houston central, that's a ten-four. I've gotta run. Love you, Mom. 'Bye."

Grace had already checked her email and there was nothing from Stephanie. It was beginning to worry her. After a couple of weeks of multiple daily emails, this "silence" was unnerving. She had a bad feeling that something had happened to the poor woman. Given what she'd been told about the parents and the husband, Billy could've beaten and raped her in front of them, and her mother and father would've cheered him on.

Vinnie had left half an hour earlier, saying, "I've got some work that has to be finished. I'll call you later. Okay?"

"Yup. Okay. Be careful on the road, and thanks for all your help, Vin."

"Please. Don't thank me. Hugs and kisses would be good."

Shortly after he'd gone, Dolly had phoned to say, "I'll be a little late, but I'll be there. I'm just gettin' a jump-start from Herbert."

"That's fine. Thanks for letting me know, Dolly."

"Tell Mr. Gus not to be fussin'."

"Right." Grace laughed. "As if that would stop him."

Dolly's melodious laughter came over the line. "It's true. But tell him anyway. I'll be there soon."

The moment she put down the receiver, Gus started bellowing from the bedroom.

Going to the doorway, Grace said quietly, "What are you yelling about?"

"Where is everybody?" her brother asked angrily.

"Vin just left. Dolly's on her way. And Nicky will be home later."

"I need my pills."

"Which ones?" Grace asked, trying only

to take shallow breaths; the room was overhot and the air smelled bad. "Why don't I open the window a bit?" she offered. "Let some fresh air in here."

"I *like* the air in here," he snapped. "I need my Darvocet."

"How many are you taking a day?" she asked, reaching for the prescription vial.

"As many as I need! Just give me one, Grace. I'm not in the mood to play twenty questions."

In silence, she gave him the pill, then held the water glass. After he'd swallowed the medication, he lay back against the pillows with a grimace and closed his eyes.

"You're having a flare," she guessed. "You tried to hide it so we could have the party."

"What does it matter?" he said tiredly.

"I guess it doesn't," she replied. "I'll get your breakfast started. Dolly should be here inside half an hour. Herbert was giving her a jump."

Gus let out a bark of laughter and opened his eyes.

Realizing what she'd said, Grace laughed, too.

"That Herbert's got to be a happy man," Gus said merrily.

"One would think so. Want anything in particular? Cereal? Bacon and eggs?"

"Just some O.J., toast and coffee, please." His eyes closed again, but he was smiling.

By seven-thirty that evening, she hadn't heard from either Nicky or Stephanie. She was becoming increasingly worried about Stephanie. And she was annoyed with Nicky, so she called her on her cellphone.

When Nicky answered, Grace said, "Where are you, Nicks? I was starting to get very worried."

"I'm on my way. We're just passing Hartford."

"Oh hell! I don't want you driving and talking on the cellphone."

"I'm fine!"

"It is *not* fine to drive and talk on the phone. You'll be here, what, about nine?"

"Should be."

"Okay. I'm hanging up. Love you, Nicks. Please be careful."

"I'm *very* careful, Mom. I don't know why you make such a fuss about me talking on the phone. But never mind. I'll see you later. Love you, too."

"Either turn off the phone or pull over to talk, please. You're the only Nicky I've got."

"Okay, okay. But let a little logic into your life, Mom. If I didn't have the phone turned on, you wouldn't have been able to reach me.

And you'd be in full panic mode right now."

"True. But I've reached you, so promise me you'll turn it off now."

"I promise. 'Bye."

Nicky probably wouldn't show up much before eleven, Grace knew. She was never on time, except for classes. And even then she was probably the last one into the room. No doubt it was a little genetic tic she'd inherited from Brownie who'd hadn't once in the course of their relationship showed up where he was supposed to be at the appointed time. Since Grace was invariably early for everything, lateness was always a cause of concern for her — which was why Dolly and Lucia and even Vinnie always took a minute to phone and let her know if they were going to be delayed.

As she headed downstairs to clean up the kitchen, she had a terrible sense of foreboding. She just knew that Stephanie was in trouble. She couldn't stop thinking about it, and throughout the evening she kept running upstairs to check her email.

Gus finally said, "What on earth is wrong?"

"That young woman I told you about," Grace explained. "I haven't heard from her since New Year's Eve."

"Maybe she's busy."

"She wasn't too busy to email me five

times that day, Gus. I think something's happened to her. Her sick sadistic husband has probably messed with her again."

"You worry too much," he said, turning his attention back to the TV screen.

"Yes, I do. It's what I do best, really."

"Do I detect sarcasm?"

"Nope. Truth."

"Ah! Well, that's all right then. This show is definitely going down the tubes. It's validating my thesis that, *Seinfeld*, *Law and Order*, and one or two others notwithstanding, no show maintains its quality after the second season. The characters lose their charm and become cartoonish. I'm going to stop watching this. The writing's turned formulaic."

"I agree. But you've said that every week this year and you still keep on watching."

"I'm an optimist," he said. "I want to believe it'll magically go back to being a good show."

"You're the one with the thesis," she reminded him. "Clearly, it's been proved."

"The problem is, Gracie, that along with my being optimistic, I'm a man of habit. This show has become a habit. So I'll rely on you to remind me not to watch it next week."

"I will be happy to do that."

He smiled over at her. "When's Nicky due?"

"About an hour ago."

He gave a little shake of his head. "Which means she'll be home in a couple of hours." Fumbling with the remote, he managed to turn off the TV. "I'm going to go to bed now."

"Okay, then, mister. Let's do it."

Subject: re: How are you?
Date: Wed, 3 Jan 2001 12:24:14 -0100
From: Stephanie Baine <baine_stephanie@spotmail.com>
To: Grace <gloring@homecable.com>

Dear Grace:

Sorry I haven't written. It's been madness here. My parents left first thing in the morning after the party. My mother called once they made it home, and informed me that she was so glad to be away from all of the turmoil at our house, and back to the calm of hers. I wanted to tell her that she was a huge cause of all the upset, but I haven't reached the point of being able to tell off my Mom yet.

Billy has today off and is out on one of his runs. His friends were making jokes about his weight and he's in a tizzy. I don't think that his friends are too enamored with him either. They treat him similar to the way he treats me. Out of all of the couples he invited to our party, only 2 couples came. The rest were all my friends.

This whole situation is really wearing me down. Part of my problem is lack of sleep, but I'm so depressed right now. I've been staying up late and waking up early. Same old nightmare problem. I've been reading after I have one, but I never get tired enough to go back to sleep. The hours are catching up with me and I'm chronically fatigued. Also very whiny. I feel like slapping myself about now, so I don't blame you if you do too.

Okay, so about the party. As the night went on Billy got creepier, and every time that I would walk by he would grab me or grope me. I was ready to get sick all over him. He's made me a wreck, and I'm jumping at every little sound that I hear. After my parents left, I was cleaning up the house and he came sneaking up behind me, knife in hand, and grabbed me. I'm ashamed to say that I screamed. Then he said that he was just pretending to be the guy from Psycho, and how could I be upset about that, it's one of those classic movies that I always bore him with. He was laughing his head off, saying how "cute" it was that I'm so jumpy. He's crazier than I could ever have dreamed.

Usually after he pulls an extremely nasty stunt like that, he lays off for a few days, probably hoping that I'll let my guard down. But no. He came in an hour later and told me that he was sorry for scaring me, what he was really trying to do was turn me on. He said that I was so obsessed with knives, and he can't understand the "fascination" I have with them. When I wouldn't answer him, he says at least I try to give you what I think you want, and it's not my fault that you're hopelessly screwed up. I told him to go to hell, and he says, so that does mean that knives don't turn you on after all? By the end of that convo I was freaking big time. The sick bastard should be killed!

He has been a nightmare, pretty much from the beginning. He's always followed me around, tried to listen in on my phone conversations, etc. Whenever I'd tell him that I wanted some privacy, he'd tell me that married people don't need privacy, and what am I doing that I don't want him to know about. As far as all his other antics, he's pulled them from the beginning too.

He honed in on my biggest fear and has always used knives to torment me, used to drag me into stores that sold them, show me catalog pictures of them and ask me to call up and order them for him. I always refused, so naturally he would tell me what a screwed up bitch I was. You can't imagine some of the stunts that he used to pull every New Year's Eve until I got smart and invited my parents to spend the holidays with us. I was convinced everything was my fault, and if I were a "normal" person, none of this stuff would faze me. Of course he and my mother were encouraging me to believe that.

Warning bells were going off in my head when I married him, but I ignored them. One of the things that bothered me was how obsessed he was with what happened to me and how he wanted all the lurid details. He conned me by saying that he just wanted to know about everything so that he never did anything to upset me, and that it was good for me to talk about it. He said he thought it was funny that I was worried about him being obsessed with it when there was no one more obsessed than me with what had happened. I couldn't think of any argument there. I see now that that was the beginning of him turning everything back on me.

I should have walked out on him the first night we were married, when he said that he had a lot to learn from me, because I'd done things he'd only read about. Then he laughed and said that was a joke, don't get mad. He knew I'd never been with anyone but him. I've never forgiven him for saying that, but as always, dear old mom assured me that I'm way too sensitive and he was just trying to make me laugh so I wouldn't be nervous. I don't know why I didn't leave him way before this, except that I believed this was what I was going to get from anybody, and I deserved everything that I got.

I still haven't recovered emotionally from Monday. You probably won't be too shocked, considering I haven't recovered from something that happened 18 years ago either. I just got back from the doctor. I have some injuries, but he gave me medicine and antibiotics, so I'll be fine. I'm not up to talking about the whole thing yet, so I'll write back later. I'm wiped out. They gave me a shot of valium, and I'm going to go to sleep for a while.

Love, Steph

I knew it! Grace thought, instantly angry and worried. Heaven only knew what else that sick bastard had done, but Grace had no doubt he'd raped Stephanie again. And this time he'd done damage serious enough to warrant a doctor's visit.

Stephanie had to get out of that house, away from that man. But clearly she was terrified, not to mention brainwashed, and it was rarely easy to convince women to leave their homes. They invariably had all kinds of reasons for staying. Usually it was financial necessity involving children. But since Stephanie had no children, that wasn't an issue. Habit was, though. And so were fear and shame and self-blame.

Outraged, Grace wanted to send off a response at once, but she decided to wait for more details from Stephanie, to find out what exactly had transpired.

Frustrated and hamstrung, she studied the carpet for several minutes, always seeing some new detail she hadn't previously noticed — a calming exercise — then went downstairs to prepare lunch. She could hear the water chugging through the pipes, which meant Nicky was finally up. A champion sleeper, was Nicky. Gus had observed many times over the years that she could probably sleep through an earthquake.

While Grace made ham and cheese sandwiches on multi-grain bread with dill mustard for herself and Gus (Nicky would come down and make herself some tasteless but healthy breakfast), she considered Stephanie's having written "honed" instead of "homed." The first time she'd used it, Grace had dismissed it as a typo. But after the second time, she realized Steph thought it was the correct word. Telling herself this was no time to be giving the woman language lessons, Grace found herself wishing she could talk to the poor soul. She knew her name and where she lived. After lunch, she'd do an Internet search. If she found a number, she'd phone and speak to Stephanie, give her a chance to voice her fears, and then Grace would stress how important it was to get away from her husband while there was still time. The level of violence in that household was escalating fast. It might reach its peak at any moment, which meant that Stephanie's life could well be at risk.

>ten

Grace had at least a dozen search engines bookmarked just for finding phone numbers. The results were often out of date on one site but current on another, which meant doing several searches to cross-check the listings. But if the person she was trying to locate had an unlisted number, nothing would come up.

There was a listing for a William Baine, but it was downstate, in Richmond, nowhere near Arlington. Without a street address, Grace couldn't do a reverse lookup. And a search on Stephanie's email address didn't turn up a thing. Grace hadn't expected it would. Spotmail was the largest free email service in the world. People could log on from almost anywhere to access or send their messages. It was, at best, only remotely possible that details about a Spotmail user would come up in a search. So, stymied, and unable even to think about working on her manuscript until she heard from Stephanie again, Grace played game after game of Tetris, and waited.

At last, midafternoon, the icon on her desktop started flashing and she at once went to her inbox.

Subject:
Date: Wed, 3 Jan 2001 15:19:11 -0400
From: Stephanie Baine <baine_stephanie@spotmail.com>
To: Grace <gloring@homecable.com>

Dear Grace:

I can't get over how badly he hurt me. I'm just glad that it's over now, and I'm fixed, physically anyway. Emotionally, I'm worse than ever. I have to wonder how long it's going to take to recover from all of this. I'm such a nutbar today.

Going to the doctor was one of the harder things that I've had to do, but I finally confided in Sandy, told her what's been going on and what happened after new year's, and she dragged me right off to her doctor. I was beating myself up because I thought I should have been calmer about the whole thing. It's not like this is the first time I've been through this. But I was shaking so bad at the beginning that they literally couldn't do an exam, so they gave me a shot of valium. This doctor was kind, not like the usual military sadists. I even had a nice nurse. She held my hand and kept talking till the valium kicked in. I can't believe what a wimp I was, but at least it's over. The doctor said I had a bruised cervix and quite a few tears. He was appalled by how much damage Billy had done to me. He was the nicest man, told me that he had a wife and two daughters, and when he sees stuff like this, it makes him ashamed to be a man. I was in shock over his saying that.

I'm still wiped out, and feel like shit. It's been raining here all day, so I've been trying to keep it together but I'm not doing a great job. I hope that you're not losing respect for me as we speak. I'm being such a whiny, weak thing, and I'm sorry. I know that there's no excuse for it and that I need to pull myself together soon. Feel free to ignore my ranting and raving. I've been trying to calm down and watch TV, read, something, but I'm a mess.

I talked to my phone pal early this morning before Sandy came over. You were right about me having nothing to worry about. My pal was super nice, and she's all for my getting a divorce. She thinks Billy's very dangerous. I had to go into all the details of what went on with him this time. It wasn't easy, but I did it. I was on the phone with her for over an hour. It was very draining but good to have someone to talk to. I asked her how long did she think that I would need counseling, and she warned me to be prepared for the long haul because I have a lot of damage to undo. I always wonder what she's really thinking, is she shocked, disgusted, etc., by what she's hearing. It's so weird because on the one hand, I feel relieved to unburden myself, and at the same time reliving it makes me feel dirty and ashamed and all I want to do is get off the phone and take a shower. I sound like a loon, I know. Please don't be disgusted with me. I'm trying to sort my life out, and you're the one whose opinion I value the most, so I want to do it with you at my side.

This afternoon I talked to a lawyer Sandy recommended. (She knows all the right people to call. She's amazing. Wasn't even surprised when I told her about Billy, said she'd guessed ages ago.) The lawyer's going to call the doctor and get a copy of his notes from today, also copies of my medical records from the military doctor I usually see. He's treated me for a lot of those "accidents" Billy's always having.

According to the lawyer, the laws in this state are very screwed up. The easiest way for me to get a divorce is to persuade Billy not to contest it, and even then, we have to wait a year, and after the year is up, then it takes 2 to 3 months to become final. If I leave the house before that year is up, he can claim desertion. If he contests the divorce, then we have to go in front of a judge, and he can order counseling, make life hard for me. I told the lawyer a little about the psychological abuse and the other stuff, but if Billy denies it, or claims that he didn't understand that he was doing anything wrong, the judge will order counseling for him individually, and then marriage counseling for both of us.

I'm ready to scream. I can't believe that I live in such a backward place. I'm terrified that when I give the lawyer examples of all Billy's stupid stunts, like waving knives around, etc., he's going to tell me that I'm overreacting and need to toughen up. That's what Billy always says whenever I confront him. He says what a weakling I am for letting stuff like that upset me, he was just having fun. Same thing with my Mom. She's always said it's a sign that I need a shrink, because normal people are not afraid of knives or violent TV shows, etc. She keeps saying I'm one of the most neurotic people who ever lived. What if the lawyer thinks the same thing? What if I can't find anyone who doesn't think that? I'm going over every stupid thing my mother has ever said to me, and worrying that this lawyer is going to think along the same lines — that I'm not capable of having a normal relationship because of what happened, that I blame all men for my troubles and hate them for no reason. I'm worried Billy will get a lawyer and they'll force me to see a shrink because I'm neurotic and out of control. I warned you that I was anguishing today, worrying about all these awful scenarios. I want to be free, and I'm taking the steps to get that accomplished. But, the process is terrifying to me. And Billy's always saying he'll never let me go because he "loves" me so much. I don't believe the love part, but I do believe the "never let me go" part. I think he's insane and I'm very afraid of him, especially after what he did to me once my parents were gone.

So I'm going to see the lawyer tomorrow, and it's taking every ounce of courage that I have. No one wants out of this mess more than me but I'm very scared. Wish me luck tomorrow, and hope this guy understands what a creep I married, and finds a way to get me out of this nightmare.

Love, Steph.

PS: I'm sorry this is so long and rambling.

Subject: re

Date: Wed, 3 Jan 2001 17:26:20 -0100
From: Grace Loring
<gloring@homecable.com>
To: Stephanie Baine
<baine_stephanie@spotmail.com>

Dear Steph:

I'm so sorry about everything. It seems that you underestimated Billy from the beginning. But how could you know what he was? He conned you. You went into the marriage thinking he was going to protect you. You had no way of knowing that he was merely pretending to be what you wanted because he had a very sick hidden agenda.

It sounds as if he married you so he could have his own personal victim — someone he could abuse with impunity, because you had no ability to resist his attacks. You'd been too well programmed by your horrible parents; you were made to believe that you were somehow at fault for what happened. He knew it, tapped into it, and has been abusing you with it every way possible since day one. It's a fairly complex structure, Steph, that has taken years and years to build. You don't deserve any of this, and you need to believe that. Your difficulty in believing in your own innocence is what gives your parents and Billy the power to hurt you over and over. I don't know about your father, but your mother and Billy obviously revel in seeing you suffer. This is, without question, all about power and its misuse.

You said: >He doesn't know that I have you to help me, he'd die if he did, or kill me, I don't know which.< Are you serious? Do you now believe him to be capable of even more extreme violence? If you think that's a possibility, it paves the way for a restraining order, among other things — although they're notoriously unsuccessful at keeping lunatics away from vulnerable women. One way or another, though, you've got to get Billy out of the house.

When you see the lawyer, tell him that I have a file of your emails documenting many instances of abuse. If he can use them to help you, give him my

197

email address and have him get in touch with me, then I'll forward them to him. They can't be downloaded and sent because downloaded emails can be edited. But forwarded emails would arrive intact, with the headers in place.

Could you tell Billy that you're going to visit relatives, or friends, or something and then check into a nearby motel for a mental health break? You could call your parents and say you're visiting friends for a few days. Then, during the day, you could leave blocked messages for Billy on your home phone so the caller ID won't give away your location. The thing is, you need to get out of there. Can you do that? You could have everything packed and be out of there in no time flat. Discuss it with the lawyer tomorrow, see what he has to say. Billy's out of control and you need to get away from him, even if it's just for a little while.

And by the way, in case I ever need to know, please give me your phone pal's name and number (and yours and Sandy's, too). I think she and I should know how to reach each other. I'm not saying that to scare you, Steph. But I realized last night that I don't know how to reach you or anyone you know.

I think your deciding to save your own life (for the second time) has pushed Billy over the edge because he knows he's losing you, and his only weapon is force (emotional, psychological and physical). He's going to try to scare you into staying. You must not go into panic mode. Find out what your legal position is, then sit down and strategize. No matter how you do it, you've got to get away from this man.

Again, I can't tell you how sorry I am that this has happened, Steph. Please believe that none of it is your fault. And keep me posted. I'm very concerned about you.

Hugs, Grace

Subject:
Date: Wed, 3 Jan 2001 18:06:12 -0300
From: Stephanie Baine <baine_stephanie@spotmail.com>
To: Grace

<gloring@homecable.com>

Dear Grace:

I wish I could just pack up and go. But, like you, I can't drive in the dark. Night is rough for me just being in the house, but being in a car on the highway, I couldn't. Plus I'm terrified of motels. Don't ask me why, I don't know. I don't feel safe in them. You can tell me a thousand times how safe they are, etc. It won't help. I can handle Billy, for now. He's going to destroy my mind, temporarily, but once I'm away from him, I'll get it back. Right now I'm scared of what the lawyer's going to think when I tell him all this stuff.

It's terrible not feeling safe in your own home. I can't wait until Billy is out of here for good and I can change all of the locks. I'm not as frantic and crazy as I was earlier, just mildly panicked and depressed. I hate to keep saying that, but I can't seem to snap out of it. It seems like all last week Billy would pull something awful, I'd start to recover and then he'd go and do something worse to knock me back down. I have no doubt that he could sense when I was starting to get over his stunts and he wasn't going to let me be relaxed or happy. Sorry to be free associating like this when I'm sure you have a lot of your own stuff going on. I'm battling off flashbacks and hoping that talking to you will help. It has a little, so now I'm going to get out of your cyber hair, and go try to read for a while. Write when you can.

Love, Steph.

Grace's frustration had ratcheted up a few notches by the time she'd finished reading this email. It bothered her that Stephanie's fear of what was outside her house was keeping her locked in harm's way as a result of what was *inside* her house. It took a lot of time to undo the kind of brainwashing this woman had undergone, but the problem, Grace knew, was that time wasn't as available to her right now as she appeared to think. Any abusive man who told a woman, "I'll never let you go," usually meant it — to the point of death, if necessary. Billy was going to go on full offensive now, to keep Stephanie cowed and submissive. Her only hope was the lawyer. With luck he'd be smart and set the wheels turning at once to get Billy removed from the house, with a restraining order to keep him at a distance. These things would, by no means, assure Stephanie's safety, but it was a solid opening move. Luckily, from the sound of it, there were no financial issues. Stephanie seemed to have enough money.

Of course, if she did manage to get Billy out of the house the likelihood was that his assaults would escalate exponentially, which would leave few, if any, places where Stephanie would be safe. It was just madness that she couldn't, by law, leave the state.

Grace had imagined that being so close to D.C., Virginia would have sensible laws on the books for the protection of women and children. But the divorce procedure Steph had outlined was positively Draconian. Perhaps there were considerations given for extenuating circumstances. After dinner, she'd tell Stephanie to ask her lawyer about that.

Subject: re
Date: Wed, 3 Jan 2001 20:59:10 -0200
From: Grace Loring
<gloring@homecable.com>

To: Stephanie Baine
<baine_stephanie@spotmail.com>

Dear Steph:

You're suffering from sensory overload. And this man is trying his damnedest to make you crazy. It's natural that you'd feel the fallout from the ongoing attacks of one sort or another.

If you truly feel you can't leave, when Billy comes home tonight, have a knife (or a good-sized pair of scissors) ready, hold it by your side just where he can see it and you tell him, "You know, if I kill you I'll get off because it'll be justified homicide. This is the first and last time I'm going to tell you. If you think I'm kidding, go ahead and try coming anywhere near me." Then give the knife or scissors a little twitch, put it/them away and go about your business. Calm, cool and sober.

I really don't know what else you can do with someone so cruel, so devoid of feeling — except to keep showing him your weapon, and saying something along the lines of, "I can defend myself, if I have to. So quit while you're ahead, or one morning you're just not going to wake up." The thing is you've got to stay cool. Keep him off balance. Let him think you're nuts. Who cares? Anything to make him leave you alone.

Stop hating yourself. You're only human and you're just beginning to see that you're living with someone who has no limits. So sleep with a weapon from now on — a knife, a hammer, pepper spray, whatever. If he comes near you, let him have it. Once you're rid of this man, your life will be infinitely easier. But you can't let him intimidate you.

Tomorrow you'll see the lawyer and get the ball rolling. For now, don't give in and play victim. Have a drink if it helps, then get some sleep on the sofa. And tomorrow come out fight- ing. You're too smart to fall into the self-pity pit just when you're about to claim your freedom.

Let me know how it goes.

Hugs, Grace.

"Are you coming down to watch the movie or not?" Nicky asked tiredly from the doorway as Grace hit the "Send" button. Startled, feeling guilty, she knocked her mouse off the desk and bent to retrieve it from the floor. "We've been waiting for you for over an hour. I had everything set up in Dad's room but he was falling asleep, so I switched to the VCR in the living room."

"Shit, I forgot. Sorry. I'll be right there, Nicks."

"What're you doing, anyway, that you're so wrapped up in?" Nicky asked, leaning against the door.

"An abused woman in Virginia I'm trying to help."

"Oh!" Nicky nodded and moved away, saying, "Come, if you're coming. The video's due back at eleven and I don't want to rack up any more late fees."

"I'm coming right now."

Closing the browser, Grace turned off the desk lamp and hurried downstairs to see if Gus needed anything. He was already asleep. She gathered the newspapers from around the bed, straightened his blanket, and went to the kitchen to grab a bottle of ginger beer from the refrigerator.

Settled finally in front of the set, sharing a bowl of microwaved popcorn with her daughter, she couldn't stop wondering every few minutes how, or if, Stephanie was going to make it safely through the night.

>eleven

Grace could scarcely remember a single detail of the movie the next morning. When Vinnie called near noon, she had trouble concentrating. She should've asked Stephanie what time her appointment was with the lawyer. Grace wanted very much to know what had transpired.

"You're not listening to me, sweetcheeks," Vinnie was saying.

"Actually, you're right. I'm not. I can't talk now, Vin. I'm waiting for an email from Stephanie, and I've got to go make Gus's lunch in a minute."

"You're not going to come back to the city with me, are you?"

"Do I have to let you know right now?"

"It'd be nice, but no. I figure since you're not coming, I might as well go home this afternoon."

"So soon?" she asked, focusing at last on the conversation.

"I have things to do," he said gently, as if speaking to a child. "I'll go do them. That way, I can get back sooner."

"How long will you be gone?" Disappointment thickened her throat, making it hard to speak.

"Who knows? A couple of weeks, maybe more, maybe less. Depends on the kind of incentives I get to shlep back up here to goyish land."

"What kind of incentives would you like?" she asked, trying for a playful tone but feeling a depth of sadness that threatened to bring tears.

"An offer you'll make me. I'll decide."

"Here we go with the immigrant shtick again," she complained, as she double-clicked on the Solitaire icon and started a game; anything for distraction. She hadn't expected this.

"What's with the clickety-clack? You're working while we're talking?"

"Not working, just playing."

"That Tetris *mishigas?*"

"No, Solitaire."

"Oh, that's a comfort," he said wryly. "So I'm waiting to hear about the incentives."

"I think inducements might be the more appropriate word."

"We're going to haggle over semantics here? Please, just make me an offer."

"I wish you weren't going," she said, choked. "I'll miss you, Vin. I guess I thought you'd stay for a while longer."

"We'll talk on the phone."

"It won't be the same."

"Listen, do us both a favor and get your friends over to lend a hand with Gus. In the meantime, be a good little *maideleh*. A couple of weeks and I'll be back."

"Okay, *boychik*. I really will miss you."

"We'll be missing each other, so you'll phone and I'll phone."

"Don't make me chase you," she warned.

"Hah! That's a good one. When did you ever?"

"Hah! Never. But just don't this time. Okay? You promise?"

"Hand to heart."

"I love you, Vin," she said, with the odd, near panicky feeling that she might never see him again. "I really do."

"You think I don't know that?" he said. "You think I don't *kvell* just thinking about you?"

"Really?"

"Cute, you are. But a genius, you're not. Who else could I possibly love?"

"Lots of women. They probably line up to throw themselves at you."

He laughed. "Not in this lifetime. We'll

talk, sweetcheeks. I love you, too."

" 'Bye, Vin."

After the call, she wasn't in the mood for games, nor was she in the mood to go downstairs and make lunch. But all at once, there was a fluttering in the pit of her stomach that invariably heralded her need/desire to write. It was solace; her refuge, her hiding place. She couldn't stand the thought of Vinnie being beyond her immediate reach. She needed to know what was happening with Stephanie. And she simply couldn't, just that minute, go downstairs and busy herself preparing yet another meal. So she did what she'd always done when matters began spiraling out of her control: She clicked open the folder with the manuscript-in-progress, pushed the soundtrack from *Cinema Paradiso* into the CD slot on the hard drive, listened to the opening bars, then started writing, words shooting onto the screen as her fingers moved frantically over the keys. Hiding in plain sight.

"I figured you were on a roll, so I did Dad's lunch," Nicky said quietly.

Grace was so deep into the work that it took a moment or two for her daughter's words to register. Then she glanced at the clock. It was after four. The light outside was almost gone. She'd been working for more than three hours. Automatically saving her work, she turned to look at her daughter.

"Thank you, Nicks. I appreciate it. I'm actually getting some work done and forgot all about lunch."

"I figured. So Dad's about to have his nap and I'm heading over to pick up Migs. We're gonna go eat, then catch a movie. We both want to see *Hidden Crouching, Crouching Hidden*, whatever."

Grace laughed. Nicky was forever altering titles or the names of bands, stores, everyday items. Grace's favorite of her daughter's rearrangements was Blootie and The Hofish; her second favorite was a coff of hot cuppee and/or a choc of hot cuplette. "It's had great reviews," she said at last.

"I loved *The Ice Storm* and *Sensible Old Brits* or whatever, so I figure this'll be good, too."

"I wish I was going with you," Grace said.

"So take a night off and come. It's not like you couldn't use a break."

"I can't, Nicks."

"Oh, you could. You just won't. It's okay" — Nicky held up a hand — "I understand. But you should get out, you know. You never go anywhere anymore. It's not good."

"I know." Grace sighed. "It's just . . . all

the arranging. By the time I get everything organized, I'm not in the mood to go out."

"It's not good," Nicky said again.

"Vinnie's going home this afternoon."

"Megadowner. When's he coming back?"

"A couple of weeks, give or take."

"You ought to be going with him. I definitely do not understand this relationship."

"That makes three of us; four including Gus; five, if you count Jerry."

"You'll go FUBAR if you don't take some down-time, Mom. Seriously."

"I'm already FUBAR. Thanks for pretending not to notice and for doing lunch, sweetheart. Say hi to Migs for me."

"Okay, go ahead and dismiss me. But I'm right."

"Yes, you are," Grace agreed. "I'm not dismissing you, honestly. I just can't do anything right now. Aside from needing to get this damned book finished, I really don't want to take the chance of not being able to get back here in a hurry, if I have to. Manhattan's a long way away."

"Not that long. It's bogus logic, but I'm not going to argue. We'll just wind up doing the circular samba, and I'm totally not into that. So I'll see you later." Nicky gave her mother a kiss and went clomping off down the stairs. For a slender young woman,

Nicky usually sounded like a two-hundred-pound weight lifter as she raced around the old frame house.

A few minutes later, the front door closed. Turning back, Grace saw that Nicky had left a handful of Jolly Ranchers next to the keyboard. No accident. Nicky knew her mother's weaknesses. Grace sorted through them, found a watermelon one and popped it into her mouth as she scrolled through the document on the screen, gratified to see she'd done the better part of a chapter.

Nothing came from Stephanie that night.

Grace was sitting at the kitchen table, trying to read the hard copy of that day's work, when Nicky got home.

"Cool movie, Mom," she said, opening the refrigerator door, staring at its contents for several moments, then closing the door again. Sitting down opposite her mother, she said, "Really beautiful stuff. You'd like it. I thought it was going to be a period Jackie Chan–type thing, but it wasn't at all. It was like this cosmic ballet. Migs says hi."

"Cosmic ballet?"

"Yeah. Awesome choreography and special effects, cool music. Except for the song over the end titles. That was way weird.

Techno-rock-mod. Bizarre. Didn't fit the flick at all. Only thing I didn't like, really. You should see it; you'd like it. Very restrained. People were actually clapping at the end. How often does that happen?"

"Hardly ever. Sounds great."

"Major awards, guaranteed. I'm going to bed. Everything okay?" Nicky looked at the pages on the table. "Get a lot done?"

"Almost a whole chapter."

"Good. So how come you don't look happy?"

"I was waiting to hear from this woman I've been emailing, but nothing came. I'm kind of worried about her."

"As if you don't have enough to worry about. I think Vinnie's right: You *are* Jewish. You excel at the two most Jewish things I can think of: guilt and worry."

Grace laughed, then said, "If I am, you know what that makes you?"

"Yup. He already told me I'm a living contradiction in terms: a shiksa princess. I kind of like it. There aren't a whole lot of us, you know. This woman's not your problem, Mom."

"Maybe not. That doesn't mean I don't care what happens to her."

"See! You worry about everybody, even people you don't know. Maybe you need to pull it in a little, save some for yourself."

"Some what?"

"Energy, emotion," Nicky said, mildly exasperated. "It's not as if you've got all that much to spare."

"I've got enough," Grace defended herself.

"Whatever you say. I'm going up. Love you, Mom."

"Love you, too, baby girl. Sleep well."

There was no word from Stephanie the next day or the day after. By the weekend, Grace was certain something terrible had happened. Each night when she climbed into bed, no matter how tired she was, she'd fall asleep only to awaken after a couple of hours, frightened when she considered the many possible reasons for Stephanie's silence. Unable to go back to sleep, she'd switch on the computer to check her email. Nothing. She'd shut everything down and try again to sleep, but couldn't. At last, she'd sit up, turn on the light and read. Some nights after two or three hours, she was able to sleep for another hour or two. But most nights she couldn't. She'd read, finish one book, and at once start another.

During the days, between preparing meals for Gus, she worked steadily on the manuscript, sinking like a stone into the narrative; hiding out in the word-construction she was creating.

The only relief came when Vinnie phoned, usually midday, to chat for half an hour. He was cheerful; he was funny; he was the personification of relief, and she waited for those calls with great anticipation. But the moment she put down the receiver, she became apprehensive once more, wishing Stephanie had given her a phone number, an address, something.

At last, after nearly two weeks of silence, inspiration struck. Mentally cursing herself for not having thought of it sooner, she did an online newspaper search and found the *Alexandria Journal* online. She scrolled through the sections, expecting to see something about a crazed husband killing his wife. But most of the news was wire-fed — primarily political items about bills before Congress or the Senate. The local news was minimal at best.

She was beginning to think that Gus had been right: She should never have become involved. Because now she couldn't stop thinking about it, each day speculating on what might have befallen Stephanie Baine.

>twelve

As the days passed and her work proceeded at a recently unprecedented pace, Grace's concern gradually slid from the forefront of her mind. It wasn't possible to remain focused on Stephanie without any input. And, somewhat ashamedly relieved to have taken a step back from the intense horror of the woman's plight, she went about her household chores on autopilot, anxious always to get back upstairs to the manuscript.

It had been a long time since she'd been quite so engrossed in her work, and it was gratifying to see the printout growing thicker daily as she reached the climax of the story. She barreled ahead, as anxious as any reader to find out what would happen next.

From time to time, she paused in the kitchen to look out at the snow that seemed to have been falling nonstop since Vinnie left, awed by the totality of the enclosing whiteness, by the muffled quality of the sounds inside as well as outside the house.

The attic skylight had been opaque with a thick layer of frozen snow for days. As a result, the room was in a kind of perpetual twilight that, too often, had her craving a nap at ten in the morning or just after lunch. The accumulating snow gave her a not unpleasant sense of isolation. It could be, and was, broken merely by her stepping out onto the front porch to see the snowed-over houses up and down the street, the thick sculpted mounds cocooning automobiles left unstarted for days. Each morning, as she opened the door to get the *New York Times* off the mat, she was shocked into complete wakefulness by the piercingly cold, snow-laden air. And retrieving the *Brattleboro Reformer* every afternoon had the same effect.

During the day, if she paused — fingers poised on the keyboard — to gaze up at the whitened expanse of the skylight, her thoughts lit on Stephanie and she hoped that the young woman had managed to escape and was safely hidden somewhere. Just a moment or two, and then she was drawn back to the architectural challenge of moving her characters and the plotline forward to a conclusion. She had managed to burrow deep into the connective tissue of the structure and, like a spider, was spinning more and more threads to maintain its cohesive design. Later, once this first draft was completed, she'd insert what she thought of as "the frills," the bits of description (of rooms, of clothing, of climate) that added meat to the bare bones of the narrative. For now, the pleasure was in overseeing the whole, moving it along; both an architect and an engineer subcontracted to establish the various systems that would ultimately comprise the whole.

Early on Monday morning of the third week of Stephanie's silence, two things happened. First, the sun suddenly came out, brightening the interior of the house and her mood so that, as she gazed out the kitchen window, she smiled reflexively at hearing Dolly's laughter coming from Gus's bathroom. Then, some inaudible remark by Gus had the woman laughing even harder.

Second, Vinnie called at just before ten to say, "So guess who can't get to his house because the *gonif* didn't bother to plow the driveway, so it's three feet deep in snow?"

"You're *back?*" she exclaimed, looking up to see a tiny, spreading circle of clear glass where the sun was melting some of the snow on the skylight.

"I'm sitting in Mocha Joe's, drinking

triple espressos and getting profoundly, possibly critically, buzzed while I try to get that ratbastard on the phone to tell him to clear my goddamn driveway. When he has done that, I will take a particular, even singular pleasure in wrapping my hands around his scrawny neck and strangling him. Or, better yet, I'll *bury* him in the snow he finally clears — which will be of mountainous proportions. And how are you, *maideleh?*"

"Give me fifteen minutes. I'll come right down."

"That would improve my mood no end. But don't even *think* about driving. The roads in town are a mess. And if the old 'Bird weren't so sturdy, I'd never have made it down the Maple Valley turnoff. Ninety-one was fine, all lanes open. Five's clear and so is nine, but the minute you hit the off-roads or the city streets, such *tsures.*"

"I'll walk. Fifteen minutes, twenty tops. Don't you go anywhere." She hung up and went racing downstairs to her brother's room. "Vinnie's back. I'm going to go meet him for a coffee. Will you be okay for an hour or so? I'll bring you back a sandwich."

Gus grinned. "Take your time. And there's no need to bribe me. But since you offered, nothing new-age, if you don't mind.

220

No messy sprouts or tomatoes. A *real* sandwich, please."

"No messy sprouts, no tomatoes." She hurried to give him a kiss, then asked, "You need anything before I go?"

"Not a thing. Go! You're so hyper you're practically vibrating."

"I'll have my cellphone turned on, in case you need me."

"Go!" He waved her away with a twisted, flopping hand. "Tell your boyfriend to drop by when he gets time."

"My *boyfriend!*" she scoffed.

"What do *you* call him?" he challenged.

"Vinnie," she shot back.

That won her a smile. "Okay. Just tell him I wouldn't mind seeing him."

"All right, I will. If you need me, just hit the speed-dial button. Okay?"

"Gracie, go! I won't need you."

It was hard work to move with any speed down the narrow snow-packed path that had been cleared on High Street. Normally it was less than a fifteen-minute walk to Main, the center of town, but she felt as if it was taking hours. The sun had no warmth and the cold air penetrated her lungs like a scalpel so that breathing was painful. Yet she was sweating from her effort to hurry and highly exhilarated as she rounded the corner onto Main. Opening the door of Mocha Joe's, she was met with a blast of aromatic warmth that had her eyes and nose instantly watering as she clomped down the stairs in the boots Nicky referred to as "snowbunny clodhoppers." She went past the counter to the table at the far end where Vinnie had risen to his feet and stood with his arms dramatically thrown wide.

"Sweetcheeks!" Beaming, he wrapped her in his arms, lifting her several inches off the floor. "A sight for sore eyes, you are. Look how cute!" he said, setting her down and holding her away by the shoulders. "A twelve-year-old, you look like, in the little yellow hat. With pom-poms yet. And where did you get this nice puffy thing that makes you look like a Michelin ad?"

"This 'nice puffy thing' was something Nicky just had to have," she explained, unzipping the nearly weightless down jacket. "It took her almost ninety minutes to buy it up the street at Sam's. Everybody who works there had to give their opinion, as well as half a dozen customers. Three hundred dollars, and she wore it twice. I couldn't stand seeing it just hanging in the closet, so I started wearing it a few weeks ago. You know what she said when she noticed? 'It suits you, Mom. Have it as a present from me.' I'll be right back. I'm just going to order a coffee."

"Sit," he said. "Take a breath. I already ordered. They started making it when you came through the door."

"Making what?"

"So suspicious." He reached across the table and pinched her cheek. "Mocha latte with three shots, extra chocolate."

"Damn, you're good. Thank you." She smiled at him, still winded. "Hi, Vin."

"Hi, yourself, toots. Sit and rest a minute while I try this *yeshuvnik* again."

"Yesh-what?"

"Farmer," he translated, hitting the redial on his cellphone. "Again, the answering machine," he told her, then waited for the message to finish. "Listen, Leroy. I don't hear from you by noon to say that my driveway's been cleared, consider yourself unemployed, not to mention being in the top spot on my shit list. I've left my cell number three times now. Noon I hear from you, or I get myself someone reliable who actually does what he's paid to do." He disconnected, saying, "He's probably in the barn committing unspeakable acts with the animals. Ah! Here's your fancy-schmancy coffee."

The young waiter carefully placed the brimming oversized cup on the table in front of Grace, saying, "We've got some fabulous cinnamon muffins with walnuts and a hint of lemon zest. Or would you like an almond biscotto? It'd go perfectly with your latte."

"This is fine, thanks."

"Another triple, Mr. Steinberg?"

"Better just make it a single, Lon, or I'll stroke out right here in front of your customers, which wouldn't be good for business."

The waiter laughed appreciatively as he removed Vinnie's empty cup and went off to make another espresso.

"What'll you do if you don't hear from the *yeshuvnik?*" she asked.

He shrugged. "Who knows? Maybe check into the Colonel Williams for a night or two."

"Don't do that. Come stay with us. We've got all kinds of room, and anyway Gus wants to see you."

He grinned again and gave her cheek another pinch. "I was hoping you'd say that. Such a sweetheart, you are."

"I missed you," she said softly. "I *really* missed you."

"Ditto, ditto. You're the love of my life. You know that?"

She just stared at him, that New Year's

Eve feeling rushing back, bringing with it the threat of tears.

"What, you think I'm kidding?"

"No. I don't know what I think."

"Sure you do," he said. "You think I'm a fifty-five-year-old fat guy with a swell career and even sweller delusions."

"You're the least deluded person I've ever known, Vin. And you're not fat. You're just — comfortable, cuddly."

"Hah! You're wild about me."

"Hah! You wish." She looked down at the surface of her coffee and said, "Actually, I am."

"So, okay. I'm a happy man here. The *gonif* ratbastard lets me down, I come camp out with you until I can get somebody to plow the driveway."

"Good." She looked up at him. "Great!"

"So, the Princess is back at school?"

"This morning. You wouldn't believe her room."

"Sure I would. I was a teenager once. You, of course, were not."

"Hey! I grew up with August Junior and Lydia. Two more anally retentive people never lived. Being a slob was not an option in that household. Anything that got left on the floor went into the trash. I lost a lot of important stuff that way — school newsletters, an autographed photo of The Monkees, lots of stuff."

"The Monkees? Better it should go in the trash."

"Important stuff," she repeated. "Programs for shows I saw, concert ticket stubs, even my tenth grade yearbook."

"Oy, poor deprived *maideleh*. My heart bleeds."

"You think it was easy?"

"Never," he said, lightly mocking. "Such a hardship, picking up after yourself."

"Go ahead and make fun of me. I'll get you back when you least expect it. Listen, don't let me forget to pick up a sandwich for Gus. I promised I'd bring him back something. So where's your car?"

"In the big lot. I knew it, at least, would be plowed. How's your street?"

"Passable, and our driveway's clear. You can park."

"Here you go, Mr. Steinberg," Lon said, returning with Vinnie's coffee.

"Better bring me the tab when you get a minute, Lon."

"No problem, Mr. Steinberg. I'll just get it now."

"Nice kid," Vinnie observed. "Lousy painter, but a sweetheart. He graduated last June and he's taking this year off while he decides about his future. I'm encouraging him to do a post-grad photography course. He's got a good eye, but oil is not his medium. And his watercolors look like what's left on the floor of an inner city ER after a Saturday night gang fight. So how goes the book?"

"Another two or three chapters and it's done."

"Fantastic! Then you'll have time to play with Uncle Vinnie."

"No," she corrected him. "I'll do the second draft and *then* I'll have time to play with Uncle Vinnie."

"So you'll type faster."

She laughed, then found herself unable to look away from his very blue, very knowing eyes as she drank some of her coffee. Her throat soothed, she said, "Remind me to get Gus's sandwich."

"I'll remember to remind you just when I get to the register to pay for mine."

"I don't care *when* you remember, just remember."

He leaned to one side, chin in hand, saying, "Such a cutie. I could eat you up with a spoon. When I go back to the city, you'll come with."

"Maybe. We'll see."

"You'll come with," he repeated. "The

book'll be finished and you'll bring it to Miles in person."

"We'll see."

"We'll go see every show, eat out morning, noon and night. We'll shlep around SoNo and look at lousy pretend-art; I'll take you dancing. You'll be out of your mind happy."

"This is shaping up to be one of those offers I can't refuse." She smiled at him.

"You betcha, cupcake. You think Uncle Vinnie doesn't know the difference between incentive and inducement? *Believe* me! Uncle Vinnie *knows*. You'll come with."

"Probably."

"Hah! I knew you would."

"Well, hah! You were right."

>thirteen

"It's the Vinster!" Nicky cried, dumping her coat and backpack in the front hall before running to the kitchen to throw her arms around the man. "What're you doing?" she asked, giving him a hard hug.

"I'm doing dinner," he said, lifting her chin with his fist. "Oy! So gorgeous. Are the boys climbing all over each other to get to you?"

"As if." She made a face.

"*Shmegeggis,*" he declared. "They know nothing. Thirty years ago, sweetheart, I'd have been scrambling to get to you."

"That's because you've got a brain. The guys're scared of me," she said, shrugging.

"At college, the guys're stupid. They're so busy drinking and smoking funny cigarettes they don't know what's what. But out there, in the real world, they're not so stupid. Wait and see. You'd better take those boots off or your mother will do you an injury."

"Where is she?"

"Upstairs." He made typing motions with his fingers.

"And Dad's napping?"

"Right."

"So it's just us. Cool. We can talk."

She ran back to the front hall to push off her boots and returned to see Vinnie wiping the slush off the linoleum with a fistful of paper towels.

"I'd have done that," she protested.

"It's done." He tossed the wet towels into the trash, asking, "You want some coffee, tea?"

"I'll put the kettle on," she said. "So what're you cooking?"

"Pasta, what else? Throw a bunch of stuff in a pot with some red wine, pour it over fusilli and, kaboom, dinner."

"No meat?"

"I don't know who lives here?" he replied.

"Sounds good, then. Are you staying over?"

"It's a problem?" he asked, chopping green peppers.

"Never. It's the bomb. But how come you're not at the barn?"

"Don't ask," he said, holding the cutting board over the pot and using the knife edge to push the green peppers into it. "Couldn't get the driveway cleared."

"I thought there was some guy who does it for you."

"I thought so, too. Couldn't even get the

scrawny *mamzer* to return my calls today."

"What's a mumzer?"

"A ratbastard by my standards," he answered, slicing Portobello mushrooms.

"Good word. I've gotta remember that."

"So tell me why the schoolboys are afraid of you."

She shrugged again. "It's bullcrap. You tell me why you and Mom aren't more of a thing."

He laughed. "A thing. We're a *thing,* just maybe not the *kind* of thing *you* think of as a *thing.*"

"You could give a person a headache," she said, searching through a cupboard filled with several dozen boxes of different kinds of tea, at last selecting one labeled Calm.

"That's going to do you anything?" he asked, pointing his knife at the box before using it to push the mushrooms off the cutting board into the pot.

"I like it. It's got chamomile blossoms, and" — she read from the back of the package — "hibiscus flowers, spearmint, rose petals, blackberry leaves, peppermint, safflower, lemon balm, lemon grass, natural flavors and the mumbled chantings of a certified tea shaman." She was laughing by the time she finished.

"A salad, you're drinking."

"I never actually read the ingredients before. Now I'm not so sure."

"A certified tea shaman. *Gevalt*." He reached for a large Bermuda onion and began peeling it. "For this, you paid how much?"

"I don't know. Six bucks? Whatever. It's good, really. You should try it."

He shook his head. "I'll save myself for a nice glass of red wine with dinner, something containing only grapes, no salad."

"So how long are you staying?"

"Who knows? Finding someone to plow that driveway at this juncture could take days."

"Mom could give you the number of the guy who does ours."

"Already did. He doesn't go outside of town, couldn't recommend anyone, either."

She hoisted herself up onto the counter and sat with her hands braced on either side, her legs dangling. "Good," she declared. "It'll be like a dorm. I'll go rent some videos. After dinner, we'll have popcorn and watch movies."

"Might be just the two of us," he cautioned. "Your mother's getting to the end of her manuscript and doesn't want to stop for anything, and Gus plans to watch some nature show on PBS." Lowering his voice, he said, "I can't stand those shows. Lugubrious voice-overs while scorpions eat rattlesnakes, lions tear gazelles apart. *Feh*."

"Double *feh*," she agreed. "I can't stand them, either. This is way cool, Vin."

"You think so, huh?"

"Definitely. Bet Dad's psyched, too."

"Oh, hugely. He launched himself into an hour-long dialectic, complete with verbal footnotes, on the hermeneutical invalidity of some weighty tome he's just finished. I was beyond lost. My eyes were starting to glaze. But he was happy as a clam. So fine."

"What book?"

"Oy! You actually want to know?"

"As a matter of fact, I do."

"Then you'll have to take a look at the top book on the bedside reading mountain because I got so lost in the polysyllables I can't even remember. He talks good, your uncle."

"He talks great. He is beyond smart."

"This is true. He is also beyond my comprehending."

"That is such gar-*bahj*, Vinster. Don't try to kid a kidder."

"Listen to this!" he said to the ceiling. "My own lines, she's using on me."

"Get over yourself," she said, slipping down from the counter to unplug the kettle and pour hot water over the tea bag she'd dropped into a mug.

"I'd need a ladder," he quipped, attacking the onion with a flourish of his knife. "So show me. When you add water, you get re-constituted flowers and veggies?"

"Away!" she said, shielding the mug with her body. "I'm not showing you."

"Hah! A cupful of blossoms and petals you've got."

"Tea! It's tea! Look!" She held out the mug.

"Whaddya know!" he said in mock wonder. "It's a bever-*ahj*."

"I'm going up to get changed," she said, "and then we'll talk movies."

"Sounds like a plan."

While she got Gus into his pajamas, Lucia chattered away about the weather and how hard it was getting around town with all the snow. Nicky, Grace and Vinnie lingered at the kitchen table, listening. Nicky was pick-ing the last bits of arugula from the salad bowl, Grace was nibbling on the heel of the baguette, and Vinnie, sipping his wine, was contentedly admiring mother and daughter.

"Good thing you're within walking dis-tance," they heard Gus say.

"It's the truth, Mr. Loring. Else I'd never

be gettin' here. The car's under a good two feet of snow, froze solid."

"As I said, it's a good thing you're nearby."

"So, Nicks." Grace at last broke the silence in the kitchen. "What movies did you rent?"

"I got Vinnie's and my all-time fave, *Waiting for Guffman*."

On cue, Vinnie said, "Salt vaw-ta," and Nicky laughed.

"I also got *Groundhog Day*, which I happen to think is the best Bill Murray flick ever."

"How can you watch the same movie over and over?" Grace asked her daughter.

"If I like it, it's easy."

"And we all know how easy *I* am," Vinnie said.

"True. So you two watch the movies and I'll clear up in here, then get a bit more work done," Grace said.

"We'll help," Vinnie offered.

"You cooked. I'll do the cleanup."

"A hard bargain she drives, your mother." He smiled over at Nicky.

"You cue up the movie," she told him, "and I'll nuke the popcorn."

"Maybe the popcorn could wait a while," Vinnie said, patting his abdomen.

"Okay, then. *I'll* cue up the movie and you

shmooze with Mom." She went off to the living room.

Grace continued to sit at the table, sweeping the bread crumbs into a pile with her hand. "It's nice having you here, Vin."

"I like it. If we worked at it, we could get a little habit going."

"We might, if there weren't so many complications."

"Complications only exist if you acknowledge them. Work past them as a matter of routine and they're not complications anymore, they're just things you do."

"That was profound. I think I like the immigrant shtick better." She got up and began stacking the plates. "Take your wine and go watch the movies."

"Bossy," he murmured.

"You betcha. Got a lot of *routine* things to do."

"Okay!" He held up a hand. "I'm going."

"Thanks for cooking, Vin, and for buying more food than we'll ever be able to eat."

"Hey! Next to giant drugstores where I can wander the aisles for hours, finding products I never knew I needed, what I love best is a supermarket the size of a football stadium. Granted, I compromised today at the Co-op. But I can do damage even in a small market."

"I noticed."

Moving close to her, he whispered, "You gonna come play with Uncle Vinnie later?"

"Wouldn't miss it. Now go watch the movie and let me finish up here so I can get back to work. No work, no play."

"Ooooo! I'm going, I'm going."

With a start, Grace opened her eyes. According to the clock it was just after six. And according to the warmth at her back, she'd actually slept for almost five hours with someone in her bed. Vinnie couldn't have moved at all or she'd never have been able to sleep for so long. Amazing, she thought, easing away and turning over to study him in the snowlight caught in the room.

The miracle man. He didn't thrash about, didn't snore; he just lay serenely still, his breathing barely audible. Maybe he'd have to stay here for several days before someone could be found to clear his driveway, and they'd have another chance to try out this arrangement, see if she was able to sleep for a second or even a third night with Vinnie in her bed. But it was selfish to hope his driveway would remain unplowed in order that she might use him, in essence, as a guinea pig. He had work to do, too; commissions for covers and illustrations, and, of course, the never-ending project of the barn itself.

The first thing he'd done after closing on the property was to have the most energy-efficient oil furnace he could find installed, along with all new ductwork; he'd also had the old inadequate fifty-gallon oil tank dug up and replaced by a two-hundred-gallon one.

"Three things I can't stand," he'd told her as he held open the door for her on the night they'd met nearly four years after he'd bought the barn. "Being cold inside a house, lousy appliances and previously owned bathrooms. Most people look for the books or the art on the walls when they visit somebody's home for the first time. Me, I check first the appliances, then the bathroom. If everything's nice and clean, I can relax and enjoy. If the stove or the bathroom's *shmutzik*, I don't want to know from this person who's living in a *chazzer-shtal* — which is a pigpen, since I can see you're ready to ask. I'm putting my money on your bathroom, sweetcheeks."

Before he'd even consider bringing a single piece of furniture in (as if fearful of contaminating his possessions), he'd hired the best contractor in the area to gut and renovate the bathroom as well as the kitchen — which occupied the entire area beneath the hayloft. At first sight, Grace found the results startling: a vast, high-tech chrome and butcher block kitchen, and — mercifully enclosed (Grace believed in privacy in certain areas and was relieved to learn that Vinnie did, too) — an ultramodern all-white, fully tiled (walls, ceiling and floor) bathroom contained within the perennial work-in-progress that was the barn. Some area or other was invariably curtained by heavy gauge plastic sheeting because every spring Vinnie attacked another section of the structure. Ultimately, he alone removed many of the weathered exterior boards, then went to great pains to make the replacements as authentic as possible.

Then he'd moved inside and began adding studs on the interior walls that gradually climbed thirty feet to the peak of the roof on one side, and sixteen feet to the hayloft on the other. Insulation got packed between the studs, drywall went over that and then, ever the perfectionist, he covered the drywall with raw tongue-and-groove oak paneling. Wearing a face mask, he smoothed down each newly completed section with an electric sander, then stained and sealed it. In the eleven years he'd owned the barn, he'd managed to redo all the structural walls and insulate them. The golden oak interior paneling gave the dwelling cohesiveness; the kitchen no longer seemed misplaced beneath the heavy beams of the hayloft.

His current project was the hayloft itself which would, when finished, be the bedroom. He'd already had a local carpenter he knew and trusted install subflooring up there, along with a proper staircase instead of the old, splintery homemade ladder — which Vinnie had saved, planning to refinish it, too. "It's solid maple. Once upon a time, the poor farmer who grew stones on this land made this ladder with his own hands. It's a work of art. And when it's cleaned up, it'll be beautiful. I'm thinking I'll suspend it from the underside of the loft, put big S-hooks on the rungs and hang stuff there."

When she'd asked, "What stuff?" he replied, "I'll think of things." Grace had no doubt that he would, once he'd completed this year's project: laying hardwood over the subflooring in the loft, and then building a huge storage/closet unit. "Then," he'd declared the previous summer, "I'll think about the windows."

She was certain he'd choose exactly the right spot to place an immense window offering a splendid view of the property. And after that, no doubt he'd tackle the area that was now the bedroom. He was a man who never ran short of ideas.

Smiling, she turned back onto her side, remembering how lovingly Vinnie had handled the old, hand-hewn ladder, and how he'd been able to see the beauty and value in something most people would have simply thrown away.

>fourteen

When next she opened her eyes, it was almost eight-thirty. Jumping out of bed, she grabbed her robe, jammed her feet into her slippers, and ran down to the kitchen to find Vinnie, dressed and fresh-shaven, hair still wet from the shower, sitting at the table, drinking coffee and reading the business section of the *Times*.

At once setting aside the paper, he said, "Dolly's been and gone. The Princess just left for school, and Leroy-the-*gonif* phoned maybe half an hour ago to say the driveway's clear. Sit. I'll get you coffee. I just made a fresh pot."

She sat down, with a flatness of tone she couldn't conceal, saying, "So you're leaving."

"Not forever. You'll come over tonight. The house'll be nice and warm by then."

"I can't —"

"All arranged," he cut her off. "We'll go to Panda North. I've got a craving for scallion pancakes."

"But I've got to work —"

"You'll work all day. Tonight, scallion

pancakes, lemon chicken, spare ribs, shrimp fried rice." He set the coffee in front of her, then resumed his seat. "Everything you love. I'll come get you at seven. Okay?"

She thought for a moment, then said, "Okay."

"Good. Drink before it gets cold."

He wasn't going to raise the subject, she realized. Any other man would've been taking bows for having managed to sleep through the night in her bed. But not Vinnie. If she didn't mention it, he wouldn't.

"You're a nice man, Alvin Steinberg."

"And you also are a nice person, Graceleh."

"Thank you."

"Very welcome."

"I was hoping you'd have to stay for a few days."

"I know. I was hoping, too. But so it goes. The *shnorrer* had to grow a work ethic all of a sudden."

"Will you phone me later?"

"That's permission?" he asked.

"Yes."

"So I'll phone you later."

The phone rang at five past nine, just after Vinnie left. Grace glanced at the caller ID. Anonymous. Probably another telemarketer. She ignored it and let the answering machine field the call. Naturally, when she checked before heading upstairs, no message had been left.

Subject: This is Sandy
Date: Wed, 31 Jan 2001 09:04:10 -0500
From: Stephanie Baine <baine_stephanie@spotmail.com>
To: Grace <gloring@homecable.com>

Dear Miss Loring:

This is Sandy, Stephie's friend. I don't know how to do email so I hope you'll excuse me if I mess up. Also I'm very nervous but Stephie asked me to get in touch with you to tell you what all has been going on here. I don't have Stephie's vocabulary and don't know how to speak in euphemisms. I don't even know if I spelled that word right. I didn't go to college like she did. I didn't even finish high school, hated it and dropped out. Anyway, that sick bastard damn near killed her. What she did was self-defense, but they wanted to charge her with murder.

Her lawyer argued and got the charge reduced to manslaughter. But they shouldn't be allowed to get away with that!! She shouldn't have been charged with anything. She should have got a medal!! If you could've heard her scream in the middle of the night last night you'd have got a gun and gone after him too. She was in jail for four days because of the weekend and no hearings or something, which was horrible for the poor girl. But the judge granted bail and she had some money hidden away, so we were able to get her out and bring her home. She was in the shower at least ten times a day for the first week, falling asleep for a couple of hours on the sofa in her clothes, and then waking up not knowing where she was. She won't say a word about what happened to anyone, except for her lawyer, who's been really great and keeps telling her she's got a good chance at getting off. She is so upset and exhausted after weeks of not sleeping at night that I gave her some valium and finally she went to sleep around three this morning. She's still sleeping and I'm glad because she is worn right out and still scared to death even though that bastard is finally dead, which he should have been a long time ago. I've been staying with her, looking out for her because she's terrified to stay here alone.

She said for me to ask if maybe you saved any of her emails because the lawyer says they could be evidence to prove she was abused. I really hope you do and that you can send them to me. I don't have my own email so Stephie said to use hers. Dear God! We have to help her. I'm praying that you did keep those emails and can send them. It'll help her a lot. The lawyer says they're like a dairy and they'll show she was defending herself. Sorry that I talked so much, I just wanted to let you know everything. Thank you for trying to help Stephie. She told me how kind you've been, giving her good advice and getting her to phone that hotline and everything.

Stephie sends her love and says to

say she's very sorry. I hope this gets to you okay.

Sandy

The email moved Grace to write a reply at once.

Subject: re: This is Sandy
Date: Wed, 31 Jan 2001 10:22:00 -0400
From: Grace Loring <gloring@homecable.com>
To: Stephanie Baine <baine_stephanie@spotmail.com>

Dear Sandy:

Thank you for getting in touch and letting me know that Stephanie is all right. Do me a favor and fill me in on the details. All I can gather from your email is that she shot(?) Billy and has been charged with manslaughter, which is a considerable step down from murder. I'd very much appreciate it if you could give me some more information so I can get a clearer picture of what you've told me.

As for Stephanie's emails, yes I do have them. However, there's a problem with sending them to you online that Stephanie's lawyer would certainly understand. It's a kind of "chain of evidence" issue. You see, once an email has been downloaded, it can be edited and changed. The same thing applies to returning them to the original sender. The only way these emails would have value as a form of "diary," would be if I forwarded each of them, complete with their headers, to the lawyer. Once he received them, he could then, with a witness present, print them out in full and have them notarized to verify their integrity. In other words, since the emails are from Stephanie to me, if they were then sent directly from me to the lawyer, all the headers would prove that they hadn't been sent back to her and altered in any way. It sounds complicated, but it's quite simple. The headers on an email show where it came from and where and when it was received. So Stephanie's emails to me would have that information, and my forwarding them to the lawyer would also contain this information. I know this because I've done research on the issue quite recently.

So, the best way to do this is to have the lawyer contact me directly and we can then arrange between us for a transfer of the emails, if they're of any value.

Please tell Stephanie that I'm terribly sorry. I'm sure this has been a nightmare for her. And tell her, too, that when she's up to it, I'd really like to hear from her.

Best regards,

Grace.

After her reply had disappeared from the screen, Grace sat looking at the Messenger window. She felt agitated, unnerved, wondering why there hadn't been anything in the *Alexandria Journal* about the shooting. But then, she reasoned, if it had happened early in the month, it would have been old news by the time she'd looked at the newspaper online. She couldn't remember if the site had an archives search engine and decided to take a look.

There wasn't a thing about a domestic shooting in the archives. Bemused, she closed the browser window. It was entirely possible that she'd selected the wrong key words for the search, but she'd tried a number of different ones before giving up. It didn't really matter, yet she'd have liked to read whatever newspaper reports there might have been.

It was shocking, really, to think that this young woman had actually killed her husband; shocking to realize that someone she knew had had to go to such an extreme to defend herself. It scarcely seemed real. And now those emails detailing Stephanie's abuse might play a significant role in justifying her self-defense. But what about Grace's replies? She had a nagging sense that she may have urged Stephanie down that path. And while she'd saved Stephanie's emails, she hadn't saved her own. Luckily, she hadn't emptied the "Sent" folder in well over a month. Opening the browser again, she named a new folder "replies," and then began scrolling through the "sent" emails, dragging each of her replies to Stephanie into the new folder. When she was finished, she had more than two dozen of them.

Starting at the beginning she began to read what she'd written. She found nothing exceptional until she came to the one she'd sent on the third of January. And then she broke into a sweat:

> If you truly feel you can't leave, when Billy comes home tonight, have a knife (or a good-sized pair of scissors) ready, hold it by your side just where he can see it and you tell him, "You know, if I kill you I'll get off because it'll be justified homicide. This is the first and last time I'm going to tell you. If you think I'm kidding, go ahead and try coming anywhere near me." Then give the knife or scissors a little twitch, put it/them away and go about your business. Calm, cool and sober.

You know, if I kill you I'll get off because it'll be justified homicide. She reread the paragraph and this sentence in particular several times, considering the implications of what she'd said. Could she be held accountable for inciting someone to violence? Had Stephanie saved Grace's replies? She distinctly remembered advising Stephanie to trash all her incoming mail, on the off chance that Billy might access her files. But had Stephanie done that? And did it matter? She, Grace, hadn't killed anyone, nor had she advised Stephanie to do more than threaten the man with a knife or a pair of scissors in order to make him back off. She'd never said anything about a gun. But perhaps she'd planted the idea in the young woman's mind. And since Stephanie had a well-grounded fear of knives, perhaps a gun was a more logical choice of weapon. God! This was frightening. Grace didn't know what to think.

Don't anticipate! she told herself. Wait to hear from the lawyer and go from there. But still . . . She needed to talk about this. But to whom? Gus might be sympathetic, but she had no doubt he'd say he'd warned her not to get involved; he'd be implacable, in full I-told-you-so mode. No blame *per se,* but she'd feel it. Vinnie would be completely sympathetic but he'd be unable to offer any viable counsel. The only person she could think of who'd be both knowledgeable and objective was Jerry. He was a law enforcement officer, a state trooper. Still, the laws of Vermont were no doubt very different from the laws of Virginia — which, based on what Stephanie had told her, stemmed from the dark ages. *God!* She couldn't think what to do. Once again closing the browser, she got up and went downstairs to make a fresh pot of coffee. She needed a good dose of caffeine to jump-start her brain, get it wrapped around the idea that a woman who'd sought her out for help had ended up killing her husband. That he had deserved his fate was, in some ways, immaterial. All she could hope was that Sandy would get back to her quickly with additional information. The more Grace knew, the better able she'd be to know how to proceed. For the present, all she could do was wait.

Another anonymous call came in at 11:15. Again she ignored it. Again there was no message.

She got one paragraph written, knew it was no good and deleted it. After reviewing the chapter-in-progress, she sat, trying to find the next sequential step in the narrative. Nothing came. She had no idea where she'd been intending to go. She felt flattened, frightened. Was she in any way responsible for what had happened? Had she overstepped the bounds and given Stephanie Baine bad, even dangerous, advice? Wrapping her arms around herself, she gazed into space, needing some form of absolution. Her brain felt as if it had been neatly severed: half believed she'd done her best and couldn't be held accountable for what had taken place in the Baine household, and half felt horribly guilty, with the sickening sense that she'd unwittingly thrown gasoline on a fire.

>fifteen

"How could it even remotely be considered your fault? Did you put a gun in this woman's hand?" Vinnie asked from across the table at Panda North.

"No, but I did put a suggestion in her head."

"*Please*. You told her to defend herself. Completely sensible advice under the circumstances. How does that make you responsible?"

"I didn't say I'm responsible, Vin. I just feel . . . as if I should've been more low-key, less . . . I don't know. I've never known anyone who actually killed another person — for whatever reason. It's scary."

"That I understand. But it still doesn't put you in the driver's seat, sweetcheeks."

"Logically, I know that's true. But I can't help how I feel. I just wish I *knew* more."

"So this Sandy person will write back and you'll know more."

"I thought I'd get a reply right away."

"The woman said, did she not, that she

255

doesn't know how to do email?"

"That is what she said."

"So why're you expecting someone who doesn't know how it works to be sitting, waiting, ready to fire off an answer bim-bam-boom? Eat, please."

"I'm really not hungry."

"Eat! You'll be hungry once you start. Look at all this beautiful food. It's practically singing that you should eat it."

She picked up a slice of scallion pancake, took a bite, and realized he was right. Suddenly, she was famished.

"See! Some things I know," he said with a smile.

"There are lots of things you know. I just wish *I* knew what to do about this situation."

"You'll get an email with more facts. When you get it you'll talk to Jerry, and you'll figure it out. Here, have some lovely chicken."

"Are you *serious?*" Nicky asked the next evening.

"Completely."

"She *killed* her husband?"

"It was self-defense, Nicks."

"Yeah, but still. She couldn't've just left him?"

"She probably felt that she couldn't."

"Whatever. But that's *extreme,* Mom. I

mean, we all go around saying, 'Oh, I could just kill whoever.' It doesn't mean you're actually going to do it."

"If someone's beaten long enough and hard enough, whether physically or psychologically, there's no saying what that person will do. Some women just go on, year after year, taking it and one day get beaten to death, or they become so brainwashed that they interpret abuse as a sign of love. If they're not being screamed at or battered, the man in question doesn't love them anymore. Some just reach their limit and one day realize they can't take another minute of it and they snap. Either they escape or they fight back. I guess Stephanie snapped and killed him before he could kill her."

"Now you're all weirded out by the whole thing."

"I am," Grace confessed. "I've been waiting all day for her friend Sandy to email me again, but so far nothing."

"Well, if she's looking after this Stephanie, who's in an advanced state of freak-out, maybe she hasn't had time. You're not going to sit up all night, waiting, are you?"

"No, I'm not going to do that."

"When're you going to talk to Uncle Jerry?"

"Once I've got more information. I don't even know what I want to say to him yet,

Nicks. When I've got some hard facts, I'll have a lot of questions. But there's no point in phoning him until I've got specifics."

"Makes sense, I guess. You want me to hang with you for a while?"

"No thanks, baby girl. Go to bed. I'm going up in a minute myself. Just don't mention this to Gus. Okay? I really don't want him to do a little verbal tap-dance on my conscience."

"He wouldn't do that."

"He'd *definitely* do that. He told me from the get-go not to get involved, and I told him in so many words that he didn't know his ass from his elbow. He was probably right, but I didn't think so at the time. Eventually I'll tell him the whole story, because I always wind up telling him everything. I just don't want to do it now."

"Poor Mama," Nicky cooed, giving her mother a kiss. "I'm sorry it so totally turned to shit. But it's not your fault. You shouldn't feel guilty."

"Can't be helped. It's probably those Jewish antecedents Vin likes to insist I had."

"Still, you shouldn't feel that way. You were just trying to help. How could you know it'd all turn to rat doo-doo?"

That earned her a laugh. "You're too funny," Grace said.

"The day I can't make you laugh is the day I start worrying seriously about your mental health. 'Night, Mom."

Just before one A.M. Grace shut down the computer and got ready for bed. This was, she thought, starting to feel like a replay of the aftermath of Steph's last email, when Grace waited day after day for word — initially anxious, then gradually becoming resigned to the ongoing silence. Except that this time a man was dead and his wife was being charged with manslaughter. Why the hell hadn't Sandy written back? It made Grace angry. If the situation was so dire, urgency ought to have been the order of the day. So what possible reason could there be for the delay?

As she brushed her teeth, she decided that perhaps it was a matter of Sandy and Steph having a problem connecting with the lawyer; lawyers could be notoriously difficult to reach. It was the only answer Grace could think of that made sense. And satisfied that this was most likely the case, her anger dissolved, for the moment leaving only her ongoing, somewhat inexplicable fear.

Once in bed, she reached for the mystery she was currently reading, found her place and settled in for the usual half-hour session that culminated in her being sufficiently drowsy to go to sleep.

An hour later, she was still reading, still wide-awake, and hungry. Taking the book with her, she went down to the kitchen to study the contents of the refrigerator, hoping to find something that looked appetizing. Nothing. She opened the cupboards, one after the other, and with a sigh reached for a bag of potato chips. With the chips and a tin of V-8, she sat at the table and munched her way through half the bag and all the juice as she read several more chapters. A glance at the clock as she rinsed the tin for the recycling box told her it was two-thirty. The chips back in the cupboard, she returned upstairs.

Muttering, "What the hell," she turned on the computer, reading a couple more pages of the mystery while she waited for the machine to boot up. The icon was flashing: email. She clicked on the inbox. Spam, spam and more spam. Too disgusted to bother with copying and pasting the things over to the SpamCop site, she shut everything down and went back to bed to read some more.

At last, just before four A.M., as her eyes were beginning to glaze, she got to the end of the book and turned out the light. She was awakened by the telephone at eight. Anonymous. Relentless telemarketers. Her bank was the worst culprit. On the rare occasions when she picked up on an anonymous call, it was inevitably some barely coherent paid slave launching into a script about the many new services her bank was offering. She cut them off curtly every time with, "Thanks, but I'm not interested. When are you going to take my name off your list?"

"Why are you grumping around today?" Gus asked when she brought his lunch tray.

"I didn't get to sleep until four. I'm tired, that's all."

"Too much excitement in your life," he said drolly, "what with Vinnie back in town."

"Right. That's it exactly."

For a change, she sat down to eat with him in the living room.

"Next to your grilled cheese, I love your salmon salad and cucumber on white the best," he said. "Delish, Gracie."

"Hmmn," she murmured, all but falling asleep as she chewed.

"Might be a good idea to take a nap this afternoon," he advised. "Unless you're planning to sleep right there with your face in the plate."

"Remember that old Mary Hartman episode where the guy drowned in his soup?" she said with a grin.

"A thing of beauty. I cherish that episode. It's right up there near the top of my all-time favorites list, just below the frilly shirt episode on *Seinfeld*."

"That one's not even *on* my list."

"Probably a guy thing," he said, as a fair amount of the innards of the half-sandwich he lifted to his mouth landed on his bib.

"Probably," she agreed, averting her eyes. Sometimes, watching him eat could wipe out her appetite. And then, of course, she was swamped by shame — which was why she usually ate lunch alone in the kitchen. It was safe to eat dinner together because they both watched the nightly news. But unless there was an afternoon game of some sort, Gus didn't turn on the TV until after six and it would've been unforgivably rude of her not to look over at him every so often.

"So how long is Vinnie staying this time?" he asked as he put down the sandwich and with both palms lifted his lightweight plastic cup of juice.

"I didn't think to ask. A few weeks, I'd imagine." As she spoke, she realized all at once that she hated it when Vinnie was away. Odd, but his absences were something she'd tolerated for seven years as a form of punctuation in her life. He was gone; she shut her mind to thoughts of him. He came back; she opened her mind again. But since New Year's Eve everything had changed and it was no longer either convenient or easy to wall off thoughts of him. *You're the love of my life. You know that?* Without warning, her throat was burning and she was on the verge of tears. You're the love of *my* life, she thought. What have I been doing all this time? What was I thinking?

"What's the matter?" Gus asked, looking at her with his brows drawn together.

Not trusting herself to speak, she shrugged and took a small bite of her sandwich.

"I don't believe you," her brother persisted. "Something's wrong. I know you, Grace."

"Honestly, I'm just tired. I'll definitely take a nap after lunch."

"I've seen you tired and I've seen you bothered. I know the difference."

"Leave it, please, Gus. It's nothing, really."

"You know that I appreciate everything you've done for me, don't you?"

"Of course I do," she said thickly.

"If you ever feel I'm taking you for granted, you have to tell me."

"I've never felt that and I never will. Look at all you've done for me and Nicky!"

"That's not on the same level."

"It's exactly the same," she argued.

"It isn't, not remotely, but I'll drop it. Just know that I'm grateful, Gracie. I don't always remember to say thank you when I should, but I'd never have been able to get by without you."

She nodded, managed a shaky smile, and took another bite of her sandwich in order not to have to speak.

She slept from three until five that afternoon and awakened with a fierce headache. After taking a couple of Excedrin Migraine tablets, she checked her email. Nothing from Sandy or Stephanie, and she was back to being angry. This was starting to get on her nerves in a big way.

"The hell with this!" she declared. Determined not to allow that distant drama to wreak havoc on her life and her work, she clicked open the manuscript. If it was the last thing she ever did, she was going to get this book finished.

Another anonymous phone call came in just after six while she was making dinner. "You're starting to piss me off," she whispered to the ID screen on the kitchen phone. "Give it up! I'm not going to answer."

>sixteen

There was not a word from Sandy or Stephanie the next day. It was maddening. Grace felt as if she'd become caught up in some incomprehensible game without rules, and she didn't like it. The frustration of not knowing what was going on down in Virginia was bound to overwhelm her, if she allowed it. So she closed her mind to the matter and concentrated on the manuscript, stopping only to prepare a meal, to throw another load of laundry into the washer or the dryer, or to talk to Vinnie on the phone. She gobbled her lunch standing at the kitchen counter while Gus ate off his tray in the living room. She drank a second cup of coffee, waiting for her brother to call out, "I'm finished." Then she dashed in, removed his bib, grabbed the tray and deposited them on the kitchen counter before taking the stairs two at a time back to the top of the house.

Dinner was the only time that day when she took a break of more than half an hour. She, Gus and Nicky watched the news to-

265

gether in the living room, the three of them eating off trays and commenting about the events of the day during the commercial breaks. Afterward, she chatted distractedly with Nicky while they cleaned up the kitchen and loaded the dishwasher. Nicky was going out to meet Migs and some of her other friends for a drink at The Common Ground. "Or maybe Café Beyond. We haven't decided yet."

"Wherever you get to, I don't want you drinking and driving," Grace warned, as she always did.

"I'm not an idiot, Mom. I'll have maybe two drinks max. If I get wasted, I'll leave the car and walk home. Okay?"

"No, you'll phone me and I'll come pick you up."

"Whatever. You're in a totally snaky mood. You know that?"

"Yes, I am. And yes, I know. Just be careful."

"I will be careful. And you go take a chill pill, maybe have a drink. Might do you good. Better yet, invite *Il Magnifico* to come for a sleepover."

Grace laughed and said, "If I finish this chapter early enough, I just might do that."

"Almost finished?" Nicky asked meaning-fully, with a waggle of her eyebrows.

"Close but not that close. Have fun and say hi to Migs and the gang for me."

"Aye, Captain. I'll do that thing, Captain." Then, more seriously, she said, "You need to bring it down a notch or two, Mom. You're way hyper."

"I just want to finish this book. Then I'll bring it down a whole bunch of notches."

"You'd better. You're scary when you get like this, like you're gonna stroke out or something. Really."

"You have my word I will not stroke out."

"Better not," Nicky said warningly. "Dad and I would be week-old toast without you."

"I love you, baby girl. Go!"

"I'm already gone." She got to the hall, turned around, came back and said, "At least *phone* Vin. He'll make you laugh."

"I'll do that. *Later.*"

The stack of printed pages was growing higher; she was moving at a steady clip toward the end of the book and was anxious to get there. Yet, true to her nature, she couldn't hurry the writing itself.

Several times in the course of any given working day she'd have to stop to do some bit of research, either offline (poring through the sizable stack of library books piled here and there around the room) or online (doing advanced searches that led her from one website to another until she found what she wanted). But the end was within sight — three more chapters at the outside — and at the rate she was going she'd have the draft finished within a week. The rewrite would take no time at all because, always, once she got to the end of a manuscript she knew exactly what had to be added, or removed, from start to finish, to make the whole thing hold together. Rewriting was the fun part, the easy part. That wouldn't take more than another week to ten days. And then she'd be free to spend time with Vinnie, to go down to New York once the weather cleared, to watch videos in the evening with Nicky and Gus, to do all the things that had been on hold for far too long. She longed for the luxury of time to herself, to use as she wished. That would be her "chill pill."

On the morning of the second day when, again, there was no email from either of the women in Virginia, she reached over and turned off the modem. Until she finished the manuscript, she'd only check for email twice a day — first thing in the morning, and after dinner. If she reacted like a Pavlovian puppy every time the icon flashed at the top of her screen, she'd just waste energy and lose track of the narrative by opening the browser to find yet another piece of spam or an email from some fan or friend that could easily wait for a few hours. Satisfied with this decision, she got on with the current chapter, interrupted twice — once at nine forty-five and once at eleven — by anonymous calls. She really was going to have to put a block on the line to stop these irritating intrusions. She'd been meaning to do it for months but kept forgetting, and they seemed to be proliferating.

Midmorning of the third day, the email she'd been waiting for was there when she turned on the modem.

Subject: Sandy Again
Date: Sat, 3 Feb 2001 07:42:15 -0200
From: Stephanie Baine
<baine_stephanie@spotmail.com>
To: Grace
<gloring@homecable.com>

Dear Grace:

We've been trying but haven't been able to get ahold of the lawyer. Stephie's phoned a bunch of times and left messages but he's been in court or in a meeting or something.

Now it's the weekend and she's wondering if you could please just send the emails back to her. The thing is she did like you said to and kept deleting everything in case Billy got into her email account, so she only has copies of the last couple of emails she wrote you. She's been real sick, puking all the time and taking showers nonstop, and scratching at herself so her arms are all shredded from her nails. It's been pretty scary around here and the poor girl is up most of the night every night just sitting on the sofa, with all her clothes on, wearing extra sweaters and two pairs of sox, covered up with blankets because she's freezing all the time and scared to go to sleep. Then she'll fall asleep in the daylight and wake up an hour later screaming. I'm real worried about her. But she said to say she's going to write to you today. Sorry I didn't email sooner but we were hoping to hear from the lawyer.

Sincerely, Sandy.

Subject: re: Sandy Again
Date: Sat, 3 Feb 2001 08:32:18 -0800

From: Grace Loring
<gloring@homecable.com>
To: Stephanie Baine
<baine_stephanie@spotmail.com>

Dear Sandy:

As I explained, the emails aren't going to have any legal value if I just send them back to Stephanie. It would be much better for her case if they went to her lawyer. If she would like it, I can get in touch with him directly and arrange to send him the emails. All I need is the name and phone number of his office.

I'm sorry to hear Steph is in such rough shape, although it's not surprising under the circumstances. Even if one is defending herself, it's still horrifying to be the cause of someone's death. I'm sure she feels terribly guilty. Please give her my best wishes and tell her I'll look forward to hearing from her when she's able to write.

Best regards,

Grace

After replying to several other emails, Grace closed the browser and turned off the modem, wondering if Sandy hadn't properly conveyed to Stephanie the information Grace had given her about the "chain of evidence" with respect to the emails. They would have some probative value in Stephanie's possession, but not to the same degree that they would have if they were sent directly to the lawyer.

Something was off-kilter about the whole situation but she wasn't going to allow herself to speculate on it. She needed to get on with the book. That, for the moment, was her first priority.

"Come out tonight," Vinnie said. "We'll eat and go see a movie. And don't give me any *tsouris*. I already talked to the Princess and she's all set to have her goyish friends over; they'll order in and feed and entertain Guseleh. Besides, you'll *kvell* when you see the beautiful floor I made."

"You've already put down the floor?"

"It's down. It's not stained yet, but such a floor. It could make a person weep, it's so gorgeous."

"How could I resist?" Grace said. "I get sweaty just thinking about a gorgeous floor."

"Sarcasm, you give me?"

"Oh, heaven forfend. No, no. What you're hearing is genuine, unbridled excitement."

"That's all right, then. I'll come for you at seven. A little chitchat with your *meshugeneh* brother and the Princess, then we'll eat Indian and go catch the late show of *Cast Away*."

"You're not serious. You want to watch a couple of hours' worth of a FedEx commercial?"

"Says who, it's a commercial?"

"The resident critic."

"Tell the Princess she knows from nothing. I've got serious money here says you'll love it."

"Who's betting?" Grace asked.

"Don't get all literal on me. You'll see it, you'll love it."

"Fine."

"No more arguing?" he asked, feigning surprise.

"Not from me, *boychik*."

"Good. Seven."

"You got it."

"Oy! I could eat you up right through the phone."

"Save it for later," she said and hung up smiling.

When she arrived home just before two in the morning, she found a Post-it message

Nicky had left on her keyboard.

Lisa Keeran or Kernan(?) called, says it's URGENT she talk to you. She'll call again in the A.M. Did you have fun with Vinster? How about that Fedex commercial? Love ya, Ma, N.

"You *liked* it?" Nicky looked horrified.

"I loved it. I can't think of another actor who could've done what Hanks did."

"Come *on*. It was just a big long promo for FedEx."

"No, it wasn't, Nicks. It was about a lot of things, one of them being a kind of company loyalty that's on the endangered species list. It's the way things used to be: People signed on with a company and stayed there for their entire working lives. In return, the company took care of their employees with health insurance and pension plans, annual picnics, Christmas parties. The movie was also about the depths of human resources and the will to survive. Plus, it had the best special effects I've seen in ages."

"Are you sure we saw the same flick?"

"Positive. Why didn't you like it?"

Focusing on the soy milk she was pouring over her organic oatmeal, Nicky thought for a few moments. "Why did it have to be FedEx?"

"Would it have been more acceptable to you if it'd been Airborne Express or UPS or the postal service?"

"Maybe. I don't know. To me it was just a whole lot of free advertising."

"Excuse me, baby girl. One of their planes crashed; not exactly an ad for the company. I think you missed the point."

"Maybe. I might check it out again when it goes to video. Could be one of those movies that's better on a small screen."

"That's possible. But it worked for me on the big one. So tell me about this woman who called."

"I could hardly hear her. But she sounded Southern and kind of out of breath, said she's been trying to get you for days."

"Why didn't she leave a message?" Grace asked, wondering if this was her recent persistent anonymous caller.

"She said it was impossible to explain in a message, that she really needs to talk to you. Something about her brother and his wife. Didn't make a whole lot of sense to me."

"Did a number come up on the caller ID?"

"I didn't even look; I just picked up. She said she couldn't leave a number, but she'd phone back this afternoon or tomorrow."

"You know I never pick up anonymous calls, Nicks."

"So if I'm home, I'll answer. It's no biggie. Probably one of your battered women, looking for some one-to-one advice. Wouldn't be the first time that'd happened, would it? Anyway, if somebody wants to find you, it isn't all that hard. I mean, one trip to the library to look through the reference books would do it. You know that."

"I know. And it's too late in the day to do anything about it except to get Gus's number taken out of the phone book and have it unlisted finally."

"Dad wouldn't mind," Nicky said.

"No, he probably wouldn't. It just never seemed right to do that to him. When he was still at the college, he encouraged the kids to phone him if they needed help, or just to talk. But now . . . I think the time has come to make the change."

Grace walked over to the phone and scrolled through the calls. Vinnie, Migs, Jerry, Anonymous. She deleted the numbers, wondering who this woman could possibly be. The name meant nothing to her. Nicky was undoubtedly right in thinking that it was one of her readers looking for help or advice.

>seventeen

Sunday morning, after getting Gus bathed and dressed, Dolly stopped in the kitchen to say, "How you doin', Miz Grace?"

Grace put aside the hard copy she was correcting with a fine-point felt-tip pen, saying, "I'm fine. Have you got time for some coffee?"

"That'd be good," Dolly said. "Got the day free for a change."

"That *is* a change. I don't know how you do it."

"Gotta work," Dolly said matter-of-factly, sliding into a chair as Grace brought a cup to the table for the woman. "You make good coffee, Miz Grace," she said with a smile, holding the cup with both hands and breathing in its aroma before taking a sip. "Miss Nicky still sleepin'?"

"Naturally."

"Nice to be young, huh?"

"It certainly is. How are you, Dolly?"

"Tired. But we all are, isn't that right?"

"True. So how are you going to spend

your day off?"

Dolly emitted one of her lovely laughs. "Laundry and cleanin', grocery shoppin'. Just a big holiday."

Grace smiled. "If I ever win the lottery, I'll hire you to work only for us and you can have all the time off you want."

"I'd like that a whole lot. I'll be hopin' you win. You buy the tickets?"

"Hardly ever."

Both women laughed. Then Dolly said, "That new 'scription seems to be helping. Mr. Gus is movin' a lot better. You notice that?"

"Actually, I haven't. I've been so busy with this book that I only come down to make a meal, then run right back up again. But that's very good to hear, especially since the Arava is ten dollars a pill."

"My lord," Dolly said, appalled. "That's a *lot* of money, way more than the Celebrex."

"If it works, it's worth every penny."

"I guess so. He's not complainin' so much gettin' in and outta the bath, or when I'm dressin' him. But seems to me a sin, the money those people chargin' for pills."

"I couldn't agree more."

"Are you okay, Miz Grace? You talk about me, but you're always workin' so hard every single day, never takin' any time to yourself."

"Oh, I do take time. I was out last night. Vinnie and I had dinner and went to the movies."

"Well, good! You need some freedom now 'n' then. You're good to your brother. He's lucky to have you."

"He's been good to *us*, Dolly. It's only fair."

"You and me both know what's fair hardly ever gets considered." She drank the last of her coffee and got up to carry the cup to the sink. " 'Preciate that, Miz Grace. I'll be goin' now."

"See you tomorrow. Enjoy your day off."

Dolly laughed again. "Sure will, once I'm done with the marketin' and the laundry and what-all. Be ready for bed by then. 'Bye, my dear."

Before heading upstairs, Grace stopped in her brother's room to ask, "Do you think the Arava's helping?"

"Hard to say. I guess I feel a bit better."

"Good. I'm heading up to take a shower, then get some more work done. I'm within shouting distance of the end of this manuscript. You need anything?"

"Some more coffee, please."

"No problem." She got his cup from the bedside table, refilled it in the kitchen and brought it back. "Anything else?"

"I'm fine, thanks."

"Okay, see you in a while." She paused to kiss him on the forehead. "Love you, big brother."

"Love you, too, little tyrant."

Laughing, she went on her way.

After inputting the corrections she'd made on the hard copy, she picked up where she'd left off. When she glanced at the clock at the top of the screen and saw that it was almost 1:30, she exclaimed, "Oh, shit!" hurriedly saved the document, and went rushing downstairs.

"Sorry," she told Gus from the living room doorway. "You must be starving. I'll get lunch right away."

"I'm okay," he said mildly. "I figured you were on a roll."

"I was. I'm really sorry. Five minutes. Okay?"

"Sure. Take your time."

"Where's Nicky anyway?"

"Went out a couple of hours ago to meet some of the kids for brunch."

"She's got quite the social life," Grace observed.

"She sure does," Gus agreed. "I remember having one."

"Me, too," she sympathized. "You'd have it back if you gave in and called people now and then, let them visit."

He made a face and she let the matter drop.

When the phone rang just as she was taking her first bite of the turkey on whole wheat sandwich, she glanced at the caller ID, saw it was anonymous and ignored it.

"You want me to get that?" Gus called from the living room.

"Hell, no!" Grace called back, carrying her sandwich to the doorway. "And since when do you answer the phone?"

"Since never. I just thought I might if you couldn't get to it."

"It's yet another anonymous call, and you know I don't answer those. Listen, while we're on the subject, would you have any objection to my getting a new unlisted phone number?"

"Nope, none."

"Okay, good. Thanks, Gus."

He nodded, his mouth full, and she went back to finish her lunch in the kitchen.

On impulse, just after five she phoned Vinnie.

"Want to come eat with us?" she asked.

"You're *phoning* me. Wait! I've gotta write this down in my diary."

"Very funny. You want to come or not?"

"What're we having?"

"My special London broil in coconut milk with sun-dried tomatoes."

"I'm on my way. Should I bring my jammies?"

She had to pause and think about that. "I'd really like to say yes, but not tonight, Vin. I'm on a roll here. I'm so close to the end."

"Okay. I understand. I'm on my way."

"See you soon."

She hung up and went to knock on Nicky's door. When she didn't get a response, she opened the door to see her daughter dancing around the room to the music coming through her headphones. Grace leaned against the door frame and watched until, in midturn, Nicky saw her and stopped dead, whipping off the headphones.

"Total heart attack!" she declared, going over to turn off her boombox.

"I did knock."

"Whatever. I'm still in heart failure mode. What's up?"

"Do me a favor and make a salad while I finish off what I'm doing. Vin's on his way for dinner."

"What're we having?"

"*You're* having salad. *We're* having London broil."

"That thing you do with the coconut milk?"

"Yup."

"Maybe I'll have just a leetle teeny tiny bit."

"Maybe, if ~~past~~ history is anything to go by, you'll have a lot."

Her expression sheepish, Nicky said, "Well, it's good. It doesn't taste like meat."

"I'll never tell, if you won't. Will I have to come back in fifteen minutes to remind you, or will you make the salad?" Grace asked.

"I'll do it now. And as soon as I find where you stash your chill pills, I'm gonna dose your coffee, get your mood altered but good."

"Oh, I'm quaking in my boots."

"Ah, the famous snowbunny clodhoppers."

With a laugh, Grace went to the stairs, saying, "Make the salad now, please."

"I *said* I would. Break-time here, please. As in, could I catch one?" Gathering her hair in both hands, she wound it into a knot, then grabbed a scrunchy from the top of the chest of drawers and fastened it around the knot. "Snaky, snaky. Ma needs a chill pill big time."

Monday morning as she was emerging from the bathroom after her shower, Nicky yelled, "Mom, that Lisa woman's on the phone again. I've got her on hold."

"For Pete's sake! It's not even eight o'clock in the morning. Tell her if she can't leave a number, she'll have to call me tomorrow morning at nine. I can't talk to her right now. And see if you can find out what she wants."

"Okay, will do, boss."

This Lisa was beyond persistent. But she was going to have to wait. One more full day's work and Grace would have the last chapter done. Nothing was going to slow her down when she was almost at the end.

Nicky appeared in the doorway, saying, "That woman sounds tightly wound, kind of different from before. Weird. Anyway, she said she can't leave a number so she'll call again at nine on the dot tomorrow."

"If the number hasn't been changed by then," Grace said, pulling jeans on over her silk long johns. "I'm getting on that right after breakfast is out of the way."

Nicky snorted. "As *if*, Mom. It'll take at least a couple or three days. This is *Vermont*, remember?"

"So it'll take a couple of days and I'll talk to this Lisa person tomorrow."

"Almost finished, huh?" Nicky asked.

"Within touching distance. Aren't you going to be late?" Grace asked, taking in Nicky's half-dressed state.

"My class isn't until ten this morning. Now, *where* are those chill pills?" She went off, pretending to scratch her head in puzzlement.

After getting her jeans zipped, Grace jotted a note to herself:

Call phone co.

Subject:
Date: Mon, 5 Feb 2001 07:50:15 -0400
From: Stephanie Baine <baine_stephanie@spotmail.com>
To: Grace <gloring@homecable.com>

Dear Grace:

After everything that's happened, I'm in full panic mode, just thinking about Billy and the possible consequences. It's raining here, and I'm still pretty exhausted. Just thinking about that night is enough to make me psycho. I'm hanging on by a thread. I hate being cold and shivering because it reminds me of what it was like while I was being held captive all those years ago. It was really cold then and I remember not being able to get warm. I used to like the cold prior to that event, it's a novelty in the south. Now I hate being all bundled up in heavy sweaters, coats, etc., it taps into my claustrophobia. When it's really hot and the sun is beating down on me, I almost feel like it's burning all of the filth off of me. The last couple of weeks have been stress- ful beyond belief. I'm so up and down, one minute fine, the next depressed as hell. I've got a sweat shirt and long pants on, but my skin is still crawling and I can't get warm. I don't know what to do to stop it, except to stay zoned on Valium. I'm so ready to give up that it's not funny, but I know I can't. I didn't talk to the lawyer on Friday, he was in court during my window of opportunity to talk to him. I'll try today, but I don't have a lot of hope of ever being free, will prob- ably end up being sent away. I've been trying to be stoic, but I'm dying inside. The past is coming back to haunt me in a big way, and I feel like I'm losing my mind. I don't want you to totally hate me, but I feel so crazy and can't figure out how to climb out from the pit. I feel so alone, so dirty and disgusting and terrified. I would be forever grateful if you could send me the emails. They might be what saves me. Sorry to be so whiney. And thank you again for everything you've done for me. You're the only one, aside from Sandy, who's been a real friend.

Love, Steph

Grace found herself feeling an unexpected and surprising dislike of this woman. All at once Stephanie struck her as incredibly narcissistic and self-indulgent. Why the hell didn't she just pass along the lawyer's name and number? Even if she wasn't able to reach the man, what was to stop her from giving Grace the contact information? Her behavior was making things unnecessarily complicated; it certainly wasn't helping matters. If those emails were of value to her defense, why didn't she just supply the information and let matters proceed? This was time-wasting, annoying. Having to work hard to view Stephanie's dilemma in a sympathetic light, she dashed off a quick reply.

Subject: re
Date: Mon, 5 Feb 2001 08:58:12 -0200
From: Grace Loring

<gloring@homecable.com>
To: Stephanie Baine
<baine_stephanie@spotmail.com>
Dear Stephanie:

As I explained to your friend, the emails aren't going to have any legal value if I simply send them back to you. It will be better for your case if they go directly to your lawyer. Just give me his name and phone number and I'll get in touch with him to make the arrangements.

I'm very sorry about everything that's happened. I can't begin to imagine how you must feel. Just hang in and get some rest, if you can. As soon as I get the contact information from you, I'll forward the emails to your lawyer.
Try to take it easy.

Best, Grace

>eighteen

"Want me to make Dad's dinner?" Nicky asked.

Startled, Grace glanced at the top of her screen. She'd done it again. It was six-forty and she'd been so hard at work she'd forgotten about dinner.

"Sorry, didn't mean to scare you. But Dad's making hungry noises."

"It's okay. Listen, could you take that pot from last night out of the fridge and put it on a burner set low? I'll be right down. Are you in or out this evening?"

"I'm in. I've got some reading to do for my postmodern lit class tomorrow. I'll throw some veggies together, 'cause there's not all that much of the London broil left."

"Thanks, Nicks. It'll just take me two minutes to save this."

"I gave Dad some cheese and crackers to keep him happy," she said and went clomping down the stairs.

Grace reread the last sentence, typed a note about what she wanted to say next, then saved the document. Two or three more hours and the draft would be finished; she'd be able to take deep breaths again, watch videos, relax, spend time with Vinnie.

Just as they'd started to eat, the telephone rang. Gus and Nicky both looked at Grace.

"If it's anonymous, we're not answering," she said.

Nicky got up to check, said, "Anonymous," and returned to her place on the floor beside the sofa.

"This has to be an all-time record," Gus said. "We've never had so many of those calls before."

"They promised me the new number would be on by noon tomorrow," Grace said.

"Is it a good number?" Nicky asked.

"A good number?" Grace looked over at her.

"You know. A *good* number. Something like 254-2540."

"You mean an easy number. I don't remember. It's written down on the pad next to the computer."

"I'll check it out after we eat. I've got to let everybody know."

"Most of your friends call you on your cell," Grace pointed out.

"Some still call me on this line."

"Better let the school know," Gus told his sister, "and Jerry, too. And we mustn't forget about Vinnie."

"Like that would happen," Nicky said with a grin. "And you've got *your* cellphone, too, Mom. We are *such* the new-age family. Oh, and I'm getting that cool new iBook. Have you seen it?"

Grace shook her head.

"It's way better than the old one, not as clunky, very sleek and way thin, weighs almost nothing; it'll fit right into my backpack. I'm going to order the new one online tonight. If I do it before seven Pacific time, they'll overnight it and it'll be here tomorrow. Then I can transfer all my files and give Migs the other one tomorrow night. She really needs it. She doesn't even *have* a computer. I don't know anybody else who doesn't have one."

"Sounds like a plan," Grace said.

"You're not even listening," Nicky accused.

"Sleek, not clunky. Old one to Migs," Grace said, her eyes on Tom Brokaw.

"Okay, so you're halfway listening. When're you going to upgrade to a G4?"

"Probably never. My G3 is perfectly fine, thank you. I've got all the megahertz and RAM I'll ever need."

"So how close are you to finishing?" Gus asked.

"A few hours."

"That's great. Are you happy with it?"

"I'll know once I read the whole thing through. But I think so. There are a few places where I need to polish, add some detail. Nothing major."

They finished eating in silence, watching the news. Grace gave her brother a sliced apple and a sugar-free cookie, then perched on the edge of her chair, waiting for him to finish. Nicky dumped her plate in the sink, then took off upstairs to order her new iBook. For a few seconds, Grace was irritated by the fact that Nicky hadn't offered to help clean up the kitchen, but it passed. Nicky had never mastered the art of loading the dishwasher, with the result that, at best, she could only ever get half the dishes into the machine. Grace could do it better and faster by herself.

At last, Gus said, "I'm finished," and Grace got up to remove his bib and lift the tray from his lap. "It was very good. Thank you," he said.

"You're welcome," Grace replied. Gus never forgot to thank her for each meal she presented to him, and she appreciated it because there were days when she wished she'd never again have to cook on demand.

★ ★ ★

Precisely at nine the next morning the telephone rang, and Grace jumped. Anonymous. Then, remembering, she picked up.

A soft, hesitant voice, said, "Is that Grace Loring?"

"Who's calling?"

"This is Lisa Kernan. Could I speak to Grace, please? It's really important."

The woman had a slight Southern accent and sounded timid.

"This is Grace."

"Oh, I'm *so* glad I've finally reached you. I'm Billy Baine's sister, and I really need to talk to you about what's happened."

"I'm listening," Grace said warily.

"Is there any chance we could talk in person? I'm not comfortable discussing this over the phone. I know it's a huge imposition and I appreciate your taking the time even to talk to me. The thing is, I live in Boston and I could get to Brattleboro in about two hours."

"What exactly is there to talk about?" Grace asked.

"I'm trying to help Stephanie," the woman said. "I'd really feel better if we could talk in person."

"I don't know —" Grace began.

"*Please!* Just meet and talk with me.

Stephanie's in trouble and I can't sit by and do nothing."

"Tell you what. I could meet you for coffee tomorrow afternoon. It's the best I can do. I've got a book to finish and I'm on a deadline."

"That'll be fine," the woman said eagerly.

"Do you know Brattleboro at all?"

"Not really. But tell me where and I'll be there."

Grace thought for a second or two, then said, "I'll meet you at two at the Vermont Country Deli. It's on Western Avenue, which is actually Route 9, just outside of town."

"I'll map it online and meet you there at two. Thank you *so* much. I really appreciate this."

"How will I know you?" Grace thought to ask.

"I'll carry a copy of *Hit or Miss*. How would that be?"

"Fine. I'll see you tomorrow."

Grace hung up, wondering why she'd agreed to meet this woman. Curiosity, she decided. She wanted to know what Billy Baine's sister would have to say about him. Obviously, she wasn't going to defend him if she wanted to help Stephanie.

"You don't have classes this afternoon,

do you?" Grace asked Nicky the next morning.

"Nope. Why?"

"I've got to go meet this woman at the Country Deli at two."

"What woman?"

"She's the sister-in-law of the woman in Virginia who's been emailing me."

"Oh! The Lisa person?"

"That's right."

"And? What's the deal?"

"I'd feel better about going out if you stayed home with Gus for a couple of hours while I'm gone."

"Okay, sure. I'll hang with Dad. But seriously. What's up with this? Why are you meeting her?"

"She wants to talk about her brother."

"I don't get it," Nicky said.

"Me, neither. But it's neutral ground, and I'm curious."

"Kind of a dumb reason, Mom. Take your cellphone," Nicky advised. "This sounds kind of hinky to me."

"Why?"

"I don't know. It just does. Take your cellphone. And don't forget to turn it on, the way you usually do."

"Okay, I'll take it and I'll turn it on. Any other instructions?"

"Sometimes you're kind of naive, you know that?"

Grace laughed. "You think so, do you?"

"I'm serious. This woman could be anybody. You're a famous writer. People do nutty stuff when it comes to famous people."

"Nicky, ninety-nine percent of writers are basically invisible. Most people would have no clue who I am."

"Yeah," Nicky argued. "But this woman's tracked you down. She's got your phone number —"

"Until tomorrow," Grace interrupted.

"— and your address. It's *way* hinky, and I want you to be careful."

"I will be careful. I will take my cellphone and I will turn it on. I'm going to be in a public place, Nicks. Nothing's going to happen."

"Okay, but I really don't like it. I'm with Dad on this one. I don't think you should've ever got involved with this Stephanie person."

"You and Gus have discussed this?" Grace was thrown. "When? Why?"

"Because it's the *Internet*, Mom. You can't really be sure who's on the other end. There's no way to know."

"And you think I'm so stupid that I'd buy into just anything?"

"You're not one bit stupid, but you really are kind of naive. You trust people."

"Of course I do. I've been helping abused women for years. They need someone —"

"I know all that. And you've helped a lot of people. You're a good person. Nobody's arguing that fact. But Dad and I agree: this doesn't feel right. So just please be careful. Okay?"

"Fine, okay."

Grace had only just taken a seat with a view of the door when a slim but quite tall, fair-haired woman entered with a copy of *Hit or Miss* in her hand. Grace waved and the woman made her way over.

"This is so good of you," she said in a voice that was little more than a whisper. "Thank you for agreeing to meet me."

She was so nervous that her cheek actually twitched when she tried to smile at Grace.

"Sit down. Do you want some coffee?"

"Ah, I'd rather have tea."

"Okay. Any particular kind?"

"Sorry?"

"Regular, herbal, Earl Grey?"

"Oh. Herbal, any kind. Thank you. I can get it."

"Just sit. I'll be right back." Grace got up

and went to the counter at the front, ordered the beverages and glanced back at the table while she waited. Lisa put the book and her handbag on the table and unbuttoned her coat but kept it on. Grace thought she must be freezing. The coat looked lightweight and the woman was wearing street shoes, not boots. Boston winters were sometimes worse than they were in Vermont. Either Lisa had dressed for the occasion or she'd removed her boots and put on the shoes before getting out of the car — perhaps to make a good impression.

Back at the table, Grace set the steaming cup of Red Zinger in front of the woman, then Grace studied her as she drank some of her coffee. Pretty and quite young, with an unsettled quality to her eyes that were a rather watery blue; blond hair that had had some help in arriving at its present color: fine and straight, it was side-parted and fell precisely to her jawline. She had a flawless pale complexion, light eyebrows, a small tidy nose and a tremulous mouth. Her only makeup was some mascara, a hint of blush, and an unbecoming too-pink lipstick. Vinnie would've had a field day, describing this young woman as the ultimate prototypical shiksa.

"I'm very nervous," Lisa said. "I can't believe I'm actually sitting here with you."

"Well, you are," Grace said, always uncomfortable when people tripped on the threshold of her so-called fame. She was anxious to get to the reason for this meeting so she could wrap it up and get home to start the rewrite. "So, why don't you tell me what this is about."

Lisa held her hands around her cup and stared down at it for a moment. "My brother was not a good person," she said, looking briefly at Grace then away again. "I always knew that. So did my parents. It was my dad who pushed him to go into the service. He thought it would give Billy discipline, some control of his impulses. And Billy liked being in the military. He loved it, loved being in charge of other guys, bossing people around; he loved his uniform, his rank — he got to be a lieutenant in the navy — all of it. But everybody hated him. He was a sadistic bully, but charming to anyone senior in rank or to people he thought were worth his time. After his last tour, the rank and file got together and went to the captain. They said if they had to serve under Billy again they'd all leave the service. So Billy got reassigned to shore duty. He was furious. He'd always thought he'd get to be an admiral, or at least a captain." Lisa paused, looked again at the cup between her hands and finally drank some of her tea.

"I warned Stephie not to marry him," she continued. "But she didn't believe me. He was in full charm mode with her, so she went ahead and married him. From the start it was a nightmare. Maybe a year later, when I went down to visit them, she told me about some of the things he'd done to her. I begged her to leave, said she could come stay with me in Boston. But she has these *horrible* parents, especially her mother. Did she tell you about them?"

Grace nodded.

"So then you know," Lisa went on. "No way was her mother going to let Stephie leave him. Her mother was in *love* with Billy, I swear. It was sick. Her father couldn't stand him, but he was military, too, and into discipline in a big way. You got married, you stayed married. Because of what happened when she was sixteen, Steph was pretty well brainwashed. Between her parents and Billy she really didn't have much of a chance. She was scared of everything. I think the bravest thing she's ever done in her life was getting in touch with you after I sent her a copy of your book, because I thought it might help her to see things more clearly. She says you've helped her so much." Lisa looked directly into Grace's eyes for the first time. "You've done more for her than anyone ever has."

"I merely gave her some common-sense advice," Grace said. "And I let her tell me her problems."

"That's a lot," Lisa insisted. "Anyway, now this. It's a horror story. If she lived in any other state, I don't think she'd have been charged at all. But Virginia. The laws are beyond ridiculous."

"They certainly don't protect women, according to what Stephanie has told me."

"Not a bit. You'd think being so close to D.C. . . . . Well, you already know all that. What I'd like to ask . . . This is very difficult. But could you please give me copies of Stephie's emails? I know it's a lot to ask, but if you could print them out with the headers —"

"Look, I've explained this several times —"

"But it's so important —"

"I can't —"

Just then Grace heard a muted ringing and realized it was her cellphone. "Excuse me," she said, digging the phone out of her bag.

"Mom? It's me. Be chill. Okay? There's a woman here who says she's Lisa Kernan and she needs to see you."

Glancing at the woman on the other side of the table, Grace felt suddenly queasy. "I see," she said calmly. "Could you give Uncle Jerry a call? I'll come right home."

"Already called and clued him in," Nicky said. "He's on his way. She's sitting in the living room talking to Dad. Be cool, get outta there, and get back here. And keep your phone on just in case. Okay?"

"Okay. I'm on my way."

"I've got to go," Grace told the woman calling herself Lisa Kernan. "There's a problem at home."

"But the emails —"

"It's a family emergency," Grace said, grabbing her jacket and bag. "I'm sorry. I know you drove all this way to talk but, aside from every other consideration, it would take time to print out the emails. I'm on a deadline and really can't spare the extra time right now. Call me tomorrow and I'll see what I can do about getting them to you. Sorry, but I've *really* got to go."

Pulling on her jacket as she went, fishing the car keys from her pocket, Grace raced out to the car. What the *hell* was going on? she wondered, as she jabbed the key into the ignition. Thank heaven Nicky had had the presence of mind to call Jerry. *Two* Lisa Kernans? Maybe Gus and Nicky were right and she was naive or just plain stupid. She'd managed to get herself involved in something crazy. Beyond crazy. She waited for an opening in the traffic, then accelerated out of the parking lot and onto the road, sliding on the slippery pavement. Taking a deep breath, telling herself to slow down, she gently corrected out of the slide. Her right knee was jiggling and she had to keep glancing at the speedometer to hold the car at a steady speed.

>nineteen

Nicky was sitting at the foot of the stairs, waiting for her, when Grace came bursting through the door.

"Where is she?" Grace asked, winded.

"Jerry was nearby and came right over, said would she mind going to the barracks with him to verify her ID. She said no problem and went off with him in the cruiser. Did *you* ask to see that *other* woman's ID?"

"It never occurred to me," Grace confessed, putting away her jacket. "Please don't tell me it was dumb, Nicks. I know it was. I now admit that I am every bit as naive as you claim. I just wish I knew what was going on. None of this makes any sense."

"This Lisa said she talked to me on the phone. And she did sound familiar. But the second time she called, she sounded different, so maybe that was the *other* Lisa. This is all sooooo weird," Nicky said, as the doorbell rang.

"What now?" Grace wondered aloud.

Grace opened the door to see the woman

she'd just met at the Country Deli, and said sharply, "Did you follow me?"

"I'm sorry, but I had to."

Nicky, who was concealed by the open door, pulled out her cellphone, pressed the speed dial, listened to make sure the connection got made, then dropped the phone, speaker side out, into the bib pocket of her overalls.

"This is really not a convenient time. We've got a family situation —" Grace began.

"Please, just give me five minutes," the woman interrupted, stepping inside and closing the door before Grace had a chance to stop her.

"Wow!" Nicky said in an overloud valley girl voice Grace had only heard her use when she was joking around. "Cool shoes. What are they, Ferragamo?"

"Oh!" The woman glanced down at her feet then up at Nicky. "Thanks."

"But aren't your feet like totally *freezing?* It's way cold out, and there's like a foot of snow."

"Not really."

"The coat's Calvin Klein. Right?"

"Ye . . ."

"I *love* Calvin Klein. But I sort of like

305

Donna Karan better. Of the like classic American designers, that is, ya *know*. The Italians are like more daring, more hip. Ya *know?* And you've got, ohmagod, like my absolutely *favorite* Kate Spade bag from last year. Ultra cool. Not as up there as Prada, but totally decent. Ya know? Mega tough to decide whether to go with the Spade or the Prada. But good call, rilly."

"Thanks." The woman was gazing at Nicky with something like awe.

Grace, too, was staring at her daughter, realizing that Nicky was playing for time with a performance that would have been hilarious, under any other circumstances. And why was she holding her head at such an odd angle? It looked as if she was talking to her chest.

"And those're Fogal tights," Nicky raced on. "Am I right? I'm right. They're the total best, but now and then you'll get a dud pair and they run as soon as you touch them. Which is *such* a complete bummer. I mean, forty bucks *fazoom,* right down the toilet, pardon my crudity. But have you had that *happen?* Oh, check it out! You've got the Cartier tank watch. I'm absolutely, *totally* torn, deciding between that and the Panthère, but I'm really kinda young, ya *know,* for gold and diamonds and stuff, so

I'm having a monster tough time deciding which —"

"Look, could you knock off the Elsa Klench routine and" — the woman directed herself to Grace — "could we hone in on the issue here, please?"

Nicky let out a shriek of laughter. "Way funny! You're a scream!" she declared, giving the woman a shove on the upper arm with the flat of her hand. "Elsa *Klench*. I totally loved her fashion gigs. It's such a downer she's not —"

"Be quiet!"

"Ooops! Like sorry." Nicky giggled and clapped a hand over her mouth.

Grace felt as if all the air had been sucked out of her body as she looked hard at the woman.

Hone. *Hone*. HONE.

The author of those emails detailing episodes of horrific abuse was standing in her front hall, pretending to be someone else. Had it all been a hoax or was it real? If it was real, had the experience sent her over the edge? And had she come all the way here directly from Virginia? Or had she been staying somewhere nearby, emailing from a laptop or somebody else's machine? Every library had computers, and Spotmail was accessible from anywhere.

Reading Grace's expression, the woman asked, "What's wrong?"

With Nicky very close to her side now, Grace said, "I don't know who you are, but you are not Lisa Kernan."

Suddenly the woman underwent a remarkable transformation. Her voice dropping by an octave and losing its tentative quality, she said, "No, I'm not. Lisa is my sister-in-law. Look, I *need* the emails." Her features no longer appeared quite so young or so pretty. And a flush had taken hold of her pale complexion. "Just print them out for me and I'll be gone. Thirty or forty pages, an hour at most, if you've got an ink-jet, half an hour if you've got a laser printer."

"What is the *point* of this bizarre exercise?" Grace asked. "And who the hell are you, anyway?"

"I don't know how, but you've already figured that out, haven't you? I'm Stephanie. How *did* you know?"

"*Hone,*" Grace said numbly. "The correct word is *home*. One homes, not hones, in on something."

"Hone, home. Whatever. Why couldn't you just do what I asked and send me the emails? Why did you have to make everything so difficult?"

"Why wouldn't you give me your lawyer's

name and number?" Grace countered.

"I *told* you. I haven't been able to get hold of him. I'm only trying to save time. You give me the emails, I fly home today and give them to the lawyer. Done, finished, and I'm out of your life."

"So you flew up here, rented or borrowed a car, and pretended to be somebody else. Explain the point of that to me, if you can."

"Will you just, please, *do* it?"

"Why won't you answer the question?" Nicky asked in her normal voice.

"You stay out of this, if you know what's good for you."

"What's *good* for me? Who writes your dialogue? That is *so* lame. There were kids in my sophomore lit. class who could write better stuff."

"A little personality change here," Stephanie said snidely. "Who are *you?* Sybil?"

"Right. That's it exactly. I'm Sybil," Nicky shot back. "Don't leave home without us."

"What's going on? What's the fuss?" Gus called from the living room.

"It's okay, Dad," Nicky said, popping over to the living room doorway. "We're just talking with a friend of Mom's." Dropping her chin, so her mouth was even closer to the cellphone, she said, "It's Lisa Kernan. You know? The woman Mom went to meet at the deli, the one who's been calling."

"Oh!" Gus said and went back to his book.

"What's the urgent family problem, anyway?" Stephanie asked, stepping into the doorway to look at Gus.

"My dad is disabled," Nicky said protectively.

"He looks okay to me. Kind of crippled, but okay. And I thought your parents were divorced."

"Our *family* is none of your *business*. Why are you here hassling my mom? What's your deal, anyway?"

"I'm going to make this nice and simple," Stephanie said to Grace, reaching into her bag. "You are going to give me those emails. I'm not leaving here without them." With that, she pulled a small gun out of her bag.

"Jeez Louise!" Nicky exclaimed, her chin lowered again. "You're going to *shoot* us if we don't give them to you?"

"Something like that," Stephanie said, glancing over at Gus who hadn't looked up from his book.

"My dad's hard of hearing," Nicky said.

"How come he's all twisted and bashed up? What's wrong with him?"

"He has rheumatoid arthritis," Grace said stiffly.

"He looks a thousand years old."

Infuriated, Nicky said, "You shut up, you stupid bitch! You march in here, making demands, all rigged out in knock-off crap, as if it'd fool anyone who actually *knows*." Pointing at the woman's wrist, she said, "They sell those lame-ass fake Cartiers on the street in Manhattan for fifteen bucks, ten if you bargain hard enough. And Ferragamo shoes, sure. You *wish*. Every single thing you've got on is a knock-off, except for the tights. And you probably had to save for weeks to buy those. The gun's probably by Mattel or one of those other top gun makers. And what's so goddamned important about those emails that you'd come all the way here and pull this shit on my mom?"

"The gun is very real. I promise you that. And you're really starting to bug me, girlfriend. So shut up, unless you want to find out just how real this is." Stephanie lifted the gun and pointed it at Grace. "I want them, and you are going to print them out for me right now."

"You're nuts —" Nicky started.

"Fine. Anything to get you the hell out of here," Grace interrupted. "I'll print them out for you." She took a step toward the stairs and Stephanie blocked her way, asking, "Where are you going?"

"Upstairs. To my computer."

"Unh-unh. No way I'm letting you out of my sight. You go!" she told Nicky.

"Fine."

"They're in a folder called StephMail," Grace told her daughter who hadn't moved.

Stephanie glanced again into the living room to find that Gus was looking back at her. Then he smiled, and said, "Hello."

Nonplussed, Stephanie automatically said, "Hello."

From behind her, Nicky signaled to Gus with one hand, indicating he should keep talking, while pointing to the cellphone in her overall pocket with her other hand.

"Have you come to get a book autographed?" Gus asked pleasantly.

"Um, yes."

Just then the front door flew open and Jerry stood framed in the doorway, a small blond woman beside him. The three women in the hallway turned to look over.

"Lisa, what the hell are *you* doing here?" Stephanie snapped, her gun still pointed at Grace.

"Put the gun down, miss," Jerry said quietly. There was a heavy rumbling from the living room and Gus came pushing his walker across the carpeted floor at a speed none of them would ever have believed he could achieve.

At the sound, Stephanie whirled around and fired the gun. Gus was thrown backward and landed with a terrible crash that seemed to shake the entire house.

Nicky screamed, "DAD!" and ran to him.

Without hesitating, Jerry took two steps, swept both Grace and Lisa Kernan aside with his left arm, knocking them into each other, drew his gun with his right and shot Stephanie once, twice, then again. Her expression one of utter disbelief, she stood upright for a long moment and then dropped.

Frozen on the spot, her ears ringing, deafened, and her vision gone awry as it had on New Year's Eve, Grace seemed to be looking at everything at once, as if through an extreme wide-angle lens. Nicky was on the floor, crouched beside Gus. Jerry was on his radio, undoubtedly calling for help. And on her knees by the closet door was the petite blond woman, her eyes wide and unblinking, her mouth hanging open as she, like Grace, tried to absorb the reality of what had just taken place.

All Grace could think was, it's my fault; my arrogance, my conceit brought this tragedy into our home. *How could I have done this?*

She was shocked to feel a small, warm hand close around hers. She looked down at it, then up at Lisa Kernan, who was speaking, but Grace couldn't make sense of what she was saying, couldn't hear her words.

She didn't move until a minute or two later when police and paramedics came flying into the house, filling every inch of available space. Lisa Kernan drew her over to the stairs and made Grace sit down, with her head between her knees. "You'll be all right," Lisa said. And Grace could at last hear her.

"Everything will be all right. You'll see." Lisa repeated this over and over. But it was nonsensical babble to Grace. Nothing would ever again be all right. There on the hall floor lay a dead woman in a widening pool of blood; that woman had shot Gus. And in the living room, within the sheltering arm of a trooper, Nicky sobbed, one hand reaching out as two paramedics blocked Gus from her view, crying, "Dad, Dad!" over and over, like an inconsolable child.

>twenty

The corridor had the unique hospital odor of strong disinfectant struggling to conceal the potent underlying reek of sickness. Every so often a cryptic, coded announcement came over the P.A. system, or some doctor was paged. Seated in an uncomfortable orange plastic chair, Grace tried to ignore the smell and the echoing messages as she listened to what Lisa was saying.

"I went down to Virginia for the funeral, which didn't happen until after the autopsy and Stephanie's bail hearing. By then, it was almost ten days after Billy died — after he *supposedly* tried to attack her, so she pulled out the gun she'd bought to protect herself, and shot him . . . twice, in the head." Lisa closed her eyes for a few seconds, as if to shut her mind to the image, then went on. "I had a *lot* of problems with her story of how things had happened. But I could hardly start questioning her under the circum-stances. I could, though, stay for a few days, to help 'the grieving widow,' who didn't seem to be even remotely interested in keeping up the pretense, once her show of tears for Billy's friends was over. That very night, she started taking Billy's clothes from the closet, dumping his things into big plastic garbage bags for the Salvation Army; in a hurry to erase any sign of him from the house.

"From early the next morning, for the entire three days I was there, Stephanie was on the computer nonstop, emailing constantly. One afternoon, the phone rang and she put whoever it was on hold and went to take the call in the bedroom upstairs — obviously so I wouldn't hear. I was beyond curious by that point, imagining she'd found herself a new boyfriend who was waiting in the wings, so I went to take a look at her computer which was in the den just off the kitchen. She'd closed her email but she hadn't logged off. I was terrified she'd come back at any moment, but I had to know what she was doing, so I opened her mail folders. There was an email she was writing to you that wasn't finished, with 'This is Sandy' in the subject line and I started to read it. I was really shocked that she was emailing you. I couldn't get my mind around that. And what she was writing gave me the creeps because she was pretending to be some other woman named Sandy, who was barely literate. So I opened her 'Sent' folder, but it only had four emails in it. The trash was empty. But she had another folder, and in it there were all these emails from you. I didn't have time to read them, but I was completely creeped out, and just had to know what she was up to. I could hear she was still on the phone, so I threw a disk into the drive and downloaded all the emails she'd sent you and the ones you'd sent her onto the disk, then put everything back the way it had been. In the kitchen I put the disk in the zippered pocket of my purse, then, shaking like crazy, I grabbed some stuff from the refrigerator, and started to make lunch.

"After her call, she came into the kitchen and I could feel her looking at me, but I kept on making the salad, humming to myself. I felt completely transparent, but I guess she was satisfied, because she didn't say anything, just went back to her email. The next day, I said I was going out to do some shopping, pick up a few things I'd forgotten to bring with me. Stephanie didn't care. When she wasn't on the computer, she was on the phone. She had no time for me and couldn't stand me, anyway. Every time I had ever come to visit them, which wasn't often, she'd picked fights with Billy and the climate in that house was just unbearable. Billy *hated* dissension. We both had way too much of it, growing up. He was a very calm, very even-tempered man who'd walk away from a fight, unless it was about a matter of principle. And even then, if he argued, it was quiet, logical, thoughtful. He never, ever raised his voice.

"Anyway, I found a Kinko's, booked a machine and started reading the emails I'd copied onto the disk. That's when I got really, really scared." Lisa stopped and looked down at her hands, which were tightly clenched together.

"We were twins, you know. Very close. It was always us against the world. My brother was the sweetest, gentlest man who ever lived," she said, raising her now damp eyes again. "And Stephanie had planned all along to kill him. All those things she told you: the abduction, the abuse. Those things happened to *me*, not to her. Billy had told her about me, and she was always pumping him for more and more details. He thought it was because she was sympathetic, because she made the right noises, but the whole time she was making mental notes, creating a scenario that would allow her to get away with murder." She pulled a tissue from her pocket and blotted her eyes. She blew her nose and went on.

"I *begged* him not to marry her. I knew what she was the first time I set eyes on her. She was completely egocentric; everything was about her. No one else mattered, unless she could get something from them. She married a navy officer, thinking she was taking a step up in the world, thinking Billy would stay in the service for life and eventually wind up a captain, maybe even an admiral. And she'd be an admiral's or a captain's *wife*. Big-time prestige. But Billy had done enough tours and wanted out; he wanted to be a civilian in the private sector, with a nine-to-five job so he could spend time at home, have some kids and be a family man. To Stephanie's mind that was not only a drop in status, it was also her idea of hell. She *hated* children, had no patience with them. She was one of those people who refer to babies as rugrats. I just can't bear hearing that. I love children, really love them. And, besides, she didn't care for Billy. She liked his income, the house he bought them, the car he let her buy that was way beyond what he could afford. But she always wanted more. And the way to get more and, at the same time, be free of his attention and his desire for kids was to kill him, get acquitted, then collect on his insurance and inherit his assets.

"To do this, she had to establish a pattern of abuse. So she used you as her 'wailing wall' so to speak, and she stole every detail of my life. Every single thing she told you was something that happened to me, especially how I was abused by my husband. My parents were exactly the monsters Stephanie described, especially my mother. Interestingly enough, according to Billy, she hated Stephanie the moment she set eyes on her. He had his own reasons why he thought they didn't get along. But in my opinion they were too alike: too self-centered and arrogant and uncaring. The one Christmas they visited Billy and Stephanie in Virginia was a horror show. According to my brother, if Stephanie wasn't making a scene, Mother was. He pretended to be sick and went for a long walk on Christmas day, while our mother and Stephanie were arguing in the kitchen about the right way to make the stuffing, and Dad was watching TV in the living room with the volume jacked up so he wouldn't have to hear them." She shook her head and smiled ruefully. "It was the first and last time my parents went anywhere near her. All those things she told you in her emails must have happened that year.

"So, getting back to the abuse" — she sighed and shook her head again — "it was my mother who kept pushing me to marry Peter Kernan. He was sixteen years older than me, a well-paid executive; he was charm personified, and seemed so sympathetic when I told him, over time, the details of what had happened to me at sixteen. He was always encouraging me to tell him more, then more. And while it was shameful to put words to that experience, it was also a huge relief, finally, to be able to tell somebody who seemed to give a damn.

"Meanwhile, my mother pushed and pushed and, finally, I did what she wanted and married him. I thought I'd found someone who'd be gentle with me, who'd protect me. I wasn't in love with him, but I liked him well enough. It seemed, all things considered, the sensible thing to do. So we got married.

"When he raped me on our wedding night, I phoned home and said I'd made a terrible mistake, that I needed to come home right away. But my mother told me to stop being such an idiot crybaby, that it was a wife's duty to be obedient. So what if he was 'a little rough'? A little rough," Lisa repeated. "My legs were black and blue, I could scarcely walk and bled for a week. But according to my mother I was being ridiculous and spoiled and hadn't given the marriage any kind of a chance. I was a drama queen and always had been, forever making a big fuss over things. So I stayed and tried to do everything right. But nothing I could *ever* do was right, because the man was certifiable. He was completely, totally insane. I think he'd spent his whole life looking for his perfect victim, someone he could torture at will, who'd be too stupid or too ignorant to complain, and he found me. I didn't know a thing. The only sexual experience I'd ever had was what was done to me during the abduction. Maybe my mother was right: Peter was normal and I was defective. But in my heart, I didn't believe it. Still, there was always the possibility that she was right.

"As time went on, I realized that Peter despised not only women but pretty much everyone. Secretly, I wondered from the start if he was gay because the very idea of homosexuality made him even more nuts. And usually the men who make the biggest stink about it are the people who are most drawn to it, and are trying to fight it off. He was the worst bigot, the most homophobic, right-wing lunatic I've ever encountered.

"Every single day of our marriage, he

found some way to remind me of the abduction and torment me with it. He'd leave knives on the countertop; he'd brew a pot of coffee, even though he didn't drink it, and leave it there, knowing I couldn't bear the smell, until I finally covered my nose and mouth with a dish towel and turned off the machine; he'd find some horribly violent show on TV and insist I come watch it with him. If I refused, he'd taunt me. He'd burst into the bathroom if I was taking a bath and assault me. I'd be doing the laundry and he'd sneak up behind me, throw me down and rape me. All the time, any time. If I tried to fight him, I got hurt. If I begged him not to, he'd laugh at me, and I got hurt. And the so-called 'accidents' were endless. I was so stupid. For the longest time I actually believed he was just clumsy and they really were accidents. We went to a party one night and I talked for a time to one of his associates, a very nice man. Peter didn't like that. When we were getting into the car to go home, he slammed the car door on my hand. I screamed from the pain. He told me to stop making such a big fuss. It was just an accident. But he was furious that I'd talked to another man. And when we got home, he dragged me out of the car by my hair and raped me in the garage. He'd come into the kitchen, pull open a cabinet right in front of me and bash me in the head with it, hard enough to knock me out. Oops, sorry. Accident. I'd be carrying the laundry down the stairs and he'd bump into me on the landing, making me fall down the stairs and dislocate my shoulder, crack my ankle. Oops, sorry. Didn't see you. And the worst part, the absolutely worst part, was that he and my mother talked on the phone all the time, comparing notes. I couldn't say anything to her, because she'd repeat it right back to him. Then he'd come home from the office and pound me until I dropped.

"And then I read your book." She stopped and looked at Grace for a long moment. "It was the most important thing that ever happened to me. It made me *see*. And what I saw was that Peter wasn't going to be satisfied until he managed to kill me. If I didn't do something, I was going to wind up dead. The attacks were getting worse and worse, more and more violent. I was forever going to the doctor to get patched up, or sewn up, or medicated for yet another concussion.

"I'd stay in the house all day, afraid to move, too ashamed of the bruises or the latest black eye to go out. I'd sit and listen to old Dinah Washington recordings and cry for hours. Then I'd pull myself together to make Peter's dinner and get ready for whatever assault he had dreamed up for the evening. I'd sit in the living room most of the night, terrified of the man sleeping right over my head. Sometimes, the sensors would get tripped and the outdoor lights would go on. I'd go to the window to peek out and most of the time it was this family of raccoons strolling through the back garden. It's ridiculous, but I loved those raccoons, especially the mother who'd look back at me sometimes with such *defiance*. Nobody was going to mess with her or her little ones." Lisa smiled and unclenched her hands briefly, then knitted her fingers together again.

"The only person who gave a damn was my brother. He told me over and over to pack my bags and leave, to come to live with him, let him look after me. But he didn't know Peter the way I did. Peter would have hunted me down, no matter where I went, and he'd have killed both of us. I couldn't put anyone else, but especially not Billy, at risk. Billy was the only person alive who actually cared about me, who never pretended I'd been in a car accident and didn't blame me for being stupid enough to get myself forced at knifepoint into the trunk of a car at the age of sixteen. I adored my brother. I couldn't let anything happen to him. I had to find a way to get out of that house alive, with no possibility of Peter ever coming after me.

"So after reading your book I decided I was going to have to protect myself until I could come up with a solid plan to escape to somewhere Peter would never find me. I got on the Internet and started doing research on self-defense, and found a website that had every conceivable kind of device. The one I liked best was a Taser. It was a kind of stun gun, but you didn't have to make contact. You could fire it like a gun and deliver someone an electric jolt that would drop them on the spot. So I ordered one, along with a pepper spray. The order came by over-night delivery, and I began to carry the spray and the Taser around with me. I started wearing only clothes with big pockets and al-ways had one hand in my pocket wrapped around the Taser. The next time Peter started in on me — it began every single time with a rant of some kind about how defective I was, what a fat, lazy slut I was, what a use-less stupid fool I was — I was ready. And when he'd worked himself into a frenzy and was about to come at me again with a knife, I pepper-sprayed him, then aimed the Taser at his chest and fired."

Again, Lisa stopped and took several deep breaths. Then, her voice almost inaudible, she said, "He died. The Taser triggered a heart attack, he couldn't breathe properly because of the pepper spray, and he *died*. Just a couple of minutes was all it took. I stood there in the kitchen forever, just staring at him on the floor. Hours, literally. And when he didn't move, there came a moment when I knew for certain that he was dead and I was happier than I'd ever been in my entire life. Just a moment. Then, I was terrified, absolutely terrified. I knew I was going to spend the rest of my life in jail. But when I thought about it, being in jail would be better than living with Peter. So I picked up the phone and called the police.

"The prosecutor listened to my story, looked at my medical records and declined to press charges. I couldn't believe it. He was so sympathetic. He actually said he was *sorry*. He *held* my *hand* and said he was *sorry*. I just cried and cried. It was over. I was free. My mother, of course, went wild, calling me a murderer, all kinds of horrible names. I'd killed the one person she'd ever truly loved. How could I have done that, taken Peter away from her? Sick, so sick. I put the phone down and never spoke to her or my father again. I took my clothes and left everything else in that house, told the real estate agent to take the first offer she got. I didn't care. There was nothing there I wanted. I got in my car and started driving and didn't stop, except to get gas and food to eat in the car. It was the first time I'd ever driven alone at night and I was very scared, but I did it. Every mile I put between myself and everything that had happened was like another little victory. I didn't stop until I got to Boston. By then I was so tired, so dirty, so drained in every way that I just had to stop.

"I lived in a motel for a couple of months, one of those 'efficiency' places. Nothing fancy, but clean. And the managers were very nice. I heated soup on a hotplate and watched cable TV and read, and only went out to buy more soup or more books. Then one afternoon, I decided I liked Boston. I phoned Billy and told him. 'I like it here. I'm going to stay.' He was so happy for me. He flew up and helped me find an apartment, took me to the movies and to Faneuil Hall and the market; we walked along the river, ate at all kinds of exotic restaurants. It was wonderful. He liked the city so much he even talked about getting a transfer so he could be nearer. But then he met Stephanie and that was the end of that. We'd talk often on the phone — he'd call me from his office — but we rarely saw each other.

"Eventually, the estate was settled and I inherited all of Peter's money. I bought a condo in a very secure building, and I took the training, then started doing volunteer work on the hotline for the Rape Crisis Center. It surprised me, but I felt good working the line, as if I was doing something that would make you proud." Again she offered Grace a watery smile. "I know it sounds silly, but you were so important to me. I read every book you wrote and they were personal, somehow; I felt as if I knew you, that you'd guided me to safety. And, of course, that's how Stephanie found out about you. Because I was reading one of your books the first time I went down to visit them. So," she wound down, "when I figured out that she was planning to use you to substantiate her claims of abuse so she could get away with having murdered Billy, I had to try to stop it. I wanted people to know what she'd done, wanted her to go to jail. But I never thought she'd actually come here and try to *force* you to give her what she wanted. Although I shouldn't have been surprised. She was capable of absolutely anything."

"I kept explaining to her why the emails would be useless," Grace said. "Why did she go to such extremes to get them?"

"Stephanie was a female version of Peter. She was determined to be rid of Billy, and to do that she had to establish abuse. Reality never meant much to her; it was just a technicality. I don't think the emails would've done her one bit of good. Too many people knew, and would have testified to it, what a nonviolent man my brother was. Besides, she didn't have any medical records to speak of. Just a bogus report of some bruises from a few months ago that she said were from Billy beating her but were actually from a fall she took when her heel got caught in a grating. The report wouldn't have stood up under any kind of scrutiny. But she had her storyline and she wanted those emails to back it up, and Stephanie *always* got what she wanted."

"It's crazy."

"Completely. I can't tell you how sorry I am that I brought all this down on you."

"How is it your fault?" Grace asked her, hearing an echo in her head of Vinnie saying those exact words.

"I'm the one who introduced Stephanie to your books. She was never a reader. If I hadn't talked about you, none of this would've happened. Maybe my brother would still be alive. But somehow I don't think so."

"If she was that determined to be rid of him, she'd have found someone or something else," Grace had to agree.

"Probably," Lisa said.

"I'm so sorry."

"So am I. But I'm glad Gus is going to be all right. If he'd . . . I couldn't have lived with myself."

"I know," Grace said, taking hold of Lisa's hand. "Believe me, I *know*. There was so much blood. I thought she'd killed him. And all I could think was, 'How am I going to live with myself?' I felt as if I'd die of guilt; I'd been gullible and stupid, and the result was I'd managed to get my brother killed. I knew Nicky would never forgive me. Gus is the only father she's ever known."

Lisa reached over and took hold of Grace's hand. "Everything's going to be okay now."

"Everything's going to be *different* now."

"That's true," Lisa agreed. "And I really feel badly about that."

"You're good at guilt," Grace said, finding herself able to smile. "Vinnie would proclaim you to be Jewish."

Lisa laughed. It was almost as good a laugh as Dolly's: pure and musical and contagious. Then she said, "The man I'm going to marry is Jewish, actually."

"You're getting married? That's wonderful."

"It is," she said solemnly. "In a small way it makes up for losing Billy. After four years, I finally trust Phil. He's a very gentle, very patient man. So is that officer, Jerry. He was so kind when he asked me to go with him. We were just pulling in to the station or barracks, I think he called it, when his cellphone rang. Your daughter's amazing."

"Yes, she is."

"He sat listening for a minute, then he said, 'Something's very wrong. That's not the Nicky I know. And who in hell is she talking to? I don't like this.' He turned the car around, put on the siren and took off like a rocket. When we got to where Route 9 ends, he turned off the siren. We listened to the whole thing on his speakerphone in the cruiser. It was as if Nicky knew exactly how long it would take him to get there, so she just kept talking and talking to give him enough time. Even Stephanie's gun didn't stop her. It was incredible. She was making sure Jerry had time to get there.

"When we pulled up out front of your house, he told me to stay in the car, but I just couldn't. I felt that this was all my fault. So as soon as he got out, I followed him. Nicky was so clever, so brave. And so *funny*."

332

"She is all of those things," Grace said.

"You have a nice family, Grace, good people around you. I'm glad. And you're just the way I imagined you'd be. I just wish we didn't have to meet the way we did."

"Listen, I'm grateful. You did a gutsy thing. But why wouldn't you leave a message when you called?"

"How could I have left all that stuff on an answering machine? I couldn't even think how to start. I'd been phoning Stephanie every day since I left Virginia, keeping tabs on her. When I kept getting her machine yesterday, I phoned her next door neighbor. Linda's a very nice woman who can barely stand the sight of Stephanie but she thought the world of Billy and we talked a lot after the funeral. I had coffee with her a couple of times while I was down there. So I phoned her, and when she told me she'd seen Stephanie getting into a taxi with a laptop and a suitcase, I just got in the car and drove here as fast as I could. I had a bad feeling about what she was up to. I knew in my bones she was coming here."

"You weren't wrong."

"I guess not."

Gus bellowed her name and Grace rolled her eyes. "He's feeling better already. Nothing as small as a bullet wound in the arm is going to put my brother down. I'd better get in there and see what he wants. I always thought it was tough looking after him at home. He's even worse in a hospital."

"I should be going. I want to get home before dark."

The two women stood and Grace gave Lisa a hug, saying, "Thank you, for staying over, for comforting Nicky, for explaining . . . for everything. I am *so* sorry about your brother. If I'd known . . . If only I'd known . . ."

"I think we agree that nothing would have stopped her," Lisa cut her off. "And Billy just wouldn't listen to me when I tried to tell him about Stephanie. I'm working very hard not to feel guilty. You've had to work hard at it, too. I think it comes with the territory. Don't you?"

"It probably does," Grace allowed.

"Would it be okay if I phoned you sometime, or emailed?" Lisa asked.

"If you don't phone me, I'll worry. You've got the new number, right?"

"Right."

"Good. I think I'll be emailing a lot less from now on. Drive carefully. I'll be waiting to hear from you."

"Okay. Thank you."

Gus bellowed again and Grace made a

face, then said, "I'll talk to you later. Don't forget to phone."

"You make a difference to people, you know, Grace."

"I'm not so sure about that anymore."

"No, you *do!* So please don't stop what you do. It's important. And you couldn't have known Stephanie wasn't for real. I'll call you. Say goodbye again to everybody for me. Okay? I loved meeting them all."

"Absolutely. They all loved meeting you, too."

"Thank you." Lisa pulled on her parka, slung her bag over her shoulder and headed for the elevator.

Grace watched her go, then went into Gus's private room — courtesy of Vinnie — where Nicky sat on a chair beside his bed, working on her new iBook.

"Did Lisa go?" Nicky asked.

"Unh-hunh. She said she loved meeting you."

"Ditto. She's a total sweetheart."

"I'm starving," Gus complained. "Don't they feed people here?"

"Vin and Jerry are down in the cafeteria getting some sandwiches." Grace told him. "They'll be back in a few minutes."

"What a place! Why the hell did they have to keep me overnight? When can I go home?"

"As soon as the doctor signs your release, you're out of here, Dad. I *told* you that."

"You'll have something to eat, and then we'll go home. Okay?" Grace said.

"It can't be soon enough to suit me. It stinks of hospital in here."

"That's true," Grace agreed.

"Could be 'cause it's a hospital," Nicky said. "You know, Mom, I think we should enter Dad in the Disabled Seniors Special Olympics; he'll easily win the hundred-yard walker dash."

Grace burst out laughing. After a moment, Gus laughed, too.

>epilogue

By July everything had changed. Nicky had moved down to Connecticut for the summer to stay with her friend Gin Holder in New Canaan. The two had become close since Nicky and her friends had rescued Gin in Times Square on New Year's Eve, and she had managed, through her father's business connections, to get both of them internships at a radio station in the city.

Jerry had, with everyone's blessings, cleared out Nicky's excess wardrobe and moved into the guest room. He'd hired Dolly to work five days a week exclusively for Gus (she now made breakfast and lunch and Jerry cooked dinner), and Lucia still came every evening to get Gus bathed and ready for bed. Sunday nights, Jerry saw to getting Gus showered and into his pajamas. Most evenings, they either watched a game on TV or sat and read in contented silence.

When Grace asked him how he was able to manage all this on his trooper's salary, Jerry laughed and said, "Grace, I bought a whole bunch of tech stocks and sold them all at the top of the market. The money's now in nice secure CDs. So I've got more than Gus and I will ever need. Lucky thing I'm not a greedy guy, huh?"

Grace moved her office into the vacant area of the barn where the old bedroom had been, and she traveled back and forth into the city with Vinnie. The arrangement suited them both. There were nights when she couldn't sleep with him in the bed and she took herself quietly off to the sofa. Her agent, Miles, was negotiating with a media company that wanted to launch an interactive website for victims of domestic violence, with Grace acting as host.

Her new, and probably final, book was in the production stages; her site continued to get a goodly number of hits. And the emails kept coming in. But when one arrived that asked, "Is it really you?" she now replied, "Yes, it's really me. If you need help, I'll be happy to recommend places where you will find it."

Domestic Abuse Prevention Resources U.S.A.

Domestic Violence, Family Violence, Child Abuse Page
http://www.famvi.com

National Domestic Violence Hotline
Using a national database of domestic violence shelters, other emergency shelters, legal aid and social services, this organization links people to local assistance. The hotline number is 800-799-SAFE(7233), or 800-787-3224(TDD).

National Violence Against Women Office
http://www.ojp.usdoj.gov/vawo/
Part of the U.S. Department of Justice, the office works to enforce federal criminal statutes of the 1994 Violence Against Women Act, and administers more than $270 million a year in grants to states, tribes and local communities.

National Coalition Against Domestic Violence
http://www.ncadv.org/
Since 1978, this national information and referral center has sponsored national conferences and several innovative projects, including linking scarred victims of domestic abuse with plastic surgeons, dentists and dermatologists.

Family Violence Prevention Fund
http://www.endabuse.org/
With a focus on domestic-violence education, prevention and public-policy reform, the site provides fact sheets, personal stories, information for advocacy action, and a "celebrity watch" section that tracks celebrity involvement in domestic violence.

Domestic Violence Information Center
http://www.feminist.org/other/
dv/dvhome.html
The Feminist Majority Foundation's detailed site lists resources for women victims of domestic abuse. Resources include hotlines and a list of state domestic-violence centers.

Minnesota Center Against Violence and Abuse
http://www.mincava.umn.edu/mensissu.asp
Men and Violence Electronic Clearinghouse. This site lists articles, books and sites that re-

late to men and violence, including links to organizations such as Men Against Domestic Violence and Men Overcoming Violence.

Stop Abuse for Everyone
http://www.safe4all.org.
This nonprofit organization sets up SAFE chapters for men, women and children who have been abused by an intimate partner, caregiver or family member.

Johns Hopkins Population Report
http://www.jhuccp.org/pr/llledsum.stm
Ending Violence Against Women. An in-depth report on violence against women in the United States and other countries, with recommendations on violence prevention, published in January 2000.

American Bar Association Commission on Domestic Violence
http://www.abanet.org/domviol/home.html
The ABA commission brings together leaders from business, the military, the legal community, the medical community, and domestic-violence organizations to develop a blueprint for communities to reduce domestic violence.

Sexual Assault Hotlines

Rape, Abuse & Incest National Network (RAINN)
635-B Pennsylvania Avenue, SE
Washington, DC 20003
800-656-HOPE

State Sexual Assault Coalitions

Alabama Coalition Against Rape
1415 East South Blvd.
Montgomery, AL 36116
Telephone: 334-286-5980
Fax: 334-286-5993

Alaska Network on Domestic Violence and Sexual Assault
130 Seward, Rm 209
Juneau, Alaska 99801
907-586-3650

Arizona Sexual Assault Network (AzSAN)
12 West Madison
Phoenix, Arizona 85013
Telephone: 602-258-1195
Fax: 602-258-7390

Arkansas Coalition Against Violence to Women and Children

523 Louisiana, Suite 230
Little Rock, AR 72201
800-269-4668

California Coalition Against Sexual Assault
Rape Prevention Resource Center
1611 Telegraph Avenue, Suite 1515
Oakland, CA 94612
800-9CAL-CASA
916-446-2520

Colorado Coalition Against Sexual Assault
(CCASA)
P.O. Box 18663
Denver, CO 80218
303-861-7033

Connecticut Sexual Assault Crisis Services,
Inc. (CONNSACS)
110 Connecticut Blvd.
East Hartford, CT 06108
860-282-9881

CCASAD (Coordinating Council Against
Sexual Assault in Delaware)
c/o CONTACT Delaware
P.O. Box 9525
Wilmington, DE 19809
Telephone: 302-761-9800
Fax: 302-761-4280

24-hour Helpline: 302-761-9100

Florida Council Against Sexual Violence
1311 A Paul Russell Road
Tallahassee, FL 32301
Telephone: 850-297-2000
Fax: 850-297-2002

Dekalb Rape Crisis Program
101 East Court Square, Suite B4
Decater, Georgia 30030
Telephone: 404-377-1429
Fax: 404-377-5644

Hawaii Coalition for the Prevention of Sexual Assault
741-A Sunset Avenue, Room 105
Honolulu, HI 96816
Telephone: 808-733-9038
Fax: 808-733-9032

Idaho Coalition Against Sexual & Domestic Violence
815 Park Boulevard, Suite 140
Boise, ID 83712-7738
Telephone: 208-384-0419
Fax: 208-331-0687

Illinois Coalition Against Sexual Assault (ICASA)

100 North 16th St.
Springfield, IL 62703
Telephone: 217-753-4117
Fax: 217-753-8229

Indiana Coalition Against Sexual Assault, Inc. (INCASA)
55 Monument Circle, Ste. 1224
Indianapolis, IN 46204
Telephone: 317-423-0233
Fax: 317-423-0237
General e-mail: incasa@incasa.org

Iowa Coalition Against Sexual Assault (Iowa CASA)
2603 Bell Street, Suite 102
Des Moines, IA 50321-1120
515-244-7424

Kansas Coalition Against Sexual and Domestic Violence (KCSDV)
820 SE Quincy, Suite 416B
Topeka, KS 66612
Kansas State-wide Crisis Hotline:
800-400-8864
TDD: 800-787-3224

Kentucky Association of Sexual Assault Programs, Inc.
P.O. Box 602

Frankfort, KY 40602-0602
Telephone: 502-226-2704
Fax: 502-226-2725

Louisiana Foundation Against Sexual Assault (LaFASA)
P.O. Box 40
Independence, LA 70443-0040
Telephone: 985-345-5995
Fax: 985-345-5592
Toll Free: 888-995-7273 from Louisiana. (Please note that this is a toll-free number to the office and is not a hotline.)

Maine Coalition Against Sexual Assault
3 Mulliken Court
Augusta, ME 04330
207-626-0034

Maryland Coalition Against Sexual Assault
1517 Gov. Ritchie Highway Suite 207
Arnold, MD 21012
Telephone: 410-974-4507
Fax: 410-757-4770
Toll Free: 800-983-RAPE
info@mcasa.org

Jane Doe Inc., The Massachusetts Coalition Against Sexual Assault and Domestic Violence
14 Beacon Street

Boston, MA 02108-3704
Telephone: 617-248-0922
Fax: 617-248-0902

Michigan Coalition Against Domestic &
Sexual Violence
3893 Okemos Road, Suite B-2
Okemos, MI 48864
Telephone: 517-347-7000
Fax: 517-347-1377
TTY: 517-381-8470

Minnesota Coalition Against Sexual Assault
420 N. 5th, Street Suite 690
Minneapolis, MN 55409
Telephone: 612-313-2797
Toll Free: 800-964-8847
Fax: 612-313-2799
E-mail: mncasa@msn.com

Mississippi Coalition Against Sexual Assault
Department of Health — Mississippi State
P.O. Box 4172
5455 Executive Place Drive
Jackson, MS 39296-4172
Telephone: 601-987-9011
Fax: 601-987-9166

Missouri Coalition Against Sexual Assault
P.O. Box 16771

St. Louis, MO 63105
816-931-4527
E-mail: mcasa@netdoor.com

Missouri Coalition Against Sexual Assault
3217 Broadway, Suite 500
Kansas City, MO 64111
Telephone: 816-931-4527
Fax: 816-931-4532

Nebraska Domestic Violence & Sexual Assault Coalition (NDVSAC)
825 M Street, Suite 404
Lincoln, NE 68508
Telephone: 402-476-6256
Fax: 402-476-6806
In-state Toll Free Hotline: 800-876-6238
General e-mail address: info@ndvsac.org
Administrator@ndvsac.org

Nevada Coalition Against Sexual Violence
P.O. Box 530103
Henderson, NV 89053
Telephone: 702-914-6878 (Please note that this is not a hotline number. For crisis calls, please call 1-800-656-HOPE for a local rape crisis center in Nevada.)
Fax: 702-914-6879
E-mail: tysonlow@apl.com

348

New Hampshire Coalition Against Domestic
and Sexual Violence
P.O. Box 353
Concord, NH 03302-0353
Hotline: 800-852-3388 or 800-735-2964
(TDD/Voice)
603-224-8893

New Jersey Coalition Against Sexual Assault
— NJCASA
1 Edinburg Road, 2nd floor
Trenton, NJ 08619
Telephone: 609-631-4450
Fax: 609-631-4453
E-mail: mail@njcasa.org
Hotline: 800-601-7200

New Mexico Coalition of Sexual Assault
Programs, Inc.
4004 Carlisle, NE, Suite D
Albuquerque, NM 87107
Telephone: 505-883-8020
Fax: 505-883-7530

New York State Coalition Against Sexual
Assault (NYSCASA, Inc.)
784 Washington Avenue
Albany, NY 12203
Telephone: 518-482-4222
Fax: 518-482-4248

North Carolina Coalition Against Sexual
Assault
(NCCASA)
174 Mine Lake Court, Suite 100
Raleigh, NC 27615
Telephone: 919-676-7611
Fax: 919-676-1355

North Dakota Council on Abused Women's
Services — Coalition Against Sexual Assault
in ND
418 East Rousser #320
Bismarck, ND 58501-4046
800-472-2911 (in state)
701-255-6240
701-255-1904
E-mail: NDCAWS@btigate.com

Ohio Coalition on Sexual Assault (OCOSA)
4041 N. High Street, Suite 410
Columbus, OH 43214
Telephone: 614-268-3322
Fax: 614-268-0881
E-mail: ocosa@mindspring.com

Oklahoma Coalition Against Domestic Violence and Sexual Assault
2525 NW Expressway, Suite 101
Oklahoma City, OK 73112
Telephone: 405-848-1815

Fax: 405-848-3469
Toll Free: 800-522-7233

Oregon Coalition Against Domestic and
Sexual Violence (OCADSV)
520 NW Davis Street, #310
Portland, OR 97209
Hotline: 800-OCADSV-2
503-223-7411

Pennsylvania Coalition Against Rape (PCAR)
125 Enola Drive
Enola, PA 17025
800-692-7445 (in PA)
Telephone: 717-728-9740
Fax: 717-728-9781

South Carolina Coalition Against
Domestic Violence & Sexual Assault
P.O. Box 7776
Columbia, SC 29202-7776
Hotline: 800-260-9293
803-750-1222

South Dakota Coalition Against Domestic
Violence and Sexual Abuse
P.O. Box 2000
Eagle Butte, SD 57625
Telephone: 605-964-7233
Fax: 605-964-6060

Tennessee Coalition Against Domestic and
Sexual Violence
P.O. Box 120972
Nashville, TN 37212
Telephone: 615-386-9406
Fax: 615-383-2967
Toll Free Information Line: 800-289-9018
(8 A.M.–5 P.M. M–F)
State-wide Domestic Violence and Child
Abuse Hotline: 800-356-6767
E-mail: tcadsv@telelink.net

Texas Association Against Sexual Assault
(TAASA)
One Commodore Plaza
800 Brazos, Suite 810
Austin, TX 78701
Telephone: 512-474-8161
Fax: 512-474-6490

Utah — CAUSE — Coalition of Advocates
for Utah Survivors' Empowerment
366 South 500 East, Suite 212
Salt Lake City, UT 84102
Telephone: 801-322-1500
Fax: 801-322-1250

Vermont Network Against Domestic Violence
and Sexual Assault
P.O. Box 405

Montpelier, VT 05601
Hotline: 800-489-7273 (statewide)
Telephone: 802-223-1302
Fax: 802-223-6943

Virginians Aligned Against Sexual Assault
(VAASA)
508 Dale Avenue, Suite B
Charlottesville, VA 22903-4547
Telephone: 804-979-9002
Fax: 804-979-9003

Washington Coalition of Sexual Assault
Programs
2415 Pacific Ave. SE #10-C
Olympia, WA 98501
Telephone: 360-754-7583
Fax: 360-786-8707
E-mail: wcsap@wcsap.org

West Virginia Foundation for Rape Information & Services
112 Braddock Street
Fairmont, WV 26554
304-366-9500

Wisconsin Coalition Against Sexual Assault
(WCASA)
600 Williamson Street, Suite N-2
Madison, WI 53703

Telephone/TTY: 608-257-1516
Fax: 608-257-2150
E-mail: wcasa@wcasa.org

Wyoming Coalition Against Domestic Violence & Sexual Assault
441 South Center
Casper, WY 82602
Hotline: 307-235-2814
Fax: 307-472-4307

Domestic Abuse Prevention Resources Canada

National Clearinghouse on Family Violence
http://www.hc-sc.gc.ca/hppb/
family violence/index.html

Provincial Transition House Associations

Newfoundland Provincial Association
Against Family Violence
P.O. Box 221, Station C
St. John's, NF A1C 5J2
Telephone: 709-739-6759
Fax: 709-722-0164

Prince Edward Island Transition House
Association
81 Prince Street
Charlottetown, PEI C1A 4R3
Telephone: 902-894-3354
Fax: 902-368-7180

Transition House Association of Nova Scotia
1657 Barrington Street, Suite 319
Halifax, NS B3J 2A1
Telephone: 902-429-7287
Fax: 902-425-5606

New Brunswick Coalition of Transition Houses
115 Candlewood Lane
St. John, NB E2K 1Z5
Telephone: 506-648-0481
Fax: 506-652-5651

Quebec
Federation des ressources d'hebergement pour femmes violentees et en difficulte du Quebec
1096, rue Joliette
Longueuil, PQ J4K 4W1
Telephone: 514-674-0324
Telecopieur: 514-674-0558

Regroupement provincial des maisons d'hebergement et de Transition pour femmes victimes de violence conjugale
5225, rue Berri, Bureau 304
Montreal, PQ H2J 2S4
Telephone: 514-279-2007
Telecopieur: 514-279-4109

Ontario Association of Interval and

Transition Houses
2 Carlton Street, Suite 1404
Toronto, ON M5B 1J3
Telephone: 416-977-6619
Fax: 416-977-1227

Manitoba Association of Women's Shelters
Inc.
P.O. Box 651
Dauphin, MB R7N 3B3
Telephone: 204-638-8785
Fax: 204-638-6568

Provincial Association of Transition Houses
in Saskatchewan
#418, 230 Avenue R South
Saskatoon, SK S7M 2Z1
Telephone: 306-978-6654
Fax: 306-978-6614

Alberta Council of Women's Shelters
#2-12739 Fort Road
Edmonton, AB T5A 1A7
Telephone: 403-456-7000
Fax: 403-456-7001
E-mail: acws@connect.ab.ca

British Columbia/Yukon Society of Transition Houses
1112-409 Granville Street

Vancouver, BC V6C 1T2
Telephone: 604-669-6943
Fax: 604-682-6962

Northwest Territories — N.W.T. Association
of Family Violence Prevention
Baffin Regional Agvvik Society
P.O. Box 237
Iqualuit, NWT X0A 0H0
Telephone: 819-979-4500
Fax: 819-979-0328

We hope you have enjoyed this Large Print book. Other Thorndike, Wheeler or Chivers Press Large Print books are available at your library or directly from the publishers.

For more information about current and up-coming titles, please call or write, without obligation, to:

Publisher
Thorndike Press
295 Kennedy Memorial Drive
Waterville, ME 04901
Tel. (800) 223-1244

Or visit our Web site at:
www.gale.com/thorndike
www.gale.com/wheeler

OR

Chivers Press Limited
Windsor Bridge Road
Bath BA2 3AX
England
Tel. (01225) 335336

Or visit Chivers Web site at
www.chivers.co.uk

All our Large Print titles are designed for easy reading, and all our books are made to last.